Lavender Lies Bleeding

Spice Shop Mysteries

ASSAULT AND PEPPER
GUILTY AS CINNAMON
KILLING THYME
CHAI ANOTHER DAY
THE SOLACE OF BAY LEAVES
PEPPERMINT BARKED
BETWEEN A WOK AND A DEAD PLACE
TO ERR IS CUMIN

Lavender Lies Bleeding

A SPICE SHOP MYSTERY

BY LESLIE BUDEWITZ

Published 2025 by Seventh Street Books®

Lavender Lies Bleeding. Copyright © 2025 by Leslie Ann Budewitz. All rights reserved. No part of this publication may be reproduced, stored in a retrieval system, or transmitted in any form or by any means, digital, electronic, mechanical, photocopying, recording, or otherwise, or conveyed via the Internet or a website without prior written permission of the publisher, except in the case of brief quotations embodied in critical articles and reviews.

This is a work of fiction. Characters, organizations, products, locales, and events portrayed in this novel either are products of the author's imagination or are used fictitiously. Any similarities to real persons, living or dead, is coincidental and not intended by the author.

Inquiries should be addressed to
Start Science Fiction
221 River Street, 9th Floor
Hoboken, New Jersey 07030

Phone: 212-431-5454
www.seventhstreetbooks.com

10 9 8 7 6 5 4 3 2 1

978-1-64506-086-4 (paperback)
978-1-64506-096-3 (ebook)

Printed in the United States of America

Cover image © Shutterstock: Vahe3D, Oksana Shufrych, Madlen,
Zhanna Hapanovich, Oleksandra, Danilian, New Africa, Bulatnikov,
LightField Studios, Natallia Yaumenenka, Africa Studio, StudioSmart,
Ekaterina Perlov Bass, Tatiana Popova, Osinskih Agency, Petra Schueller,
Anton Vierietin, Dmitry Kalinovsky. AdobeStock: Tony Campbell
Cover design by Paula Guran
Cover design © Start Science Fiction

In memory of Jim Frickle.
Smart, funny, generous, and much missed.

How Does Your Garden Grow?

Aka the cast, stirring things up!

AT SEATTLE SPICE

Pepper Reece—Mistress of Spice
Sandra Piniella—assistant manager and mix master
Cayenne Cooper—newly promoted to events coordinator
Kristen Gardiner—Pepper's BFF
Vanessa Rivera—the new girl, catching on fast
Arf—an Airedale, the King of Terriers

FRIENDS AND FAMILY

Nate Seward—the fisherman
Lena Reece—Mom, a free spirit
Chuck Reece—Dad, still driving that '67 Mustang

THE FLICK CHICKS

Pepper
Kristen
Laurel Halloran—widowed restaurateur and houseboat dweller
Seetha Sharma—chai-drinking massage therapist
Aimee McGillvray—owner of Rainy Day Vintage

IN SALMON FALLS

Liz Giacometti—aka Lavender Liz
Abby Delaney—self-described modern witch
Orion Fisher and Brambo—lovable, but clueless
Sara and Preston Vu—cousins with a plan
Desiree White—all business, all the time
Monica Salter—lavender-loving soccer mom

THE LAW

Sheriff Joe Aguilar—eagle-eyed skeptic

One

From ancient Egypt, Greece, and Rome to modern days, lavender's fragrance has made it one of the most popular herbs in human history, used for everything from mummification to treating insomnia to making the evening dishwashing more tolerable.

THE SCENT SEEPED IN THROUGH THE VENTS AND WINDOWS of my black Saab. Sharp and tangy, floral and sweet, it overpowered the divine aroma of my double mocha and the odor of damp dog coming from the back seat.

Lavender.

If the pervasive smell was any indication, Salmon Falls, a short drive from Seattle, should be the chillest place on earth. But even though I'm a city girl, I knew enough about small towns to catch the undercurrent in Lavender Liz's voice when she'd invited me out to chat about the annual Salmon Falls Lavender Festival. My staff and I at the Spice Shop hoped to create a similar festival, recruiting a few trusted friends. If we succeeded, we'd petition the powers that be to introduce an official Pike Place Market event. If we didn't—well, I didn't want to dwell on the hit my reputation as a savvy retailer and a Market mover and shaker would take.

Not to mention my view of myself as a woman who got things done. "Bring Cayenne out to see the farm," Liz had said, referring

2 · *Lavender Lies Bleeding*

to the salesclerk I'd recently christened events coordinator. "Then tour the town. Give her a sense of the place and what we're up to."

Since buying the venerable Spice Shop two and a half years ago, I'd worked hard to develop a strong supply pipeline, bringing in the freshest, most flavorful herbs and spices I could find. To expand what we offered both our commercial customers and curious home cooks. And whenever possible, to cultivate relationships with growers right here in Western Washington. That included "Lavender Liz" Giacometti, a woman I'd liked the moment we met. My whole staff liked and trusted her, and it would be good for Cayenne to see her on her home ground.

So, on this Thursday in early May, I'd left my assistant manager in charge of the shop. Loaded the dog in the back seat of my sputtery old Saab, picked up Cayenne, and left the city drizzle behind.

It had been a while since my last field trip, so Liz had texted me directions, warning that GPS would likely steer me wrong. My phone in hand, Cayenne read them to me now.

"'Half a mile from the highway, just after the big lavender and poppy seed farm, watch for a giant metal moose on the edge of town. Turn right,'" she read. "Oh my gosh. There it is. I've never seen such a thing."

A ten-foot-high welded sculpture made of old car parts perched on a small, flower-covered hill. As directed, I turned right onto a narrow, two-lane road.

"'Continue for two miles, until you come to Mrs. Luedtke Road.' I wonder who she was."

"My guess, one of those name-your-own road deals, way back when."

"'Left onto Mrs. Luedtke,'" Cayenne continued. "'Slow down when you see the white rail fence and watch for the sign, on the right.'"

On one side of the road, a broad swath of peonies and lupine was beginning to bloom, bordered by a strip of lavender. The splashes of color and shades of green—so many shades of green— were the antidote we all needed after winter. I sipped my mocha. Lavender's pleasant enough, but I find my comfort in chocolate and caffeine.

Leslie Budewitz · 3

A black-and-white SUV, a Falls County Sheriff's Department insignia on its side, passed us going the opposite direction, a man and woman in the front seat. Another, with a single driver, followed.

"Wonder what that's about?" Cayenne asked, but she wasn't looking at the law enforcement vehicles. She was pointing at the signs along the field mesh fence. 'Keep Your Pinky Fingers Off Our Farms.' 'Trees, Not Teacups.' 'Weeding, Not Weddings.'

"No idea." A cluster of buildings dotted each farm—here a stucco cottage from the 1930s, there a double-wide. Clapboard farmhouses. Barns in shades of red and weathered gray. A farmhouse with Tyvek siding and a shiny new roof.

We reached the white rail fence Liz had mentioned, the farm country equivalent of the storied white picket fence. Up ahead, a sign marked a narrow lane. I recognized the logo, a vintage purple truck encircled by sprigs of lavender and the name "Salmon Falls Lavender Farm." I slowed, catching a glimpse of a red-and-white sign attached to the open gate.

"'Farms are for Farming,'" I read out loud. "Well, yeah."

The curved driveway led past the field of lavender to a small cottage. Dark green trim offset the white clapboards, and the wide porch invited customers to enter, sniff, and shop. Liz's classic midcentury Chevy pickup, deep purple with a bold, rounded profile and shiny metal grill, sat to one side. A showpiece—farm art.

But the sheriff's rig beside it didn't fit the idyllic scene. Another thing I knew about small towns: Just like in the city, the presence of law enforcement usually signals trouble.

"Ohmygod." Cayenne clapped one brown, red-tipped hand over her mouth and pointed with the other. I followed her gaze.

"Holy marjoroly."

Beside the cottage stood the greenhouse, roughly twenty by thirty. If you could call it a greenhouse, with the glass in shatters and shards. The copper weathervane atop the peaked roof tilted dangerously.

All signs of trouble with a capital T.

"Stay," I told Arf, who'd sat up the moment we stopped. He's an Airedale, energetic but well trained, no thanks to me, and I was sure he needed to pee, if for no other reason than to announce his presence to other critters.

4 · *Lavender Lies Bleeding*

As Cayenne and I got out of the car, Liz came toward us, side by side with a man in a two-tone brown uniform who had a good foot on her, even without the hat.

"Pepper!" she called, picking up speed. "Cayenne! I completely forgot you were coming."

"What happened?"

"Vandals. Thieves. Who knows? Most of the glass in the greenhouse is destroyed. The ventilation system is trashed, and they seriously messed up the distilling equipment." Liz raked a hand through her short, dark curls, messier than usual. A trail of dried blood traced a long cut down the back of her hand, almost merging into the lavender flowers tattooed on the inside of her arm. A smaller, deeper cut marred her cheek. She didn't appear to notice. Her nylon cargo pants were smeared with potting soil, as was the front of her white T-shirt. Hiking shoes, no socks. No sweater. The air was cool, but she didn't appear to notice that either.

"Pepper Reece," I said, extending my hand to the uniformed sheriff. "I own the Spice Shop in Pike Place Market. This is Cayenne Cooper, who works with me. We came out to see the farm and chat with Liz."

"Sheriff Joe Aguilar, Falls County Sheriff's Department." His grip was firm, his face placid, but I had no doubt the wheels were turning behind his dark brown eyes. "Not the best morning for a tour."

"Oh, gosh, sorry," Liz said. "Where are my manners?"

"No worries," Cayenne said. "We'd be rattled, too."

Truth to that. I well remembered the horror of seeing flames lick the outside walls of my shop, smoke pouring out a shattered clerestory window, the employee I'd recently fired cackling wildly and clapping her hands as she watched from the sidewalk.

"So, who? What? Why?" I asked.

"Could be kids," Aguilar replied, though from his sideways glance at Liz, I suspected he was watching his words in front of virtual strangers. Us. "Thinking you had marijuana plants hidden among the herbs. He didn't see a security system, so in he went."

"Joe, you know my operation is completely above board," Liz said.

"I know that, but do the potheads?"

"Why steal it?" I was baffled. "Pot's legal in Washington."

Leslie Budewitz • 5

"The black market is huge," Aguilar said. "Task force just took down a family operation that used a legitimate business as a front, skirting the regulations and the taxes. They made millions. Other growers take it to states where it's not legal."

"Wow. I had no idea." I turned to Liz. "I hope your seedlings didn't get damaged. Can they survive without the greenhouse?" May weather can be unpredictable, and she'd mentioned concern about the seedlings when we talked about a visit. Where she meant to put them, I couldn't imagine, but gardeners always have room for more plants.

"Can't tell until I start cleaning up inside," she said. "What a mess."

"My team's finished with their photographs and measurements, so you're free to do what you need to do," Aguilar said. Ah. The vehicles we'd passed on our way in.

"Can we help?" We weren't dressed for it, and we had other plans, but a vendor in need is a friend indeed. Or something like that.

"No, no," she said. "I'll call someone."

"You think that boy's in the clear, you try finding him," Aguilar told her. He turned to Cayenne and me and touched his fingertips to the brim of his hat. "Ladies." Then he climbed in his vehicle and I saw him raise the car radio mic with one hand, his phone in the other. The modern tools of the detecting trade.

I glanced at Liz, astonished by the fury written all over her face.

Two

Know your herbs and your grower. For cooking, choose Lavendula angustifolia *and be sure to avoid herbs grown with pesticides or contaminated with artificial aromas.*

ONCE IT WAS CLEAR THAT THE BROKEN GLASS WAS LIMITED to the area around the greenhouse, I let Arf out of the car, keeping his leash short. Aguilar rolled through the curve to Mrs. Luedtke Road, then sped out of sight.

"He's not a bad guy, Joe. Or a bad cop. But he doesn't quite get—" Liz opened her arms and gestured to the expanse of lavender around us. "All this. Not everyone in Salmon Falls does, despite all the money and business the crop brings the community."

The reason for our visit. "So what do you think happened?" I asked. "If it's potheads, have they broken into other greenhouses?" Half the farms we'd passed had one, though none as sophisticated as Liz's. Some were artful assemblages of castoff windows and doors. Others were covered by plastic sheeting—one good gust and poof! They'd be gone.

"Not that I've heard. And they didn't take the copper, which you'd think a thief would want. Granted, those big kettles are harder to sell than wire—what thieves usually go for—but they'd bring a pile of cash."

Leslie Budewitz · 7

A different black market.

"Copper thieves?" Cayenne was surprised. "I've never heard of that. Copper always looks so homey."

"It works better than steel," Liz said. "I always do a demo later in the summer, after harvest. I hope I can do one this year. I'm going to have to replace the tubing and pound out the dents in the kettles so they don't interfere with the distilling process."

I'd bet money that when Liz said "I," she meant she would do the work herself. Not some hired hand or metalworker. Farmers are self-reliant.

"That's how you get the oil, right?" Cayenne asked.

"Yep. We force steam through the buds and leaves to extract the volatile oils. It's not a giant part of my business—mostly, I dry the buds for culinary use—but the oil helps the bottom line. Lavender is big business, here and in France. These days, a lot of the crop comes from Bulgaria and Australia. China, too. In Washington, most farms are small, even though this is where commercial production in North America began, a hundred years ago. But whether they're buying flowers or lotion or essential oil, my customers want organic, hand-grown lavender. They want to know me." She spread her hands. "And this place."

I got it. My customers, too, want to know where their food comes from. They want an assurance of quality that stems from a personal connection, if not with the grower, then with a passionate retailer.

"I can't think straight," Liz said, her curls bouncing. "Up too early without coffee. Join me?"

"I never say no, even when I probably should," I said.

"Cayenne, I have decaf," Liz said. "You're glowing, even though you're not showing."

"Thanks," Cayenne said, a protective hand on her belly. "I feel great. They told me the MS symptoms would probably go into remission when I got pregnant, and so far, so good."

I crossed my fingers that her remission would last. It had been hard to watch her struggle when the disease first hit.

We followed Liz along a stone path past the wreckage to her house, its telltale roof line that of a manufactured home. As we walked, she talked.

8 · *Lavender Lies Bleeding*

"Lavender is pretty forgiving. It needs sunshine but not a lot of water, and like all plants, as little competition as possible. Heavy-duty weed cloth is spendy, but worth every penny." She kicked stray gravel off the path. "The right blend of attention and neglect."

Cayenne rubbed a blossom between her fingers. You almost can't help yourself.

Liz pointed out the different varieties, the purple, pink, or white buds on long, thin, square stems. Some were coming on, while others were weeks from blooming. "There's always a few plants that don't make it through the winter. Temperature swings have gotten more extreme—hard on what's basically a Mediterranean plant. A bad rodent year can be devastating. One of my first years, chipmunks ate half the flowers two days before harvest."

"Is that what happened here?" I pointed to a row of small plants, clearly new. "Replacements?"

"Ahh, no." She wiped the back of her hand across her forehead, leaving a smear of blood. "That's—"

Somewhere close by, a rooster crowed.

"Now he decides to wake up," Liz said. "Usually, he's crowing long before dawn and once I hear him, there's no point trying to go back to sleep. But this morning, not a peep. If I'd woken earlier, maybe I'd have been able to stop the vandals."

"Or maybe you'd have been hurt," I said. Her eyes widened and her nostrils flared. The possibility had not occurred to her.

"You raise chickens?" Cayenne asked. "I'd love to buy some fresh eggs."

"No, not me," Liz said. We were almost at her house now. She pointed at the thick windbreak that ran along one side of the lavender farm. "Through that gap, you can see the old farmhouse. My ex, TJ Manning, and his wife, Brooke, took it over. The chickens are hers. I can text her, see if she has eggs."

The Tyvek farmhouse we'd passed on the drive in. To a baker like Cayenne, fresh eggs are gold.

"Funny how things change," Liz said, thumbs flying across her phone. "Multigenerational farms like this often have two or three houses. His great-grandparents built the farmhouse."

"The Luedtkes?" I asked, remembering the road name.

"No. I don't know who they were. I seriously itched to redo the house and move in, but TJ didn't want all the work. He never wanted to get married and he never wanted kids. So, what happens? We break up and less than a year later, he's married and pregnant and remodeling the home place. I'm not complaining. She's sweet, and probably better for him than I ever was. But still . . ."

But still, it was an old story, no less painful for being common. Liz had mentioned a guy or two in the past, but nothing serious. Hard, she'd said, to date in a small town. She'd made a few mistakes. I'd sympathized; dating in the city wasn't easy, either.

"Happily, the Manning family was willing to sell me this house and the five acres, and pretty cheap, too. They own or lease hundreds of acres." She glanced at Arf. "How is he with cats?"

"He loves them, especially with mustard." My standard stupid reply. "No, seriously. He's got the best manners, other than the occasional stinky fart. My friend Laurel's cat hisses at him every time we visit and he barely notices." He'd growled at first—no one likes being hissed at—but he got over it. The treats Laurel slips him had helped.

A pair of wooden Adirondack chairs, painted a deep purple, sat on the small front porch. We took off our shoes and followed Liz inside. The house was cute and clean and, no surprise, lavender scented.

Liz started coffee, then dashed into the bathroom while it brewed. We settled on stools at the kitchen counter to wait.

Now, she poured, sweetening each mug with a hefty dose of lavender syrup. She'd wiped the blood off her arm and face, but the shocked expression remained. I wasn't sure if our presence was comfort or intrusion.

I picked up a mug, handmade with lavender stalks carved into the clay, the top and handle a soft pinky-purple. A local potter, I imagined.

"Mmm. Good. Thanks. Hey, it's not the morning you had planned, so let's talk about festival stuff another time. Do you have staff you need to call?"

On the other side of the counter, Liz gripped her mug like a life preserver. "No. This time of year, the cottage is only open on Saturdays. In another week or two, we'll expand that, and by Memorial Day, aim for six days a week. You remember Abby who used to work summers for me."

"Used to?"

10 · *Lavender Lies Bleeding*

"Yeah. She loves the place. But she needed year-round work. Her mother is running the retail side this summer." Liz sipped her coffee. "Most of the field work is done, freeing me for other projects."

"The sheriff mentioned someone who could help you clean up?"

"Orion Fisher. Local labor for hire. He helps with planting, weeding, general upkeep. I've got a small tractor for harvest, but extra hands make it easier."

"Not the sheriff's favorite person, I take it."

"Oh, Joe—Sheriff Aguilar—got a bug in his ear. Orion and I exchanged a few words. It'll blow over. I don't even know how Joe knows about it." She fiddled with her coffee spoon. "Joe sent a deputy to talk to Orion—he lives above the carriage house behind the B&B. Does some maintenance for them. But he and his dog were both gone, so Joe thinks the worst."

"Like Pepper always says," Cayenne said. "It's a cop's job to be the suspicious type."

"What about that guy you were seeing last winter?" I asked. "I know it was off and on, but you said something about him and a farm."

"That's how we met, ages ago. But no. No way."

I had one foot resting on Arf's back, and felt the small growl creeping up his spine before I heard it. I pressed down lightly and the growl stopped. A few feet away stood a large gray tuxedo, his yellow-green eyes trained on the Airedale.

"Sir," Liz said firmly. "Go outside." The cat gave Arf a disdainful look, then disappeared through a cat door, his long gray tail upright in indignation.

"The cat's name is Sir?" Cayenne laughed. "Funny. He's beautiful."

"Thanks. He showed up a couple of years ago. No chip, no collar or tags. Just that fancy tuxedo. And a bit of an attitude. City people sometimes bring animals out to the country and dump them, figuring they can fend for themselves, or that someone will take them in. But he's actually pretty sweet. Great mouser."

"They leave them? Dogs and cats?" Cayenne was appalled. "That's terrible."

The mention of animals reminded me about the rooster that didn't crow. "This morning, you didn't hear anything? A car or truck? Glass breaking?"

Liz pressed her lips together. "I didn't want to say this in front of Joe Aguilar. Even though it's perfectly legal. But I've been having trouble sleeping—too much going on—so I took a gummy. Edible THC, for sleep. I was dead to the world."

Made sense. I hadn't tried the stuff myself, but plenty of people swore by it. The greenhouse was tucked away, not visible from the road or other farms, so it wasn't likely a neighbor had seen anything, though I was sure Aguilar and his deputies were asking. "If it wasn't this Orion Fisher, who was it?"

Liz shook her head. Then she poked her phone, bringing it to life. "Oh, man. The morning's almost gone. I've got to call my insurance agent. The glass company. Pipe supplier. Ventilation guy. And the Alliance is meeting this afternoon."

Time to go. Outside, with no sign of Sir, I let Arf off his leash and he sniffed up a storm. Liz gave us a brief tour, since it was Cayenne's first visit, pointing out the bee hives in one corner of the field, and the rustic benches and chairs where visitors could bask in the surroundings. Near the patch of new plants was a DIY outdoor photo booth, a purple Adirondack suitably positioned for picture-perfect vistas.

"A wedding photographer brought a couple out for an engagement photo shoot last weekend," Liz said. "Even without the plants in full bloom, it was so pretty, I nearly cried."

"On our way in," Cayenne said, "we saw signs hung on fences. Then one on your gate. 'Farms are for Farming.' What's that about?"

"Oh, a perennial tension in rural communities." Liz waved it off. "Happens all over. Farmland is pretty, farm towns are cute. People want to live there. But every subdivision destroys a farm and a way of life."

"'Weeding, Not Weddings'?" I quoted one of the signs.

"I give farm tours." Liz gestured toward the cottage. "I sell plants and flowers and almost anything you can make with lavender. But taking a working farm out of production and turning it into a wedding venue is completely different. Some farmers use chemicals, and they smell. Brides don't want fertilizer in the air on their big day. I tried to stay out of it, but I can't. The wrong kind of growth could interfere with—well, everything."

I clapped my leg and Arf came to heel, sitting to be hooked to his leash before we reached the greenhouse. A large area behind it had been cleared, all that remained a pile of brush.

12 · *Lavender Lies Bleeding*

"Don't go inside," she said, gesturing to the broken glass and the peat pots and seedlings that lay on the brick floor. "But you can see the pots and tubing. The steam extracts the aromatic oils out of the plants, then as it condenses and cools, separates the oil from the water. The lavender water is called hydrosol. I sell it, too."

"It's like a gardener's mad science lab," Cayenne said.

"It is kind of mad," Liz agreed. "The whole industry is evolving. There's no standardization in distilling or labeling, though the growers' association is working toward that."

It was a problem I knew well from sourcing herbs and spices.

"Thank goodness the cottage wasn't touched," Liz said as we followed her inside, where she scooped up a small knife that lay on the floor and tucked it into her pants pocket. She showed Cayenne a few of her products. "Lavender has three main uses—culinary, medicinal or aromatic, and decorative. I focus on the first, but I'd be a fool to ignore the others."

"If the greenhouse is a science lab, the cottage is a lavender fairyland." Cayenne pointed to the wall map, dotted with pushpins, a visitors' book open beneath it. "Look, Pepper. She tracks her visitors, like we have the map that shows where our spices come from."

Of course, ours also covers a crack in the plaster that no one's been able to fix.

"Every state and province except Vermont and Prince Edward Island," Liz said.

Outside, Arf nosed a stainless steel water bowl that lay upside down on the dirt path. I righted it.

"My dad would drool over that." I pointed to the gleaming purple Chevy. "And then he'd ask if you have to have a name that starts with L to run a lavender business."

We all laughed. It felt good. So did the sunshine, warming the flower buds and releasing their fragrance.

"Legally, I'm Mary Elizabeth, which is what my parents always called me. In school, I was Lizzie. But I like Liz."

It suited her. Short and to the point.

"You should come to the shop when we do our lavender festival," I said. "Be the resident expert for the day."

"I'd love that. Hold on," she said and dashed into the ruined greenhouse. Emerged not two minutes later holding a square peat pot with a gray-green seedling, a rounded mound about six inches across and just as tall. She held it out with both hands and I slipped Arf's leash from my hand to my wrist so I could take it.

Out of nowhere, Sir the cat appeared and rubbed against Cayenne's legs.

"Take care of this, Pepper," Liz said, her eyes finding mine, her voice solemn. "It's special."

A special piece of a special place. I took a deep breath, hoping its calming influence would soon be restored.

Three

In 1852, a newspaper in Olympia, the future territorial and state capital, ran an advertisement for a general store in the fledgling city to the north called the Seattle Exchange, named for the Duwamish chief. That marks the first appearance of the name Seattle in print, a far cry from the settlement's original moniker: Duwamps.

ON THE HUNT FOR EGGS, WE PULLED INTO THE FARMHOUSE driveway next to Liz's place.

"Cute," Cayenne said. "Or it will be, when they finish all this work. Wonder why the ex was willing to remodel with the second wife but not the first. Although I guess he and Liz weren't married."

"Nothing like hanging Sheetrock to test a relationship." The Saab's gears groaned as I shifted into park. "And if it wasn't that strong to begin with, might have been smart not to take on a project this size."

The house wasn't big—a story and a half, with a classic gable upstairs and a wide porch wrapping around the front and one side—but the job was huge. I could almost smell the sawdust. A new roof, deck, and siding. Modern windows, and no doubt major upgrades to the plumbing and electricity, all things I knew well after the build-out of my loft in an old cannery warehouse and tending

Leslie Budewitz · 15

to the Spice Shop. Both buildings date back more than a century. And maintaining the 1930's bungalow my ex and I had bought from his great-aunt. I wasn't kidding about Sheetrock. Living in that chaos with little kids? Eek.

Liz had told us TJ was at work, running the family's farm supply business, and it was Brooke's day to volunteer at the kids' preschool. With no humans around, the rooster had taken charge, perching on a stack of lumber. A pair of pretty black-and-white hens clucked as we climbed the porch steps and found the cooler filled with eggs. Cayenne oohed and ahhed over the rainbow colors. She has one of those faces where you can practically see her thinking.

"I'll buy," I said, "as long as you use some of those eggs to test recipes for the shop."

"Deal."

We picked up extras for staffers I knew would want them. I slipped cash into a bank envelope hidden beneath the cartons.

A good system for egg lovers. An easy target for a thief.

Back at the welded moose, we turned toward downtown Salmon Falls. Brightly colored flags and flower baskets hung on the streetlights. Outside nearly every shop and business, window boxes were in full bloom.

"I don't know about you," I said, "but I need lunch. We have plenty of time before meeting Sara to talk about festival stuff."

"I always need lunch," Cayenne said. "Now that I'm over the morning sickness, I'm hungry all the time."

No such excuse for me. I'd always wanted kids but spent my childbearing years with a man who hadn't been sure. By the time Tag was ready, my biological clock had run out. Though to give him credit, he had not immediately remarried and started a family after our divorce.

I parked the Saab across from the Lavender House B&B, a three-story brick Craftsman. Next to it, a café called Blossom beckoned.

We were seated at a table next to the tall windows, actually folding glass doors. Though the day was warm enough to sit outside, the inside chairs were comfier, a bonus for both of us. Antique chandeliers cast a warm glow over the wood and metal tables. One red brick wall held oversized photographs of lavender fields, the other

16 · *Lavender Lies Bleeding*

a display we weren't close enough to see. The early lunch crowd filled about half the seats, the chatter rising and falling.

"Wow," Cayenne said, perusing the two-sided, laminated menu. "Here I thought I'd gone herb-wild since working for you. They put herbs in *everything*."

Lavender goat cheese on crostini or in a panino. Lavender scones and shortbread. Lavender lattes, lavender Earl Grey tea, lavender limeade.

"Is a lavender latte supposed to calm you down or jazz you up?" I asked, not expecting an answer. I didn't get one.

Our server appeared, a young woman with smudged eyeliner and a dark blond side braid. Wisps of hair had come loose. I didn't need the name tag pinned to her purple-and-white ticking stripe apron to recognize her.

"Abby, hi. It's Pepper Reece, from the Spice Shop in Pike Place."

"Pepper! I knew I knew you, but couldn't come up with your name."

"We're out of context. Cayenne and I just came from the farm. Liz said you'd taken another job. She misses working with you."

"Not half as much as I miss working with her," Abby said. "Did you see—?"

"The damage? Yeah. It's bad."

She closed her eyes briefly, then forced a smile. "What can I bring you to drink?"

We both ordered the limeade, then watched Abby leave our table with a heavy step.

"I know we're here for festival ideas." Cayenne leaned forward. "But are we scouting for Spice Shop clients, too? I mean, look at this menu. They've got the lavender theme down, but they could use some variety."

"All in good time."

At the next table, two men were deep in an intense conversation— about business, to judge from their clothing and the leather portfolios that sat on the table, phones on top. And from one man's stern expression and the other's stiff back.

Abby delivered our drinks then waited, one hand gripping the other, almost strangling it. A pen and pad poked out of her apron pocket. Her gaze darted between us, as if unsure whose order to take first. Or was it more than that?

Leslie Budewitz · 17

"Ready to order? Everything here is good, I promise."

"The stuffed crepes, please," I said. "Topping them with lavender goat cheese sounds heavenly."

"My favorite." She turned to Cayenne.

"What's your second favorite? I love lavender, but . . ."

"Try the smoked salmon eggs Benedict. Our potatoes are roasted with lavender and rosemary. They're already cooked, so I can't ask for a substitution."

"That sounds great. And if the potatoes are too much, I'll give them to Pepper."

"I never met a potato I didn't love," I said. "This is Cayenne's first visit to Salmon Falls. We're planning a small lavender festival in the Market, so we're picking up ideas. Plenty of them in here." I gestured to our surroundings.

"Oh, Desiree's brilliant with the themes and decor," Abby said. "Desiree White, the owner. She owns the inn next door, too. B&B, whatever you want to call it."

"I love old buildings. I'd like to meet her, if she's around."

"No-o-o." Abby drew the word out. "She—no. I'll get this order in." She snatched up our menus and left.

"What did I say?" I asked my employee.

Cayenne's face made clear she didn't know. She'd pulled her long, black braids into a high ponytail today and the copper and silver beads in them reflected the light.

Our food came before we knew it. It was beautiful and I snapped a few quick photos. Customers often ask where we like to eat, and when we shine a spotlight on lavender, it would be great to name a few restaurants that use it well. Cayenne and Sandra, my assistant manager, were already cooking up recipes. My BFF's teenage daughters had taken up baking recently, and I hoped to entice them to test a few recipes.

But the proof is in the first bite. The crepes were thin but sturdy enough to hold the scrambled eggs, green onions, and mushrooms. And the lavender goat cheese—not too much—was divine. From Cayenne's expression as she tasted her eggs, it was clear that Blossom's kitchen was top-notch.

When our plates were empty—every last bite gone, including the roasted potatoes—another server came to clear our plates and ask what else she could bring us.

"Sorry about Abby," she said. "She's upset today. The manager sent her home."

"Oh, gosh. Sorry to hear that. I hope nothing's wrong."

"There was an incident outside of town. Sheriff came in asking questions, a few minutes before we opened."

"The damage to Liz Giacometti's greenhouse. We heard."

"They're blaming her boyfriend," the server said. "She's certain it's not him. But no one knows where he is."

"What's his name, if I can ask?"

"Orion. Orion Fisher."

WE RETURNED TO the Saab for Arf, then left the car where it was. Free on-street parking, a serious difference between big towns and small. We headed for our next appointment on foot. As in a lot of small towns, houses had been converted into law offices, insurance agencies, and retail shops, tucked in between newer buildings. A cottage next to Blossom held a real estate office.

Another, in the next block, held a gift shop called Purple Willow, although mercifully, the siding was a soft, buttery yellow. A window display caught Cayenne's eye. In a doll-sized white spindled crib, a purple teddy bear sat on a patchwork quilt done in white and shades of purple. 'Dream Bears' read a small chalkboard.

"Can we?" she asked. I nodded and looped Arf's leash through the rail, then followed her inside. Harp music drifted on the air.

While Cayenne all but drooled over the shop's baby clothes and quilts, I browsed. Lavender soap, lotion, salve. Lavender candles. Tins of lavender buds for cooking, and dried lavender wands. It wasn't all lavender. Some was calendula. Some was lavender and calendula.

"All our products are handcrafted by local artisans using locally grown herbs and flowers. I craft most of the soaps and lotions myself." The speaker was a sixty-ish woman with long gray curls, wearing a purple maxi dress and a floaty topper in shades of pink and violet shot with gold. If her stock of beaded necklaces ran low, she could sell half a dozen from around her neck and barely notice the difference.

Intricately quilted pillows filled an open trunk, reminding me of one I'd bought with my own money on a trip to the Market as a kid. It sat on the futon in my meditation space now.

Leslie Budewitz · 19

"Hmong," the shopkeeper said. "As are those baby caps with the coins and the embroidered women's clothing."

I fingered the coins, then picked up a pottery bowl that closely resembled Liz's coffee mugs. "How did Salmon Falls become the lavender capital of Washington state?"

"We've got the perfect climate. It's tough for small farms to compete in the major crops, like wheat and corn. Specialty crops like herbs and flowers and heirloom grains can be hard work, especially when it comes to developing markets, but they keep the jobs and the money close to home and keep the farmland productive. I'm Willow, by the way. Shop owner."

I remembered the signs—'Farms are for Farming.' "Just one of those tensions," Liz had said, her voice holding the same edge I detected in the shopkeeper's tone.

"I imagine the festival helps."

"To tell you the truth, by the time people wander through all the farm stalls and craft tents, then stop at the petting zoo and the kids' art booths at the park, the last thing they want to do is set foot in one more shop. But anything that boosts town boosts us. And I'm open all year." She pointed at the display of oils next to me. "Those oils are the best you'll find. Grown and distilled a stone's throw from here."

The yoga teacher whose classes I hardly ever get to had told me to try lavender oil in a diffuser or roll-on to ease my tension. Aromatherapy. I picked up a small roller bottle, Liz's logo on the label. "I'll take it."

"And I'll take this." Cayenne clutched one of the purple bears to her chest. "It's stuffed with lavender buds, for sweet dreams and a good night's sleep."

"For you or the baby?"

"You should try a lavender candle," the shopkeeper said. "Both of you. In Ayurvedic medicine, meditation often includes the practice of trataka. The student focuses on the flame of a candle, to focus the energy and quiet the mind."

My luck, I'd fall asleep and set off the smoke alarm.

Cayenne had the same thought. "Could you use a flameless candle? The battery-operated kind?"

"Oh, no. It must be a living, breathing thing. To dispel the storm clouds and calm the spirit."

We took two.

Four

"Variety is the spice of life."
—William Cowper (said "Cooper"),
English poet, 1731–1800

THE HEADQUARTERS OF THE SALMON FALLS LAVENDER Lovers' Association and Lavender Forever! Festival were located, aptly, in a tidy lavender bungalow with white trim at the edge of the business district. Flowers spilled out of window boxes. The tiny front yard, split by a concrete walkway, was bursting with herbs and flowers. A plant with bright green leaves and red stalks stood out, long red flower buds hanging down.

"Good dogs welcome," read a sign on the door.

Inside, a compact woman with shiny, shoulder-length black hair stood behind the reception counter, twisting the phone cord as she spoke. A landline, practically an endangered species, and certainly a surprise in the hands of a woman not yet thirty. She flashed us a welcoming smile and held up a finger. Then she spoke, in a language I recognized as Hmong from hearing the chatter of Hmong flower sellers and craftspeople in the Market. That's where we'd first met Sara Vu.

The office doubled as the town's tourist information center, and wall racks held brochures for activities and attractions all across the state. Fishing charters along the coast, kayak trips in the San

Leslie Budewitz · 21

Juan Islands, winery tours in the Horse Heaven Hills. Even the Batman celebration in Walla Walla, home of Adam West, the original Caped Crusader. While Cayenne browsed the racks, I studied the flyer for the Salmon Falls Lavender Festival.

Finally, Sara set the phone back in its cradle.

"My auntie," she said, fingering the silver coin that hung on a chain around her neck. Hmong, she'd told me once, though I didn't know its significance. "She wants me to look into a problem a friend of hers is having with her Social Security checks. I keep telling her, I'm busy. I have two jobs, with the festival and the association, and it's tourist season. 'You went to college,' she keeps saying, as if that makes me a social worker. Or a miracle worker."

"It's that business degree," Cayenne said. "To your auntie, that means you're good with money."

"I suppose you're right. Oops. Almost forgot." Sara plucked a dog cookie from a jar on the counter and held it up. Arf sat. She palmed it, then held it out. Like magic, it was gone.

"Sara, before we talk, there's a curious plant in the garden. Can you tell me what it is?"

We stepped outside and I pointed.

"Oh, that's *Amaranthus caudatus.* Love-lies-bleeding. By midsummer, those flowers will look like giant tassels. They're edible, and they dry beautifully."

"The flower ladies taught you well," I said, glancing at Sara. Her eyes had narrowed, her dark expression aimed over my shoulder. I followed her gaze. One of the men we'd seen in the café passed by on the sidewalk.

"Not a friend, I take it?"

"Jeffrey White." She brushed the air with her hand, dismissing her irritation—and my question—as she opened the door.

Hadn't Abby said Desiree White owned Blossom? A couple? White's a common name, but Salmon Falls is a small town. We followed Sara inside.

"Town is so cute." Cayenne settled into a purple tweed chair in Sara's office.

I took the matching chair while Sara sat behind her desk. Arf lay down beside me, resting his big head on his golden-brown paws.

Who's a good boy?

22 · *Lavender Lies Bleeding*

"Things have changed," Sara said. "Not everybody's happy about it."

One more way town was like the Market.

We asked about each other's families. Sara's grandmother still puttered around the family flower farm on the edge of Salmon Falls, but had stopped coming into Seattle, the long days picking, packing, and selling seasonal bouquets finally too much. Her parents had other jobs, but her aunties—both biological and honorary—were Market mainstays, and Sara often pitched in.

"We were out at Liz's farm," I said. "You heard about the vandalism?"

"I can hardly believe it," Sara said. "Nothing like that's ever happened here. At least not that I've heard. I'm new to running the association and festival—two years this winter—but we moved to Salmon Falls when I was a kid. And this office is practically gossip central. Not that I encourage it, but talk comes with the territory."

"You know Liz," I said. "She has two speeds—fast and faster. She'll have that place back together in no time."

"Before the sheriff has a clue what happened," Cayenne said. "She's that smart."

Sara looked from me to my staffer and back, then changed the subject. "Out here, lavender is the theme, though we have plenty of other farms and businesses. Lavender brings people to town, and that gives us a chance to feed them, house them, and sell them things they didn't know they wanted. Provide experiences, like farm tours."

"I was wondering about events," I said. "Farms can host—"

Footsteps in the outer room interrupted me. Sara rose. "Be right back."

I gathered that the visitor was asking about last-minute accommodations. Sara suggested a couple of options, then a few nearby attractions. "Make sure you go to Blossom for afternoon tea. It's not to be missed."

"No volunteer today," she said when the woman had left and she'd rejoined us. "The art center, the historical museum—we've all got the same problem. Most volunteers are older and retired, and when the pandemic hit, they cut back their social contact. Understandable, but a lot of them haven't returned."

Leslie Budewitz · 23

"You mentioned a couple of B&Bs. Which do you recommend?" Maybe Nate and I could sneak out here for a midweek getaway. My weekends would be spoken for until fall.

"Depends on the experience you're after. Poppy is out in the country. Lavender House is here in town. Desiree White owns it—she runs Blossom, too. You'd think that would be enough."

"More than enough for me," I said. "But then, here I am starting a new festival in a Market packed with them."

"Community buy-in is critical," Sara said, back in professional mode. "Remember you have to go beyond highlighting the herb and selling products. Offer hands-on stuff. A DIY perfumery. A make-and-take herb garden in a pot. Cooking classes."

Cayenne and I exchanged a quick smile, still basking in the aromatic glow of our first cooking class, focused on Italian food, a few weeks ago. Customers were clamoring for a repeat. We lacked space, so classes required a restaurant partner, but that would be easy to arrange.

"Kids' activities," Sara continued. "Can you do goat rides? Kids love making things. Cookies or sachets."

"Or their own dream pillows," Cayenne suggested.

"You must have stopped at Purple Willow," Sara said. "Willow is obsessed with dream pillows, for moms and babies. She hasn't homed in on expectant fathers yet, but when she does, don't try stopping her."

"Is that her real name?" Cayenne asked.

"Around here, you never know. For your first year, I'd focus on the farm to table angle. Farm to fork. That's the Market in a nutshell, right?"

"Right," I said. "A lot of customers are surprised to hear that you can cook with lavender. They think of it for the scent. We've been recruiting a mix of merchants and craftspeople to highlight different culinary uses, as well as the fragrance and decorative aspects."

"Great. Joint events give each participant the chance to leverage their marketing. Some people fear competition, but I see it as expanding your reach."

"That's what you always say," Cayenne said to me.

For the next few minutes, Sara tossed out more ideas. She knew what worked and what didn't. The Market connection gave us a

24 · *Lavender Lies Bleeding*

bond. Smart and savvy, she'd been learning from our vendors and merchants. Now it was our chance to learn from her.

"Come out for the next festival committee meeting," she continued. "Tuesday, week after next."

"Are you sure? No one will mind an interloper?" Especially one with her own festival dreams.

"I'm sure. And if anyone complains, I'll remind them that you're not the only Market business that buys herbs and produce in Salmon Falls."

Not until we were on our way out did I remember that I hadn't asked about the signs. Farms for farming, not teacups and weddings. Later.

I had an idea I was going to be spending a lot of time in Salmon Falls.

Five

> The first automobile arrived in Seattle in 1900. In 1904, a daylong traffic count tallied fourteen automobiles downtown—along with 3,945 horse-drawn vehicles.

"I NEED AN ANTIDOTE SMELL," CAYENNE SAID WHEN WE WERE back in the car. "Too much lavender."

"No such thing," I said. "Not in Salmon Falls. Salmon were money once. Now lavender is the cash crop."

Even though lunch hadn't worn off, we'd stopped at a bakery. We'd poked our noses into galleries and boutiques. Now, I drove slowly down Main Street, past businesses we hadn't yet explored. More cafés and coffee shops. A pub called the Draught House, where a team of sturdy horses painted on the side of the building pulled a wagon loaded with sheaves of wheat. At a turn-of-the-last-century stone bank, construction crews cut boards on sawhorses set up on the sidewalk.

Next to Lavender House Bed and Breakfast was a glorious garden tucked behind a weathered picket fence. In the back of the large corner lot stood an old stucco garage, with one of those tilt-up doors, the kind you raise and slide on runners. A chalkboard listed flower and vegetable prices, a black metal mailbox with a slot on top mounted beside it.

26 · *Lavender Lies Bleeding*

"A community garden?" I asked. "Where you pay on the honor system?"

"That's my guess," Cayenne said. "Wonder what happened to that garage. See all the char?"

She was right. Hollyhocks didn't quite hide the black soot staining the stucco wall. Had there been a fire? Curious.

We doubled back and cruised down the main drag. For midweek early in tourist season, town was pleasantly busy. Afternoon tea at Blossom appeared to be a major draw. I saw our substitute server delivering a tiered stand to a sidewalk table. No sign of Abby. I hoped the visitor Sara had steered to the B&B had taken her suggestion and was now happily enjoying scones and tea.

Next door, a big wooden sign advertised Salmon Falls Realty and Property Management. A small red-and-white sign reading 'Sold by Jeffrey!' angled across it. Jeffrey White. Why had no one commandeered that vacant lot for development? Vacant, if you didn't count the carrots and onions.

"There's so much we can do," Cayenne was saying. "I know. Keep the focus on the food. No dream bears or Ayurvedic candles. We use lavender in our herbes de Provence, and Joy's blueberry lavender Syrup is always a hit. I'd like to try making another spice blend with lavender. What would you think of an herbed lemon pepper?"

"Sounds great." I hated to stifle her brainstorming—she was so good at it. "But I thought you were lavendered out." I could relate. Our eggs and other finds were all safely stowed in the trunk, but the smell permeated the car. Probably from all the lotions and potions we'd tried, not to mention herbs in almost everything we'd eaten.

"It'll pass." She clapped her hands lightly, undaunted by my caution. "This is going to be fun."

Her joy made me smile. I love my job.

Just before the welded moose stood Manning Farm Supply, bags of compost and fertilizer stacked out front next to rows of cultivators and mulchers and other machines I couldn't identify. Liz's ex's family business? Thriving, by the looks of it.

We were almost back to the highway when we passed a man on a blue bicycle, black hair flopping as he rode, a German shepherd on a leash trotting beside him. Cycling is common out here—we'd

Leslie Budewitz · 27

passed a few helmeted cyclists in tight black shorts and DayGlo yellow shirts on the farm roads, and bike racks on the town sidewalks signaled a welcome. But this man wore olive drab work pants and sneakers, a worn army pack on his back. Homeless? A retrohippie throwback? The dog was slender but appeared healthy. I glanced in the rearview, catching a glimpse as I did of my own dog. Arf was sitting up, staring out the window silently. Did he remember that he and Sam had been homeless together for a while? Tricks of his—like a word association that had led him to save a child and then take down a fleeing scumbag, or his habit of letting out a small yip when he needed to go outside—came from training, not memory. But I had little doubt that the sight of a man in fatigues with a dog beside him stirred something deep in Arf's canine soul.

As if telling me I'd guessed right, he placed his front paws on the console and rested his head on them. I gave him a quick pat. "Good dog, Arf. Good dog."

The Saab sputtered as I pushed it toward highway speed. It had given me trouble all spring, and while my boyfriend Nate had tinkered with the engine, I'd finally taken it to a real mechanic. The verdict had not been good. But I hadn't had time to go car shopping, or figure out how to pay for a new car.

The rest of the drive, Cayenne and I tossed ideas back and forth, about lavender, the monthly cooking classes we hoped to start in the fall, and other spicy doings. I was grateful to see her taking on more responsibility and leadership. But she had a baby on the way, and an illness with symptoms that came and went. Her plans were in flux, which meant mine were, too.

Such is life in retail. Such is life, period.

THE SPICE SHOP is my happy place. Honestly, despite the nickname Pepper, bestowed by my grandfather Reece when I was four, I never imagined that my purpose in life would be running a retail shop serving up herbs and spices. I'd been coming to the Market with my mother since before I could remember, and when my life fell apart at forty, after the ink dried on the divorce papers, the loft purchase agreement, and my law firm severance package—well, I became a spice dealer. No one but my mother and Kristen, my BFF, had thought it was a good idea. Happily, they both have excellent judgment, even if I don't always want to admit it.

28 · *Lavender Lies Bleeding*

"The spice scouts returneth!" Kristen cried as Arf and I crossed the threshold. I'd dropped Cayenne off at home on Seattle's Beacon Hill—no point making her come to the shop for an hour or two—then stashed the Saab in merchant parking. Kristen had worked here part-time since I bought the place, sharing moral support and her retail experience.

The aroma is one of the first things first-timers comment on when they walk in. Me, I was grateful to see and smell something besides purple: The rich yellow of turmeric. The deep oranges and reds of the paprikas, chiles, and sumac. The pungent Tellicherry black pepper that Vanessa, our youngest staffer, was grinding fresh for a customer. We sell grinders, but not everyone has the need or space.

Arf padded to his bed behind the front counter—he's got another in my office. Market management tolerates well-behaved dogs, as long as they stay out of trouble and largely out of sight. I tucked my bag and Liz's plant in the tiny back office and grabbed my apron. Black, our shop logo on the bib—a shaker sprinkling salt into the ocean waves. I designed it myself.

"Do I reek of lavender?" I asked no one in particular. "I've been surrounded by it all day."

"Lucky you," a customer said.

"And you," I said. "Some of the daystallers and merchants, including us, are going all in on lavender in a few weeks. Spice blends, tastings, recipes."

"Sweet," she said, then we chatted about the gift sets she was debating for her sister. I asked about preferred flavors and cooking style. She made her choice, then added a jar of Puget Sound sea salt to her basket. "I can't let her have all the fun, can I?"

That's what I love to hear.

After the woman left, I stood behind the counter, surveying my domain. It's a treat for the eyes as well as the nose and tongue. Spice jars line the wall behind the counter. Artful displays fill every spare space. In the back corner sits a fabulous red Chinese apothecary stuffed with bags and boxes of tea, along with tea pots and accessories. A vintage rolling cart parked near the front counter holds the electric samovar we use to brew our signature spice tea. Nearly every customer takes a sample cup. We'd soon switch from hot tea to iced. More work for us, but anything that sells spice is worth the effort.

I hadn't made a lot of changes since buying the shop two and a half years ago, although I had expanded our supply network. The map Cayenne had mentioned hung on the front wall. It was great to see so many pins clustered around Puget Sound, representing growers within a hundred miles of the shop.

We'd also grown our book selection from a handful of spice and herb references to a full-fledged cookbook section, along with chef lit and food-related fiction. The books were Kristen's domain.

"For you," I told her, handing over my Salmon Falls finds, *The Lavender Lover's Handbook* and *Discover Cooking with Lavender.* "We had lunch at a darling place that put lavender in almost everything. Cayenne spent half the drive home on her phone, scouring menus for even more ideas. The smell was getting to her, but I bet that won't stop her from baking up a storm tonight. Oh, I almost forgot. I have farm eggs for you."

"Hey, Pepper," Vanessa said. "When I was making the deliveries this morning, I heard some news. The guy who runs the import shop in Post Alley is retiring, the one with all the silver jewelry you like. His daughter is taking over."

"I'm amazed he's hung on this long. He's one of the tenants from the hippy wave, back in the seventies." The merchants, young and idealistic, who'd seen an opportunity when the voters approved saving the Market from the bulldozer in 1971. Jane, who'd opened the Spice Shop and ran it until I came along, had been another. "We'll miss him."

"You won't miss him at the merchants' association meetings," Kristen said.

"Truth to that. But where would we be without our curmudgeons?"

"Some of the new craftspeople are doing cool stuff," Vanessa added. My smart, sweet, young staffer had become my eyes and ears since taking over morning deliveries. "There's a fused glass artist. A guy who draws people on the spot. And a woman who upscales old fabric into adorable plushies. I kinda want one."

It's great to be surrounded by so much creativity, despite the constant temptation to take too much of it home. A committee reviews applications from new artists and craftspeople, inspecting work and making studio visits, to make sure both quality and quantity measure up. Is the product unique? Will it appeal to Market goers? Can the artist handle the steady flow of foot traffic, work well with others, and interact with the public, staff, and other vendors day in and day out without losing their marbles?

"Speaking of the daystallers," I said. "Seen any more of Logan?" The pushy young man the older staffers and I had dubbed Logan the Love Bomber last spring, when he'd pestered her for weeks.

A flush rose on Vanessa's cheeks and she shook her head, one space bun beginning to unravel. "He mostly ignores me, which is fine. I think he's dating one of the cashiers from the Italian grocery, but I've also seen him flirting with the baristas in Starbucks."

"Up to his same old tricks then," Kristen said. "Which is fine, until someone gets hurt."

Vanessa pressed her lips together. The space bun loosened further, a tendril falling down the side of her face. She brushed it out of the way, then rushed to the restroom in back to fix her hair. And compose herself.

"Careful," I told Kristen. "That whole situation brought out the Universal Mother in all of us, but we agreed we need to let her handle it herself. And those other young women aren't our responsibility."

"I know. But the older my own girls get, the harder it gets. I'm missing the days when they were more interested in plushies and doll clothes than makeup and boys."

"What are they planning for your birthday?" In ten days, followed two weeks later by my own. She's blond and pretty and softhearted, and I'm, well, spiky, like my short dark hair. My brother says I style it by sticking my finger in the light socket, but even that seems like too much work. Just wash, run my fingers through it, and go.

"I told them they could make me dinner and a cake, but to keep their focus on wrapping up the school year. Can you believe we're almost forty-four?"

I could not.

As often happens late in the week, we were hit by a last-minute rush. Downtown workers swing by on their way home, shopping for the weekend. Then it was time to lock up. Vanessa helped me bring in the metal rack of herb seedlings from the sidewalk. It was looking sparse, the season about done.

"Hey, now that the customers are gone," I said to the staff. "Let me tell you what happened to Liz." I described the vandalism to the greenhouse and distillery. "She's okay, physically, and determined not to let it set her back. But it's pretty upsetting."

"And the sheriff has no idea who's behind it?" Sandra, my assistant manager, asked. Today's cheaters, in vibrant red, hung on a rainbow Pride strap she'd bought from a Market artist.

"He seemed to think a fellow who works for her occasionally might be responsible." I told them what little I knew about Orion Fisher. "She insists it couldn't possibly be him, but who else, she can't imagine."

"How can we help her?" Vanessa asked.

"Buy and sell lots of lavender," I said. "Make our mini fest a maxi success."

We zipped through closing and the staff left, the bells on the door chiming behind them. My boyfriend Nate and his brother Bron had returned from Alaska where they fish much of the year, planning to fish closer to home until fall. Tonight, they were going to a Mariners game with a group of guys, a bachelor party for a former crew member who was getting married this weekend. That left Arf and me on our own for the evening. Time to catch up on some paperwork in my office.

Liz's lavender plant was taking up precious real estate. I carried it out front to the nook, the built-in table and benches where we hold staff meetings or take a quick breather. Customers occasionally sit there, too, nursing a cup of tea, and that's fine by me.

"What's so special about you?" I asked the gift plant. "What's your secret?"

But it wasn't talking.

Six

> In the Market's early years, farmers sought easier access from the waterfront, where goods were delivered, up the hill to the stalls and shops on Pike Place. That led to a system of ramps that later became the Market's lower levels, known collectively as "Down Under."

"HOW CAN YOU BE SO LIVELY SO EARLY IN THE MORNING? What time did you get in?"

"Mmm." Nate kissed the hollow between my shoulder and collarbone. "You smell like lavender. Not that late. We're all old fishermen. Early to bed, early to rise."

"I was all about the lavender yesterday. And you're not that old." Not quite a year and a half older than me, Nate had turned forty-five last winter. He smelled a bit like beer mixed with fish and diesel. Sounds worse than it was.

After a takeout dinner and a dog walk, I'd attempted the meditation technique Willow at the gift shop had described, without much success. I hadn't gotten very far before the effects of the day's lavender exposure took over, and I'd fallen asleep around ten, the baseball game on the radio and a book in hand. One of Deanna Raybourn's Veronica Speedwell mysteries set in Victorian England. The adventurous sleuth's name—combining the Latin and common

Leslie Budewitz · 33

names for the same plant—always makes me laugh, and I wish I had half her energy. I'd barely heard Nate come into the loft and slip into bed beside me.

I noticed him now. There's a particular sweetness about making love in the morning, though I had to resist the temptation to slide back into sleep afterwards. I had a shop to run.

But I had a life, too, even though they sometimes seem like the same thing.

"Hard to believe Javier's getting married," Nate said after we'd showered and dressed and met in the kitchen by the coffee pot. Arf and I had already taken a quick spin around the block so he could relieve himself, and the dog now lay on his bed, working on a rawhide chew bone. "Last guy I'd have thought would tie the knot."

"Why? He seems genuinely crazy about Mindy, and she about him." Javier had crewed for Nate and Bron for years. Now he did finish carpentry and ran a construction crew, mainly at the winery Mindy's family owned. Its Eastside tasting room was the ideal wedding venue.

"Oh, he is. Let's just say he enjoyed the single life. You know, work hard, play hard." Nate took a bite of the eclair I'd set out for him. "Where did you get this? Best thing I've eaten in weeks."

"Better than a chili dog at the ballpark and a beer too many? In Salmon Falls." Between sips of coffee and bites of chocolate eclair with lavender cream filling, I reported the day's doings, including the damage to Liz's greenhouse.

"How much of an impact will it have on her business?"

"Hard to tell. Normally, she'd have everything planted by now, and she won't need the distillery until later in the season. But she had a greenhouse full of seedlings."

"Well, I hope the sheriff can get to the bottom of it quickly. With a name like Salmon Falls, it sounds like my kind of town."

"Cayenne had eggs Benedict with smoked salmon. She gave me a bite—you'd have loved them. Town is cute. Not sure I could live there, though. Everybody knows everything about everyone, or thinks they do."

"And that's different from the Market how?"

He had a point. Cram more than seventy-five farmers, two hundred shops and restaurants, two hundred craftspeople known

34 · *Lavender Lies Bleeding*

as daystallers, a score or more of buskers ranging from musical trios to balloon artists, plus nearly five hundred residents, into nine acres and you've got a small town within a big city. Add in ten million visitors a year, and the inevitable tensions occasionally boil over. But the joys and delights magnify, too.

"I've got eight, maybe ten, businesses willing to focus on lavender for a long weekend in mid-June."

"Isn't that early?"

"Yes, but our goal is to whet customers' appetites. We're not offering the experience of a field in full bloom. And we have to work around the Market schedule. If all goes well, I hope the PDA will take it over and put on a full-scale festival in a year or two." The Preservation and Development Authority, the Market manager, landlord, and party planner.

I wiped a bit of lavender cream from the corner of Nate's mouth with one finger. That led to other things, and before long, I had to rush to get to work. One more kiss for my human guy, then my canine guy and I headed out into the brisk morning air.

THE MAY FLOWERS were in full bloom in the Main Arcade. Twice a week, I buy flowers for the shop. Tuesday, I'd picked up red and yellow roses and creamy calla lilies from the florist at First and Pike, so starting today, my plan was to work my way down the line, buying from each of the flower ladies in turn.

"Peonies, Miss Pepper," the veteran flower seller who had the corner spot said. She held out a bouquet wrapped in newspaper. "Your favorite."

"They're all my favorites, Pengchi. Can we mix in some variety?"

The old woman nodded vigorously and got to work, opening the paper cone and splitting the bundle of peonies—white, pale pink, and deep rose—in two. Deftly, she added purple and yellow lupine, spiky liatris, and white lilies. In moments, I had an armful of spring and a smile on my face.

Okay, so I'd already been smiling, but now I had another reason.

Pengchi pulled a dog biscuit out of her apron pocket and handed it to Arf, who downed it in one bite.

A woman in a blue rubber apron bustled up to me, her dark head barely reaching my shoulder. "Oh, good, Miss Pepper, I catch you," Cua Vang said.

Leslie Budewitz · 35

"Hey, Cua. I saw Sara yesterday, in Salmon Falls," I said. "She was a big help, giving us ideas to celebrate lavender here in the Market."

"A good girl, my sister's granddaughter. Smart." She tapped the side of her head with one finger. Beneath her apron, she wore her customary flowered shirt and plaid pants. "She work hard to get us what we need, what was lost, and now all this—"

Before she could finish, two other flower sellers began barking at each other. Cua rolled her eyes, then explained. "Cart go missing again. We don't find, hard to move our buckets. We leave it out, PDA fine us."

I vaguely recalled a fuss about carts the vendors used disappearing, then being found where they shouldn't be.

The little woman shook a finger in my face. "You help her. You are a good lady. You help her."

Help Sara? With what? She hadn't mentioned any problems, beyond the loss of volunteers and concern over the damage to Liz's place. What did her auntie know that I didn't?

"Cua, what's going on?"

But between the spat about the cart and the arrival of early shoppers, each woman eager to vie for their attention, the moment for confiding was lost. Truth is, most of the sellers grow the same flowers, so there isn't much difference. Not that I would ever say so.

I let myself into the shop, juggling the bouquets, my tote bag, and Arf's leash. We wriggled around the rack of seedlings. Time to get rid of them, after this weekend. Arf stretched out in a patch of sunshine dappling the wood floor. I stored my things and arranged the flowers, one vase on the front counter and another in the nook. Then the staff began to arrive.

"Spotted a pair of cruise ships coming into Pier 66," Sandra said as she tied her apron strings. "Get your roller skates on."

Vanessa squinted, confused.

"Meaning we'll be extra busy," I said. This would be Vanessa's first tourist season in Seattle. I circled my wrist with the fingers of my other hand. "Cruise shippers usually wear colored wrist bands. They buy packaged goods, not pure spice. Lots of tea and gift sets. No liquids—most of them are flying home. They love anything with Puget Sound or Seattle or the Market in the name."

36 · *Lavender Lies Bleeding*

She nodded, a quick study.

As I'd predicted, Cayenne had put both the lavender and the fresh eggs to good use, bringing in a tray of mini cupcakes, both cake and icing delicately flavored with lavender. If I hadn't eaten that eclair with my morning coffee, I'd have had two.

"How can I top that?" Sandra said.

"No idea, but I can hardly wait to find out." Their friendly rivalry had produced a lot of good eating, and some seriously good recipes to share with customers. That reminded me to check our supply to see if we needed to reprint any of our spring favorites. I sent Arf to his bed and unlocked the front door. Time to get spicy.

I was refilling the recipe racks with copies of our ever-popular Creamy Asparagus Soup with Cumin and our Four-Ingredient Asparagus Tart when the phone in my pocket buzzed. No chance to sneak a peek as a customer approached, a gift box holding three jars of spice in hand.

"Excuse me. What's the difference between Syrian and Israeli za—how do you say it?"

"Za'atar," I said, noticing the telltale wristband poking out from her jacket cuff. "Say it with a slight stop between the first two A's. Both have white sesame seeds, sumac, and a touch of salt, but we vary the other spices. I love it on flatbread, with roasted vegetables, or as a dry rub on meats."

"Which is your favorite?"

"Oh, that's like choosing between my right hand and my left. But I'll confess a slight preference for the Syrian blend. Great on popcorn when I'm home alone."

She was sold.

A few minutes later, I poured a cup of our spice tea and sat in the nook to check my messages.

From Nate: *Love you, little darlin'!*

My mother: *Remember, brunch on Sunday!*

And one from Liz. As predicted, she was already knee deep in reconstruction, taking a break this afternoon to pick up copper pipe in the semi-industrial part of the city called SoDo. She'd be downtown after that and would stop to see me at three thirty. Typical of my no-nonsense vendor and friend, already on top of the details.

Once Vanessa returned from her deliveries, I took Arf for a quick walk, then took the stairs Down Under to talk to my co-conspirators,

Leslie Budewitz · 37

mindful of the risks of ramps on rainy days. The ramps date back to the Market's early years, the treads now well protected by nonskid strips. One exception was the narrow cattle ramp, unknown to most of the public, but Jerry the butcher had suffered a nasty fall on it a few weeks earlier, a caution to the rest of us.

First stop, the chocolate shop.

"Lavender truffles," Mary Jean, aka the Chatty Chocolatier, said when I asked if she still planned to participate in the festival. She's a fair-skinned redhead, half a foot shorter than me, and twice as talkative. "That's another word for yes."

Two words, but any time Mary Jean cuts it short, count yourself lucky.

Not that she cut it short for long. "I'm thinking we should have at least two other special items. We did pretzel sticks dipped in white chocolate with peppermint at Christmas, and a bride asked us to do them in lavender white chocolate for a wedding shower. We dressed them up with silver sugar, silver pearls, and chocolate drizzle. What about those?"

"They sound wonderful. You'll sell squillions."

"From your mouth to God's ears. That week will mark my second year in the Market, so we'll offer free samples to celebrate. I'm thinking of chocolate bark with lavender."

Two years for Mary Jean. My pal Vinny the Wine Merchant was celebrating twenty-five years with an expansion. Not to mention the comings and goings Vanessa had reported. Change was all around us.

"Lavender? In chocolate? Count me out." The protest came from a customer standing by a display of chocolate-covered fruit. "I know it's all the rage, but florals do not belong in food."

"Rose water is a common ingredient in Indian cooking. Middle Eastern cooks use both rose and orange blossom water," I said. "And chamomile tea is a popular fix for sleepless nights."

"Lavender tastes like soap," she said. "And that's where it belongs." She set down the box of chocolate-covered cherries she'd been holding and marched out.

"Sorry I cost you a sale," I said to Mary Jean.

"She wasn't going to buy anything. You can tell."

True enough. Different people react differently to flavors and scents. Some are allergic. Some people, bless them, can't stand the

38 · *Lavender Lies Bleeding*

smell of coffee. That leaves more for me. If we all liked the same thing, my shop would be very small. Our challenge, and I'm always up for it, is to help people find other options when a recipe calls for an ingredient that disagrees with them.

"For you," Mary Jean said, handing me a box of truffle rejects. She covered a yawn with the back of her hand. "Sorry. Didn't sleep well last night. By the way, the lower leg of your pants is covered with dog fur."

And so it was.

I waved goodbye. Mary Jean's comment about not sleeping well reminded me of Liz saying she'd taken a THC gummy before bed and hadn't heard a peep. That was one way to get a sound sleep.

The cheesecake baker was on board. The French bakery was planning lavender macarons. The two soap makers I'd recruited were all in.

I stopped at the deli in the Triangle Building to order lunch, then sat to watch the world go by. The Market is the definition of small business, from one-woman daystalls to family-owned operations to the group of buddies who banded together to buy the fish market where they'd all met. The pandemic had hit small businesses hard, at the same time as it had given some a boost. More people valued homegrown goods, and more people were cooking. But corporate shopping, much of it online, had grown, too. We were not out of the woods. I aimed for building resilience through diversification— the seedlings and books, our quarterly spice club and the wedding registry, and now cooking classes with a focus on spice. We'd expanded our commercial clientele—restaurants and food producers—and grown our mail-order business. Festivals were another way we Market merchants and vendors set ourselves apart. Shopping with us is a different experience. You can't get a free flower on Daffodil Day or an instant rub-on skeleton tattoo at Halloween when you shop online.

My lunch order was ready. As I crossed Pine on my way back to the shop, I saw the white canopies set up on the cobbles of Pike Place. I popped in the side door, let the staff know lunch had arrived, and slipped out the way I'd come.

In addition to the high stall produce sellers, who occupy permanent storefronts, and the daystallers with their specialty products, individual farmers are invited to set up tents during the season and

Leslie Budewitz · 39

sell on the cobblestones. Fruit and veg picked that morning, so fresh it's practically still growing.

Today, a farmer with baby spinach and other early crops had teamed up with a juicer to blend juices and smoothies to order. I accepted a taster cup of carrot-spinach juice and took a sip. Earthy, bright, and utterly refreshing. We're used to carrots raw or cooked, or even in cake, but to people raised on fruit juice, getting juice from a root vegetable seems weird at first.

A bit like first encountering a floral scent as a flavor. For some, it's intriguing. For others, it's off-putting. Depends on your mouth's sense of adventure.

This farmer was a regular, from up north, but there was a chance he'd know what was going on in Salmon Falls. One of the many upsides of working in the Market is the variety of fresh, seasonal foods that make spur-of-the-moment menu planning easy.

"How about two pounds of spinach and two of strawberries?" I said. "I've got a red onion and feta. Make a vinaigrette and voila! Salad!" Perfect with the salmon Nate planned to grill tonight.

"Two pounds of spinach will make a lot of salad," he said, throwing handfuls of greens onto the scale.

I thought of those farm eggs I'd brought home. "And a quiche. Hey, I have a question." I told him about the signs we'd seen on our field trip. "The usual stuff, or is trouble brewing?"

"Oh, who knows?" he said. "Small farms have always been the lifeblood of towns like ours. People love the charm, but sometimes it seems like all the love could kill us."

A complaint I'd heard down here more than once.

"Farmers are supposed to be salt of the earth, honest, hard-working, and all that, and most of us are," he continued. "But that doesn't mean there aren't a few who get their kicks slinging mud, especially when our way of life is threatened."

Humans, as my ex-husband the cop likes to say, with a roll of his eyes. No matter where we live or what kind of work we do, people are people.

Seven

Lavender is a member of the mint family, along with savory herbs like thyme, rosemary, and oregano.

I TOOK MY LUNCH INTO THE BACK ROOM, UPDATING OUR social media and responding to email while I ate. Then Kristen and I headed down to the Atrium, the open area in the Economy Market. There we met a rep from the PDA to figure out how much space and how many tables we'd need for the lavender crafts and other activities. I put my trusty measuring tape to good use, and a few minutes later we were back on the cobblestones, Kristen making a list of supplies on her phone as we walked.

"Kristen!" a woman called.

Though we've known each other literally all our lives, our circles have expanded over the years, and I did not know this pretty brunette in the black rain jacket. Kristen made introductions.

"My husband sells commercial espresso machines," Monica Salter said to me, gesturing with the bag in her hand. "A part that was supposed to be shipped directly to an owner came to us instead. Scott's out of town, so I'm filling in. Five-minute install and the customer will be back to perfect cappuccino every time."

"Music to my ears."

She flapped a hand in front of her face. "That horse smell. Gets me every time."

Leslie Budewitz · 41

Horses abounded in the Market in its early years, and to this day, some people swear they can smell horses near the entrance. Some call it a ghostly warning; others call it nonsense. I've never detected an equine presence, but occasionally Arf stops at this very spot for a mighty sniff and I've wondered if that's what he's picking up.

"You own the Spice Shop?" Monica continued. "Lucky you. We lived out in the country, but sometimes my mother would fill in for a friend of hers, selling produce here. When I came with her, she'd turn me loose. I always stopped for sample tea."

"Me, too," I said. "Now I get to help other people make those memories."

The three of us began walking up Pike Place. I spotted Cua watching us from the flower tables and waved, wondering if they'd found the missing cart.

"Pretty day," Monica said. "Though I guess it did rain this morning. Any excuse to wear that gorgeous coat." She wagged her eyebrows playfully at Kristen.

"You know it," Kristen replied. She likes colorful clothing and has the budget to indulge her stylish taste, like the red and orange fingertip-length coat she wore today. No one commented on mine, best described as sporty and well worn.

"Oh, there's Liz," I said as we neared the shop and I saw the lavender grower walking in. "I've got to run. Nice to meet you, Monica." Monica looked surprised by my sudden departure, but I dashed ahead, not bothering to explain.

Inside the shop, I glanced at the vintage railway clock by the front door. Liz was right on time. I watched her inhale deeply.

"You know," she said a moment later, skipping hello, "the sense of smell is so underappreciated. Some people think what I do is frivolous, that no one needs lavender. Maybe not, but taste and smell are deeply connected to our full experience of life."

Unusual to hear my practical friend wax poetic. "It's a sense people don't always appreciate, unless they lose it," I said. "So what brings you into town, besides pipe?" Liz was wearing a hiking skirt, hoodie, and hiking sandals. Not important-city-meeting clothes.

"Business meetings."

Shows what I know.

"Can we talk somewhere? Private-ish? I'm desperate for a cup of coffee, but not Starbucks, please. Too crowded."

42 · *Lavender Lies Bleeding*

The original Starbucks in the Market sits near us on Pike Place. It was not the very first Starbucks ever, though people often think so. That opened in 1971 a block north of the official Market boundary, kitty-corner from Victor Steinbrueck Park, named for the architect credited with saving the Market. When demolition forced the mermaid out a few years later, the grinders and steamers moved into the Market where they'd been attracting coffee tourists every day since. Close enough for good PR.

"I know just the place," I said.

A few minutes later, we slid into a booth on the top floor of the Corner Market at First and Pike. Liz took the seat against the wall, giving me a view of the famous red neon clock and sign. It's the same view I get from the front window of my shop, and it never gets old.

Never.

Eager as she'd seemed to talk, now she'd gone quiet. Contemplative. Could have been the influence of the warm wood glow, accentuated by the pendant lights, their Edison bulbs adding a spark of scientific intrigue. The space had once been a fancy restaurant, and in an earlier incarnation, a drop-in center for people struggling with mental illness. Around us now sat mothers and kids. A table full of students, phones out, laptops open. Business people. Coffee, conversation, contemplation.

A French press sat on the table between us. Judging the brew ready, I poured.

"I'm not letting this stop me," Liz said.

"No reason you should. Setbacks are part of doing business."

"I'm not sure the bankers understand," she said. "Though I laid it out the best I could."

"I'm sure every commercial lender on the job more than ten minutes has helped a customer recover from some kind of disaster. Fire, flood. Once they see the sheriff's report, they'll understand what you're dealing with. Won't insurance cover most of it?"

She looked up, confused. "Yes. No. I mean, the property damage, but not the rest. And no, Joe Aguilar is not investigating, not that I can see. He's certain he's identified the culprit, even if he can't find him."

"Orion?"

"He didn't do it," she said, gripping her cup and raising her eyes to stare intently at me. "I know him."

That's what we all think. We never want to think we misjudged someone. I hadn't met the man but from all my years in HR and now retail, I'd learned we could never be sure what someone would or wouldn't do when pushed.

For reasons I doubt even God knows, the Pacific Northwest seems to have more than its share of serial killers. And every time one got arrested, their neighbors and coworkers swore you'd never have known. They were the nicest guys. Relatives, even wives, denied any knowledge, though as the men's stories unfolded, as the evidence was revealed, they'd been forced to admit they'd deliberately pushed their doubts aside.

Not that we were dealing with anything like that. Thinking of those hideous crimes had given me the chills and I reached for my coffee, miraculously still hot.

"I'm sure the sheriff is investigating other possibilities," I said. "You have to admit. Leaving looks suspicious."

"But that's how he is." She leaned forward, emphasizing the point. "He comes and goes. He doesn't like to be pinned down. That's part of the problem."

"You said you were meeting with a lender. Isn't there a bank in Salmon Falls?" The only one I'd noticed had been the downtown remodel, but we'd been on the lavender trail. There was a lot I hadn't seen.

"Yes, of course, but I can't afford to let the talk slow me down." What was that about? None of my business.

"I hope you got some good ideas for the festival from Sara," she continued.

"We did. She was very generous. Hey, you and I talked about spending a few hours in the store with us, and I'd love that. What if you also set up a farm stall a day or two that weekend? I don't know who assigns those spaces, but I can find out."

"Sounds great. Any chance to talk up lavender."

"I'm on it," I said. "Something else I wanted to ask you. Obviously, senses of taste and smell vary. Some people are allergic to specific herbs and spices, like garlic. If peppers give them heartburn or an upset stomach, they get very careful. And there's the whole cilantro-tastes-like-soap thing. I understand all that, but—"

"Lavender can set some people off, too," she said.

"Right? The chocolatier and I were talking about her plans for the festival, and a customer of hers seriously did not like the idea of eating flowers. How do you deal with that?"

"Gentle persuasion. Start small—a lavender truffle goes a long way. Technically, lavender isn't a flower. It's an herb. A mint, like, well, mint, or thyme and oregano."

"I mean, I don't care for sweet potatoes," I said. "But if you tell me you want to recreate your grandmother's sweet potato pie for Thanksgiving, I'm not going to say root vegetables don't belong in dessert. I'm going to sell you nutmeg and cinnamon, and make sure you have a good vanilla, then send you on your way."

"Fortunately," Liz said, "people who seriously dislike the stuff don't come to the farm. The smell bothers some people. Maybe it triggers a bad memory. A woman once told me her husband had his mouth washed out with lavender soap when he was a kid, so she can't keep anything lavender in the house. She had to come to the farm for a fix. That's funny, about you and sweet potatoes. I love them."

"You may have my share."

"For others," she continued, "the theory is that it's physiologic, like with cilantro. Probably connected to a chemical component in the herb itself, most likely in the oils. Some varieties trigger more reactions than others."

"Really? The plants are that different?"

"Oh, yeah. I've even heard reports tracing negative reactions to specific methods of oil extraction or to plants grown in specific places."

"*Terroir*," I said. Herbs and spices share some of the vocabulary as wine tasting.

"Exactly. Natural lavender causes fewer problems than the synthetic blends sometimes used in perfumes."

"Wow. A lot more to this business than I imagined."

"You're not the only one."

Back at my shop, Liz grabbed a seedling from the rack. "Let me show you how this plant differs from the varietal I gave you yesterday." Inside, I went to grab the gift plant. It wasn't there.

"Did one of you move the plant that was sitting in the nook?" I asked my staff. Sandra was helping a customer but heard my question and mouthed "no."

Leslie Budewitz · 45

"I sold it," Vanessa said.

"You what?"

"A customer brought it to the counter. It was a larger pot than the others"—she pointed at the small black pot in Liz's hand—"but it wasn't marked so I charged her the same. I hope that was okay."

"You have to find that plant," Liz said, her tone clipped and insistent.

"Why?"

"Pepper, I'm telling you. You have to find it."

"It—it was that woman you knew," Vanessa told Kristen, her voice trembling. "The one you were talking with outside. Before you took the mail. She came in while you were out. She bought some spice tea and the plant."

"Who? Oh, Monica." Kristen dug her phone out of her apron pocket and started scrolling. "She's got kids in Savannah's class. Pepper and I ran into her on the street. I'll text her, see if we can make a trade."

Vanessa pressed her hands together in front of her lips. "What did I do wrong?"

"Nothing," I said. "Nothing worth crying over. What's the deal with this plant, Liz? Why is it so important?"

"Just get it back," Liz said. "Put it in a nice big pot with good soil. Lots of sunlight. Enough water but not too much."

"I grow a few potted herbs on the veranda, but honestly, I'm not much of a gardener." I could give it to my dad, now that my parents had moved back for half the year, giving the snowbird life a go. "But I'll try."

"I know your reputation, Pepper." Liz grabbed my hand and gripped it in both of hers. "As an investigator. If anything happens to me, promise me you'll look into it."

That was an easier promise to make than keeping the plant alive. Because nothing was going to happen to Liz.

Eight

In 2023, the most popular dog breed in the country was the French bulldog. In Washington, it was a tie between the Chihuahua and the golden retriever.

I UNLOCKED THE DOOR TO MY BUILDING AND PUSHED IT OPEN with my hip. I dropped Arf's leash and he bounded up the wide steps to the top floor, where a small landing separated my neighbor Glenn's loft and mine. I followed slowly, a baguette and a bottle of wine in my tote, the bag of produce in hand.

"Hey, little darlin'." Nate met me at the door. He took the bag and gave me a quick kiss. He'd been to the barber today, his brown hair shorter on the sides than usual, almost a fade. "That bread smells good enough to eat. You smell good enough to eat."

Thank goodness my hunny is not lavender-averse.

"Like the haircut," I said. "What a day." I slipped off my clogs, fed the dog, and put away the groceries. Sliced cheese and fruit and got out crackers. Nate uncorked the wine—a light French red Vinny had recommended that had become a house favorite. The jazz station was playing a sax tune I didn't recognize.

The loft is short on walls and long on woodsy industrial charm. A compact kitchen perfect for two sits to the left of the door. A low bookcase separates the entry and dining room, if you can call it that, from the living area. There's one bedroom, also perfect for two, and above it, via a steep wooden staircase, what the builder and my mother called the meditation room. A loft within a loft. Twelve-foot-high, multipaned windows overlook the waterfront, Puget Sound, and the Olympic range. We'd rearranged the furniture so the couch faced the view. For spring, before the western sun got too hot. Why a century-old warehouse built for the once thriving cannery business had windows, who knew? I'd only been able to afford this place because of the Viaduct, the elevated freeway that had run a few feet from my windows, blocking all signs of life. An earthquake hazard long overdue for demolition, it had finally come down, replaced by a giant traffic tunnel. My property values and taxes had soared, but so had my happiness quotient, and that's worth a lot.

I sank into the couch, cradling my wine, resting my bare feet on the old wooden crate that serves as a coffee table. Where to start, recounting a twisty, turny day?

"I'm honestly not surprised," Nate said after I'd finished my account of festival planning and the odd experience in the chocolate shop. "You should hear some of the things people say about fish."

Was there any one thing everyone liked? Probably not. Some people love the Beatles, others hate them. Some love sports and pets; others—meh. Not food—even chocolate and fried chicken have their fans and foes. And certainly not the weather.

A pot of tulips I'd brought home from the shop sat near the door. The leaves were yellowed and drooping, the bulbs ready to be tucked into my parents' garden to sleep until spring. Tulips, I decided. Everyone likes tulips. But I wasn't going to say that out loud, just so some contrarian could prove me wrong.

Nate gave me a quick update on the latest boat repairs. Bron is the better mechanic, which both brothers readily admit. The *Thalassa*, the smaller boat they keep in Puget Sound, is old and always in need of work. Now that neither of them lives aboard, I had to wonder about its future. And theirs.

Back in the kitchen, I put together the salad and Nate prepped the fish. So handy to love a man who loves to cook. Then we grabbed the bread and wine and stepped through the window to the tiny veranda.

Try doing that in a regular house. One window is hinged, the lower half lifting like the lid on a chest. I sat at the green bistro table and drank in my surroundings. Dropped a hand and fingered the herbs in their pots—parsley, sage, rosemary, and thyme. And basil and oregano.

"I need a new planter," I said. "A big one."

From his post at the grill, Nate cast me a questioning look. I told him about Liz's gift, and how Kristen had tracked it down after Vanessa sold it. "She felt terrible, but she couldn't have known. I need to drive up to Madrona tomorrow to get it back."

"What makes this plant so special?" He closed the lid on the grill and sat across from me, picking up his wine. "And why is Liz so insistent that you have it?"

"It's a mystery to me." I took a long sip.

"Might be nice to have a garden again," Nate said. He'd kept a good-sized garden when he'd been married, until his then-wife complained that it was too much work for her, with him away so much. "You still thinking of a rooftop garden?"

"Maybe. I don't know. Glenn says they had the architect look at the possibility when they did their remodel, and she assured him the building and roof are sturdy enough. It would need some kind of membrane, to prevent leaks, although if the garden is small and mostly in containers and raised beds, it could be done."

"Hmm." He sipped.

But what he was thinking behind those gorgeous green eyes—now that was the real mystery to me.

"WHY DON'T I take the dog today?" Nate asked Saturday morning. "We've got some stuff to finish up on the boat."

What stuff, I didn't ask. I tried to understand, but even after nearly a year together, boat talk was mostly blah-blah-blah to me.

"Great. He loves it." All those smells around the water. Even a gentleman canine can't resist them.

"We'll meet you back here in time to clean up for the wedding." His smile melted me. "It's been good to have a few days on shore before we head down the coast next week."

I thought so, too. Alaska trips lasted weeks, even months. Fishing these waters might mean a day trip or a week at most. For some reason, I worried less when Nate was closer to home, even though the job was just as dangerous, the waters just as deadly.

Leslie Budewitz · 49

Most mornings, Arf and I walk up the Market Steps, several wide flights of steps that lead straight into the heart of the Market, the corner where Pike Place makes its L-shaped turn. The corner is always busy, but especially at eight a.m. The flower ladies are setting out their buckets, the produce sellers are stocking their displays, the daystall vendors are unloading their vans and arranging their table space. The bakeries and coffee joints are buzzing, the air perfumed with coffee, yeast, and sugar. You can hear half a dozen languages or more, amid the clatter and clang, and smell the anticipation.

My tummy growled. Bacon cheddar croissant, it said, and I listened.

I got my croissant, then passed through the Arcade, waving and exchanging hellos. The flower ladies were busy unloading buckets of fresh blooms from the backs of their vans, so I didn't have a chance to talk to Cua, Sara Vu's aunt. Great-aunt, if I understood the family correctly. They seemed to have found the missing cart. I stepped over the hose stretched across the cobbles, water dribbling out of one end and forming a puddle. If Arf were here, he'd insist on drinking out of it.

The sun was shining, always good for business. I hoped I'd be able to slip away for an hour or so on my lavender rescue mission without too much trouble.

This was the Saturday Kristen's sixteen-year-old, Savannah, was starting. Months ago, she'd asked if she could work here part-time this summer. The plan was to give her some experience on the weekends before tourist season exploded.

Mother and daughter arrived together and we found Savannah an apron. We wear black and white, and she fit right in, her blond hair tied back like her mother's. Her gaze flitted around the shop nervously. It was all-hands-on-deck today, and I was grateful not to have to worry about Arf, even though he and Savannah adore each other.

I took a few minutes before opening to put together a thank you gift for Monica, the customer who'd bought Liz's plant by mistake. A jar of Puget Sound sea salt, another of our special Italian blend, and our custom spice tea. Then I remembered Vanessa saying she'd bought tea, so I swapped it for our Lemon Seafood Rub, a blend I'd created myself.

50 · *Lavender Lies Bleeding*

I stepped outside to pluck a lavender seedling off the rack. Ours were not nearly as tall or bushy as Liz's—no wonder it had attracted Monica's attention. I grabbed two basil plants, loving the spicy, grassy scent. You can never have too much basil.

Across Pike Place, the farmer who'd sold me the spinach yesterday was setting up his canopy, portable tables leaning against a post, buckets and coolers waiting.

"Hey, Pepper!" he called as he snapped the last leg into place and the canopy took shape. He waited for a delivery truck to pass, then crossed the cobbles. "Funny. Yesterday you asked me if I knew what was going on in Salmon Falls."

"Right. The 'Farms are for Farming' signs."

"I was at my kid's track meet after school, and the Salmon Falls team was there. A farmer I know said there's a big dustup. Somebody wants to redevelop something—I didn't get all the details—but it's gotten pretty gnarly. They want an exemption from the zoning regulations, and the farmers are up in arms."

The rub and whir of bike wheels on the cobbles caught my ear. Two Seattle Police Department bike cops zipped into view, a woman and a long-legged man. Tag Buhner, my ex-husband. He raised one gloved hand, flashed me a grin, and sped on by.

"We've dealt with the same stuff up in Skagit," my farmer pal continued. "It gets tense."

"I bet. Thanks. You hear anything else, let me know. Good luck today."

He waved and returned to his tent and tables. I took the herbs inside, pondering what it all meant. Liz's opinion on the subject was obvious, from the signs and—well, from Liz being the force that she is. But she hadn't mentioned the dispute, so I didn't think she linked it to the vandalism.

"Why," Kristen asked me, "did I think it was a good idea for me to train my daughter?"

"Same reason your dad thought it was a good idea to teach you to drive." After one too many blown tempers—his and hers—he'd begged his good buddy, my dad, to take over.

This was Savannah's first real job, other than babysitting and dog walking. I walked the floor with her, pointing out the products. Then I turned her over to Cayenne for a lesson on using the automated scale and tablet. She already knew how to make change,

Leslie Budewitz · 51

thanks to a mother who'd worked retail and playing store with her younger sister. According to my Market colleagues, counting out quarters and dimes often flummoxed new hires who'd only used a computerized cash register that told them how much change to give back. And it was worse with younger employees, who'd come of age in the credit card era.

Midmorning, I packed up my peace offerings and reclaimed my car for the drive up to Madrona. The neighborhood sits above Lake Washington, old-school classy swank mixed with new construction favoring the urban-industrial look, all but the waterfront homes jockeying for a sliver of lake view.

Monica Salter lived on a block of oversized bungalows and Craftsman-style houses. As in the nearby Capitol Hill and Montlake neighborhoods where I'd grown up, parking was scarce, and I circled twice before finding a spot on a side street near a sleek, modern, three-story. Appealing—and north of two million, minimum. I shouldered my tote, the goody bag and box of seedlings in hand, and picked my way up the sidewalk, mindful of cracks where tree roots had broken through.

Seattle is a city of hills. These houses had terraced front yards and a flight of steps, sometimes two, leading to front porches and carved wooden doors. Small lawns were framed by the ubiquitous rhododendrons and other shrubbery. I passed a man cutting his grass with a weed trimmer, so quiet it must have been electric. The smell of fresh cut grass turns us all into ten-year-olds.

The Salters' house was smaller than its neighbors. Well-kept but lived-in, in real estate speak. A stone retaining wall ran along the sidewalk. The narrow driveway was empty.

I climbed the moss-stained lower steps. I'd texted Monica to let her know I was coming, but no one appeared to be around. I took the second set of steps, wood, the white paint worn, to the porch. A white bench filled one side, a straw hat on the purple cushion. A cluster of pots brimming with herbs and flowering annuals framed the purple door.

No wonder she'd gravitated to a lavender plant. Clearly her color.

No bell. I knocked. Waited and knocked again. Checked my watch—a pink Kate Spade I'd bought myself as a splurge, a week before losing my job at the law firm. A crisis that had led directly

52 · *Lavender Lies Bleeding*

to me buying the Spice Shop. And indirectly to me being right here, right now.

Waiting for someone who wasn't home.

I didn't see Liz's plant, and I couldn't leave without it. I sat on the bench and checked my phone for a *Running late!* text. Nothing. I sent Monica one, letting her know I was here.

The next several minutes, I alternated between scrolling on my phone and watching the driveway. Finally, an older white SUV pulled in. Monica came around the back of the car. She wore a purple U Dub sweatshirt over black yoga pants and white sneakers. Purple is a popular color in these parts.

"Sorry I'm late," she said. "I was at the gym. Thanks for waiting."

"No problem. Thanks for being so gracious about the mix up."

"No big deal. Like I told Kristen, I don't care what variety of lavender I grow as long as it smells good and the bees take to it." She waved vaguely at the perennial border. "My sons were rough-housing and crashed into the garden. Teenage boys and their big feet. I took it as a sign to redo the whole thing."

At the edge of the lawn, a wheelbarrow held a pile of brush and roots. Several large shrubs and perennials waited to be planted. A bag of cedar bark lay on the walkway, giving off a faint scent reminiscent of a walk in the forest.

"It will be lovely." I pointed at the bag and box I'd left on the porch. "I brought you some basil and a few other things, as well as a new lavender seedling. Though I'm afraid it will be a while before it fills out.

"Thanks. I'll get the other plant for you."

Instead of extracting it from the cluster of pots on the lawn, as I'd expected, she disappeared into the house. A moment later, she was back with the seedling. It truly was much better looking than the one I'd brought, and I understood her reluctance to hand it over.

"You know," I said, taking the plant, "this came from a grower out in Salmon Falls. Have you ever been to the Lavender Festival? It's not for a few weeks, but I bet you could find some great plants out there."

"We haven't been to the festival in years. The town has changed so much." Her face took on a distant expression, remembering old times.

Leslie Budewitz · 53

"Oh, so you know it?"

"Yes." Her gaze snapped into focus. "We—Scott, my husband, grew up there. In fact, they just sold the family farm. His brother—well, it was business, and not mine."

And certainly not mine, but I hoped that wouldn't stop her.

"We don't get out there much anymore. Not with the kids and all their activities. The parents have passed and his brother . . ." She shook her head. "Scott wasn't looking to sell, but they got an offer from a nice couple who have great plans. So, it was time."

"Speaking of time, thanks for yours. And for being so good about all this." I gestured with Liz's peat pot.

"I understand. That plant was a gift and you wanted it back."

I walked down the driveway this time. On Monica's bumper, I saw a sticker for the Salmon Falls Lavender Festival, no doubt from a few years back when they'd had more time for such things. A nice memento.

Then I spotted another box of plants. She was going all-out, refreshing the garden. I squinted. Lavender? Funny. She'd already bought a replacement, but hadn't been able to resist another. That's how gardeners are, I guessed. Like Kristen and vintage dishes, or me and funky furniture.

A few minutes later, I unlocked my car. I arranged a safe spot for the seedling on the floor and tucked it in like a baby. A baby that had already caused more than its fair share of trouble.

"Forget I said that," I told the seedling, sending it my silent promise to make sure it lived long and prospered.

Nine

> When it came time to lay the last brick in the cobblestones on Pike Place, at the street's 1978 rededication, organizers wanted a uniquely Seattle touch. So they arranged for a very special creature to do the honors: an elephant.

BACK DOWNTOWN, I PARKED AT THE LOFT. AS I HIKED UP THE wide steps to the Market's main level, I thought about Salmon Falls. What was going on out there that had Liz lying awake at night, and Cua Vang fretting over Sara? The sole connection I knew between Liz and Sara was lavender. One grew it; the other made sure the town celebrated it.

What else?

Probably nothing, I told myself. Liz had a busy life and despite our friendship, I knew only a sliver of it. She could be anxious about any number of things, unrelated to the vandalism. Running the farm and business. Living next door to her ex. The distance—physical and emotional—from what remained of her family.

Sara too had a full plate. Who didn't? The curse of the modern age, or the inevitable result of loving what you do and being good at it? I couldn't answer that, for them or for me. As for Cua, it's the older generation's job to worry about the younger.

Speaking of. On the other side of Pike Place, Savannah emerged from the passage between the Triangle Building and the Sanitary Market. People often ask about the names of the Market buildings, most dating back a century or more. Pike Place runs at an angle, not quite parallel to First Avenue, and Post Alley cuts a jagged swath between them. One result is a curious triangular building. Shops and takeout spots occupy the ground level; above are housing and a Bolivian restaurant with phenomenal views that's been there as long as I can remember. The Sanitary Market is a serious warren, dating back to 1910, the first purpose-built building in the Market. Legend says no livestock were allowed inside; hence, the name. The truth is far less romantic: It had concrete floors, refrigerated display cases, and a drainage system.

My shop occupies the Garden Center, an art deco design from the 1930s, with salmon-pink stucco walls and forest-green trim. I'd always adored it. When I bought the Spice Shop, my mother said what I really wanted was to work in my favorite building. She was teasing, but she wasn't entirely wrong.

From the large paper bag Savannah cradled in her arms, I guessed Kristen had ordered staff lunch and sent her to pick it up. Coming toward her on the sidewalk was Logan the Love Bomber, his own lunch in hand. My alert system amped up a notch, but if he even noticed the cute teenager, I couldn't tell.

Good. One less thing to worry about.

I fell in beside her. "How's the first half day of working life?"

"Oh, I love it! The spices, the customers. Everyone's so friendly and helpful." She wrinkled her nose. "My feet kinda hurt, though. Don't tell my mom."

I looked down at her platform sandals with ankle straps and had no doubt that Kristen had warned her not to wear them. Another lesson the young have to learn on their own.

We walked to the shop together, Savannah chattering happily. We had a good crew, fingers crossed. But while Kristen and Savannah seemed to have gotten over their morning bumps and bruises, I know all about mothers and daughters, so I crossed my fingers for that, too.

"Closing should be routine," I said to Sandra midafternoon, as I untied my apron.

56 · *Lavender Lies Bleeding*

"It's retail," she said. "Nothing is ever routine. But I've been closing this shop since long before you came along. Go, go." She made shooing motions. I called my thanks to the staff, and went.

Half an hour later, I was fresh from the shower when Nate and Arf returned.

"Nice outfit," Nate said, standing in the bedroom doorway. Arf slipped past him to settle on the vintage braided rug. The door is a roll-up, garage style, giving the bedroom full view of the living room and the sky and sea beyond. I rarely bother to close it, not worried about peeping seagulls.

"Thanks, I think." I was naked, but for a silver necklace in the shape of a fish that my niece had given me, pondering a dress for the evening. We'd been asked to wear the couple's color palette, if we could, an array of soft spring pastels. Not my colors.

"Wish we had time to mess all that up," he said, gesturing toward the bed. A lacy sage-green dress I'd borrowed from Kristen lay next to a white dress with a short, flouncy skirt, splashed in bright abstract patches that to my eye evoked flowers in high summer. "But they'll be here soon and I stink."

"You definitely stink." I kissed him, swatted his behind, and playfully pushed him toward the bathroom.

"Wear the bright one," he called out. "It'll show off your legs."

"Hmm," I said to Arf. "You think so, too? Bright, it is."

Half an hour later, I walked Arf across the hall and handed him off to Other Nate. Glenn and I were original tenants in the loft conversion. Shortly after moving in, he'd met a man named Nate and later married him. Not quite a year ago, I'd met my fisherman, Nate Seward, leading to jokes about my Nate and your Nate. On our side of the landing, our neighbor was known as Other Nate. Arf adored both men, and they often took him for a few hours if we were going out.

"Nice dress," he said. "Shows off your legs."

Then we dashed down the stairs in time to see Bron and Daria pull up in the shiny new electric SUV Bron calls the pizzamobile. We slid in back, leaning forward for hit-and-miss kisses.

"Sweet rig," I said, glad they were driving. We'd have all been cramped in the Saab and I'd have been nervous about its engine. The brothers share an old pickup ideal for running around town with motors and parts and other bulky stuff in the back, but not classy enough for date night. We wouldn't all have fit anyway, not without mashing against each other like hormonal teenagers.

I ran my hand over the leather upholstery. No rips or cracks. No holes in the floor rugs, and as Bron accelerated up the hill toward the I-5 on-ramp, the gears shifted almost imperceptibly. No lurching, no grinding.

"So grown up," I said. "Business must be good."

Daria flashed me a grin. "Very."

Ever since the paper had called her wood-fired pizza the best in the state, pizza lovers had lined up to taste it for themselves. She and Bron had met cute, in rom-com terms, last December when she went to Fisherman's Terminal, a short hop from the pizzeria, in search of salmon to smoke for a Northwest flair. Bron had stopped in Seattle for a few days, between flying down from Alaska and flying back east to see the parents for Christmas. But ever since, he'd spent as much time here as he could, and I wondered if he was thinking of making a change, after fishing with Nate for nearly twenty years. Jumping ship.

Their meeting had echoes of our own, also at Fisherman's Terminal. I'd met my mother and my friend Laurel for brunch on the patio at a waterfront restaurant, then taken Arf for a walk along the docks. Exchanged a few words with a cute guy working on a gill netter. I'd been seeing someone else, determined to make it work though it clearly wasn't, and when the ax fell on that relationship, I decided to cast caution aside and go back to the marina. Only later did I discover that Nate's and my meeting had not been the coincidence I'd thought, and that I was not the only one fishing.

But it had been a lucky strike, and I knew it.

"Great that you could take a Saturday night off," I said to Daria as Bron merged the pizzamobile into traffic. "You still thinking about adding on, for some inside seating?"

"Actually, no. I'm planning to close Saturday and Sunday this summer. So my staff can enjoy the reason we all live here. So I can enjoy it."

Even from the back seat, I could feel the electricity between her and Bron. I felt the same buzz with Nate. But it never would have occurred to me to close the shop and take more time off. True, Daria liked to get out in the mountains, at Salmon Falls and beyond, hiking

58 · *Lavender Lies Bleeding*

and kayaking. That wasn't my thing. I'm a city girl, though not a lipstick-and-heels girl, the present moment excepted.

Nate squeezed my hand. I smiled at him, then gazed out the window. We were on the toll bridge now, heading to the Eastside. The day was showing off for the wedding.

Sunlight turned the waves of Lake Washington into a sea of diamonds. Was it time to consider some changes of my own? How would that even be possible? Sandra was going part-time this fall. Cayenne's plans after the baby came were unsettled. Reed was graduating in a few weeks and starting an internship on a historic preservation project in the CID, the Chinatown–International District. I'd helped him get the job and was thrilled for him. My young staffers had his hours covered, for now, but Vanessa was focused on college. If Savannah worked out, as I was sure she would, her parents had said she could work Saturdays and holidays during the school year if she kept her grades up.

I counted every day that Kristen put up with me as her boss a bonus. Hayden was doing a great job at our production facility. I'd been able to step away from everyday control over the mixing, packing, and shipping. The shift had left me free to focus on the shop, to add classes and festivals and more.

Change was happening, all right, but not the kind of change that would let me cut my hours.

I'd loved working HR, helping oversee the staff at a big Seattle law firm. I'd plunged deep into mourning when scandal and mismanagement sank the firm and took my job with it, although I could have written my own ticket in one of the new firms that sprung up afterward. But much as I'd enjoyed solving problems and making life easier for those doing the real work, it had been clear my first day as Mistress of Spice that this was the job I'd been born for. Although I had to admit, now that I'd found my passion, I'd become quite the workaholic.

Nate's here again, gone again schedule left me free to work eighty hours a week when he was away, if I wanted to, and take off early Saturday when he was home. It was working.

Or so I'd thought. Did it work for him? For us?

While I'd been reflecting, the conversation had moved on to Javier and Mindy, and the current crew members and their wives and girlfriends. Some I knew, others I'd meet soon.

Leslie Budewitz · 59

Very soon. Bron pulled up to the front of a white Victorian mansion to drop us off. This was Cascade Vista.

"Straight out of the movies," I said, eyeing the gables with their gingerbread, the carved balusters on the railing, the gleaming white paint. Though I'd drunk plenty of their wine, one of Vinny's bestsellers, I'd never been out here. "So Javier took on restoring this place and now he's marrying the boss's daughter."

"Yeah, though she's taken over all the growing operations and helps with the winemaking," Nate said. "She'll be the boss before long."

The strains of a string quartet beckoned. Bron caught up with us as we followed a slate path to the rolling back lawn. Flower beds bloomed in colors that matched the swatches tucked inside the wedding invitation. A white rail fence like the one running down Mrs. Luedtke Road in Salmon Falls separated the lawn from the vineyards on either side. On the hillside beyond, horses grazed. Pastoral barely began to describe it. Heavenly came close.

And got closer when a young woman in a white shirt, black pants, and a long black apron extended a tray of champagne flutes. No name tag needed this time; I recognized her immediately.

"Abby! Good to see you. Abby used to work for Lavender Liz," I said to Daria. "My supplier out in Salmon Falls. Now she's working at Blossom Café, which must be doing the catering."

"Blossom." Daria took a flute. "Desiree White's place?"

"Yes. Daria runs Emerald City Pizza," I said to Abby. The guys were busy greeting friends. "That's darling." I pointed to the corner of my eye, indicating the tiny pink heart Abby wore. The stick-on heart and gold eyeliner made for quite the change from the sad, distracted young woman I'd seen in the café. Not to mention the fake lashes that made me wonder how she kept her eyes open.

"I like to be a bit extra, working a wedding," Abby said, before turning to the couple behind us with her tray of champagne.

I took a sip, the bubbles dancing in my mouth. Rows of white chairs faced a white gazebo where the ceremony would take place. The string quartet sat in a semicircle in back, playing beautiful music I could not have identified if my life depended on it. Bundles of roses and other flowers tied with flowing ribbon—were they called nosegays? I wasn't sure—decorated the railing. More nosegays marked off the rows of chairs reserved for family. Round tables for eight, matching flower arrangements on each, filled the stone patio between the gazebo and the mansion. More tables—for the bridal party, no doubt—lined the wide veranda. So wide my tiny outdoor space barely deserved to share the same name.

"Let's find the gift table." I raised the bag in my hand. Mindy and her mother had come into the Spice Shop to sign up for our wedding registry. I'd put together everything on her list that hadn't already been chosen, and added some of my favorite blends. "Ahh, there it is."

"By the way, Pepper," Daria said, after we'd delivered our gifts. "I meant to tell you, that dress is great. Shows off your legs."

"Thanks. You look cute, too, though we both flouted the dress code." We were two not-quite sisters-in-law still getting to know each other. Heck, we were still getting to know our guys—and having fun doing it.

We found them chatting with old friends from the boat. Neither had paid any attention to the color palette, Nate in black pants and a charcoal gray blazer I loved, with black trim and sleeves in a soft fabric that made them easy to push up, revealing his well-muscled forearms. Bron wore brown pants and a jacket he'd scored at a thrift shop that morning. We sipped and mingled. It was a glorious early evening, the kind that made the Pacific Northwest so enticing.

"I see why she wanted us to match the flowers," I said. "So pretty."

Deep borders filled with roses surrounded the mansion, a few canes trailing up the deck rails. Wide, curved beds led you down the garden path as if it was where you'd always wanted to go.

"See how the plantings and structural features create gathering spots across the lawn," Nate said. "The birch grove. The stream and lily pond. And it's all tied together by the flower beds."

Then another former crew member arrived, prompting another flurry of greetings and introductions.

"Pepper!"

I turned to see a slender, dark-haired woman a couple of inches shorter than my five seven, a former associate at the old law firm.

"Macy Cameron!"

"You look fabulous," she said. "Selling spice clearly agrees with you."

Leslie Budewitz · 61

"Thanks. So do you." Her pale rose dress was identical to the green one I'd borrowed and rejected, and I breathed a silent sigh of relief that I'd worn the bright floral. "Still with the tipplers?"

In the big firm, she'd worked in the group of lawyers who represented wineries, breweries, and distilleries, affectionately known as the tipplers. When things fell apart, they'd formed their own boutique firm.

"Happily, yes," Macy said. "The Jarretts are clients. I've been working with Mindy on some property acquisitions."

"Doesn't your family own a winery, east of the mountains?"

"Featherhill Farm, outside Walla Walla."

"The town so nice they named it twice," we chimed in unison, native Washingtonians that we were.

"Ours is a patch of dirt carved out of an old farm." Macy waved a hand at the lawns and gardens around us, the vineyards, the mansion. "This is an experience."

That it was.

"They keep some acreage around here," she continued, "but they grow most of their grapes in the Columbia River Valley, not far from us. The land over there makes for great wine."

"I'll drink to that," I said. "Good to see you. Don't work too hard." She rolled her eyes. Working too hard was the lot of young associates in any law firm.

After a quick hug, I rejoined our foursome. I was about to tell Daria about Macy and her family winery when a tall woman sporting a chestnut ponytail stopped in her tracks in front of us. I know a lot of people—the result of working retail in a busy place like the Market and living in the same city all my forty-three years. Forty-four, in a few weeks.

But no. Her attention was on the woman at my side.

"Hello, Desiree," Daria said stiffly.

"Daria." A pause. Desiree was dressed like Abby, the server, though without the heart at the corner of her eye. Or the gold eyeliner. "It's been ages. Still tossing pizza dough?"

The lilies could have heard her disdain, if they'd had ears. Heck, they probably didn't need ears, the woman's attitude was that obvious.

62 · *Lavender Lies Bleeding*

"Yes, thank you." Daria did not make introductions. "I hear you're starting a new venture yourself. If this is your last catering gig, good to quit with a fat check in your pocket."

Ouch. Daria was a straight talker, but those words had arrows on their tips.

Desiree's eyes darkened. "Enjoy yourself," she said, then marched away.

"Ohh-kay," I said. "Spill."

"It goes back years. The woman has no loyalty. No sense of professional responsibility."

I sipped and waited.

"We were pastry chefs in the same restaurant," Daria said. "That's where women often get stuck, even if we're fully trained and can cook everything the men can. She lobbied hard for a spot in the main kitchen—we both did. Finally, she gets one, and a week later, gets a better offer in another house and takes it."

"Leaving two slots to fill, and setting everything back," I said.

"Exactly. The head chef said that proved you couldn't count on women, and it was months before he gave me the chance she blew. She kept up that kind of thing everywhere she worked, until finally she and Jeffrey bought the place in Salmon Falls." Daria took a long drink of her champagne. "Desiree claimed she'd always wanted to run her own restaurant, and that could be, but the truth is, no one in Seattle would hire her."

Neither would I, in their shoes. "Sooner or later, even the best opportunist runs out of opportunities. What's this new business you mentioned?"

"I ran into another old colleague last week. He said she's opening her own wedding venue, in Salmon Falls."

"In the B&B they own? It's next to Blossom, in an old Craftsman."

"I don't know. He said there were problems, but we didn't go into the details. Time to find our seats."

The music had changed, filling the air with a sense of expectation. Around us, guests handed empty champagne flutes to servers and filed into rows of white wooden folding chairs. Daria and I found the Seward brothers and the four of us slipped into a row on the right, as friends of the groom. I pondered her comments

Leslie Budewitz · 63

about Desiree. Did Mindy and her parents, or the winery's events manager, know Desiree planned to open a competing venue?

Then the string quartet changed its tune again. The minister took her place at the foot of the gazebo, Javier and his brother beside her in their nifty black tuxes. All eyes turned expectantly to the back of the garden. I gripped Nate's arm, any lingering thoughts of professional rivalries and ill will banished by the pure joy that is a wedding.

Ten

In many weddings, the bride stands on the left, facing the altar or celebrant, the groom on the right, a tradition dating back to the Middle Ages that allowed a man to keep his sword hand free in case trouble arrived as an uninvited guest.

THE BRIDE WAS BEAUTIFUL. THEY ALL ARE, BUT THIS ONE MORE than most, in a creamy white gown, her bouquet an echo of the flower beds. The groom looked as if he couldn't believe his luck. The minister struck the perfect balance of solemnity and celebration.

As Javier slipped the ring on Mindy's hand—Miranda, the minister called her—Nate squeezed mine and gave me a tender gaze. I drank it in. What had I done to deserve a second chance at love, with a man so strong, so good, so loyal? We'd each stood at the altar before, pledging time and troth, only to lose it. I no longer felt like a failure because I hadn't been able to make the wrong marriage work. My mother had often assured me that love doesn't keep score. It's the heart that counts.

I knew Nate's, and I knew mine. Would we ever exchange vows? I didn't know. In my heart, I already had.

"Would you care to seal it with a kiss?" the minister asked, her hands open, her broad smile saying she knew the answer. Javier took Mindy in his arms and leaned her backward. We all cheered

Leslie Budewitz · 65

and clapped and exchanged kisses of our own as the music rose and swelled.

If a wedding doesn't make your heart go all tender and mushy, I'm not sure you have one.

Baskets filled with tiny bags of lavender buds were passed down the rows, a creative substitute for the traditional wedding toss of rice or birdseed. Though there was no church or church steps, we showered the happy couple with lavender as they made their way down the aisle.

Then it was time for more champagne and mingling while the wait staff put the finishing touches on the tables. I excused myself to search out the restroom.

Once I found it—inside, past the big room set up for dancing later, through this hall, down that one, around a corner—it was every bit as elegant as I'd expected. A sitting area with plush chairs and a couch gave a woman a chance to refresh her lipstick or rest a moment. Gilt-framed mirrors; touchless faucets that looked period but weren't; soft, flattering light—all the right touches. Each stall was a tiny closet with a full-length door—no peering underneath to check for feet.

On my way back—decidedly not the way I'd come—I heard kitchen sounds and followed them, curious what kind of setup they had. Maybe we could do a class on cooking with spices out here. A waiter emerged from an open door carrying a tray of silver pitchers filled with ice water, glistening with condensation.

I peered into the room he'd left, an oversized butler's pantry lined with floor-to-ceiling cabinets, extra plates stacked on the stainless steel counters. Despite the service for one hundred and fifty already in use, the sheer bounty of glassware astonished me. Red wine, white wine, champagne, and brandy, each polished and gleaming. I'd never seen so many glasses, not even in the restaurant supply house where I buy paper cups and napkins for the shop.

I took a step inside, drawn by all the sparkle and shine.

Footsteps echoed in the hallway, followed by a woman's voice. A voice I'd heard minutes before the ceremony.

"You can't be that naive, no matter how young and cute you are."

Was she talking to me? Surely not. The footsteps stopped.

"I can't believe you'd betray Liz like that," came another female voice, shaking with disbelief and anger. Abby the server. Young and cute, for sure, but she hadn't struck me as naive.

66 · *Lavender Lies Bleeding*

"She is your friend," Abby continued, emphasizing the last word.

"Friendship doesn't mean compromising my goals," Desiree said. "I'm going ahead, no matter how hard she fights me. It will put this old mausoleum to shame. Too bad you won't be working there."

Going ahead with what? The wedding venue Daria had mentioned?

Abby gasped. "You're firing me?"

"I should have figured you'd stick up for Liz. Though after what your boyfriend did to her greenhouse, you can be sure she'll wipe her hands of you."

"He—no. He didn't. He didn't touch her greenhouse. He would never."

"See what I mean about naive? Honey, there are all kinds of things you don't know."

Her sharp footsteps resumed, coming closer. I slipped behind the door and held my breath. The china rattled as Desiree pounded past me and shoved her way through the swinging kitchen doors. I waited, my heart thumping, then peered out.

Abby slumped against the wall in the corridor, her whole body drooping. She sniffed back her tears, then raised her head when she realized she wasn't alone, eyes wide, jaw defiant.

"It's you," she said. "I thought . . ."

"You thought it was Desiree, come back to say one more nasty thing."

The pink heart at the corner of her eye had come loose and slipped part way down her cheek, like a clown's fake tear.

"Your stick-on's coming unstuck," I said. "May I?" At the mewing sound I took for yes, I plucked it off her face.

"Thanks."

"What, if I can ask, was all that about? She mentioned Liz, and Orion, who I think is your boyfriend?"

"Desiree and her husband just bought a farm they want to make into a wedding and event center," Abby said. "There's an old barn that could be pretty cool once it's fixed up. But it won't be a farm anymore, and Liz and some of the other farmers and growers are super upset. They plan to tear out the vineyard, and people are afraid it's all a smokescreen for a subdivision. Desiree petitioned the county for a zoning change or whatever it's called, and it's all a big mess."

'Farms are for Farming,' as the signs said. "Is that the betrayal you referred to? And the goals she mentioned?"

She nodded. "They've got a bunch of rental properties, and Orion's been living in one. I don't know why she said such mean things about him. He didn't damage Liz's greenhouse. He wouldn't have. He couldn't have."

What Desiree thought she knew about their tenant, I had no idea. And it wasn't the time or place to caution Abby that we never know for sure what another person is capable of, for good or ill.

"Is Orion still Sheriff Aguilar's main suspect?" I asked.

"His only suspect, far as I can tell. He's made a show of talking to everyone—TJ and Brooke. Jeffrey—Desiree's husband. Even my mother. She doesn't know anything." Abby waved a hand and I noticed a tiny heart glued to the nail of one index finger.

"Your mother? Oh, right, she's taking over your job, running the cottage."

"That's how I met Orion. He helped Liz with the planting and harvesting. And this year, all the new seedlings. Orion loves the plants. He wouldn't have done anything to harm them. Lavender is easy to propagate, but it's not easy to propagate well. He gets what she's doing. Unlike Danny, making his claims. His lies."

I was about to ask who Danny was and what lies she was referring to, but she kept going.

"I needed a year-round job, so I started working for Desiree. But I guess that's history now."

More kitchen noise. The cater waiters would be coming through, laden with trays and plates. Time to get back to my table. One last question.

"Do you think Desiree might have damaged the greenhouse? To stop Liz from interfering with her plans?"

Abby heard the kitchen sounds, too, and wiped her cheeks one more time, careful of her eyeliner. "I have to get back to work."

"But if you're fired . . ."

"If I am, she didn't mean right now. Besides, I can't leave a bride in the lurch."

That told me more about Abby's heart than any stick-on tattoo ever could.

68 · *Lavender Lies Bleeding*

I dashed back to the restroom to discard the tiny heart and wash my hands. To my surprise, Mindy sat on the couch, bent over, fiddling with her sandal strap.

"Pepper! Can you help me?"

I rinsed my hands, then sat next to her. "What happened?"

"I tried to tighten the buckle but now I can't fasten it at all. Silly skirt is getting in my way. Love your dress, by the way."

Was she teasing me for ignoring the color scheme? No—the compliment was genuine. I raised her foot to my knee and examined the strap.

"Oh, I see. New shoes. The holes aren't completely cut." I slipped her sandal off, and worked the buckle until the prong thingy went through the hole. "My first time out here. This place is fabulous."

"Thanks. Javier and his crew did a great job, even shorthanded. I wanted to do a hundred-mile dinner, where all the ingredients come from within a hundred miles. We didn't quite manage. But we've got hundred-foot wine!" She wriggled her foot to help me get the sandal back on, and I fastened it. She pushed herself up and tested it. "Pepper, you're a doll!"

We air-kissed and I left her to touch up her makeup, retracing my steps. I stopped to peek into the prep room. A cater waiter rushed past, carrying a tray of salad plates. Desiree stood at the big sink, filling pitchers. She glared at me. I hurried on.

Had she seen me earlier? I couldn't say, but if it's true that the eyes are the window to the heart, Desiree White's heart was hard as stone.

Outside, I grabbed the stair rail and stepped carefully, unused to heels. I searched for Nate. Found him, his back to me, deep in conversation with Bron and an older, balding man I didn't know.

"Pepper! Did you see that restroom? It's like straight out of a magazine. From the 1940s."

I greeted the wife of one of Nate's crewmen, a couple I quite liked.

"Right? Those mirrors made me feel seriously underdressed."

"You look great. Hey." She put her hand on my arm, signaling a serious comment on the way. "I've been wanting to tell you, Aaron and I have never seen Nate so happy. You two were meant to be together."

Leslie Budewitz · 69

She beamed and I beamed, thrilled to hear it, but wondering what prompted it. More wedding good cheer, I guessed.

I glanced back at Nate in time to see the balding man shake his hand, say something I couldn't hear, then turn to Bron, his face serious. Another shake. Then the man disappeared into the crowd. What was that about? Little mysteries everywhere.

Eleven

In its first use in print, in 1895, British gourmand Guy Beringer wrote that "brunch"—a portmanteau or mashup of breakfast and lunch—"is a hospitable meal; breakfast is not... Brunch puts you in a good temper; it makes you satisfied with yourself and your fellow-beings."

"BRUNCH IS SO CIVILIZED." MY MOTHER, LENA ISTVANFFY Reece, twirled the stem of her fluted glass between her slender fingers. We were relaxing at a Capitol Hill café, the dog still enjoying his sleepover with Glenn and Other Nate. "And I love the hint of lavender they've added to the Prosecco."

"You should smell the loft," Nate said. "It's like a lavender field. Not that I've been in a lavender field."

"What can I say?" I lifted my own glass. It's not brunch without sparkles, in my book, but just one glass. The wedding had been at a winery, after all, though none of us had overindulged, and we'd worked off a lot of calories on the dance floor. "I'm loving experimenting with it, at home and at the shop."

"My grandmother wore lavender," my dad, Chuck Reece, said. "Reeked of it and cigarette smoke. She taught me to read, and I adored her."

Leslie Budewitz · 71

My dad grew up in St. Louis, where his parents lived all their lives. We visited every summer when I was a kid. Grandpa Reece gave me my nickname, after his favorite baseball player, the great Cardinal fielder, Pepper Martin. My mother's parents were Hungarian immigrants who came to Seattle as newlyweds fresh out of their teens and died two months apart, as if unable to live without each other. I'd been a teenager myself then, and thought it both tragic and romantic, though the double loss had sent my mother and her sisters reeling.

It had been love at first sight for my parents, when he, the tall vet in his army jacket, had swept the cute little hippie chick out of the way of a moving truck at a protest march. Sitting here with them now, it was clear that the spark between them had not dimmed.

Might sound weird to call my parents my models for romance and so much more, but it's true.

"You're not going back to the shop after brunch, are you, darling?" Mom asked.

"I should."

"Come to the nursery with us instead," she said. "Your father has shrubs on his mind. And I would love to go out to the lavender farm, next time you go."

After the server took our orders, Nate turned to me. "Ever since you mentioned those smoked salmon eggs Benedict, I've been craving them. I thought for sure I'd get to have them today, but no luck."

"We'll just have to keep trying," I said. I hadn't had a chance to tell him about my conversation with Abby last night, or about Desiree and the wedding venue, so I filled them all in now.

"Sounds pretty contentious," Mom said. "So much for small-town peace and quiet."

"We see that in Costa Rica," Dad said. "People come for the pace of life, but their presence changes it. A town that's been discovered can only live off its charm for so long. Then the newcomers want a Walmart, and the residents discover they want one, too."

"Why would you need Walmart when you live in paradise?" my mother asked.

"No easy answers," I said. "With an event center, you have to ask if the local job market can support it. If not, who will work

72 · *Lavender Lies Bleeding*

there and where will they live? Those are part-time jobs, some of them seasonal. What will employees do the rest of the year? Of course, that's true of some farm jobs, too. Abby and Orion cobble together work where they can find it, but that's hardly a stable foundation. It's fine when you're young, but . . ."

I worry about such things, for my own staff and the people I know in the Market. As housing gets more expensive, life gets harder for the artists, the small-time growers, and the keepers of specialty shops. The ripple effect touches us all. I firmly believe that everyone should be able to make a living doing what they love, and that no one who works full-time should have to struggle. Idealistic, maybe, but the fruit of my family tree. My parents and Kristen's had run a Catholic peace and justice community. They'd started the free meals program at St. James Cathedral, a Montessori preschool, and dozens of other projects that had helped shape the city. I'd taken those values into my HR work, and I hoped I lived them out now.

That was why I cared about Liz and what happened in Salmon Falls.

"Then there's the effect on other businesses," Dad said. "On traffic and noise. Not to mention the loss of farmland."

"That's what has the other growers troubled," I said. "Though Liz hasn't said that was behind the vandalism. I wouldn't be surprised if there's a connection, but what, I don't know."

But I did know, and proclaim almost every week, that Sunday brunch is my favorite meal. I often share it with Laurel, drinking too much coffee, walking it off as we worked out our problems and shared the joys of our lives. Now that I was with Nate and she was sort of seeing a man who lived a few houseboats away from hers, we got together less often. With my parents here, and Laurel's son about to come home for the summer, flexibility ruled. I'd liked the routine; now I liked the variety.

Daria might be on to something, closing weekends. I hadn't founded my shop, but it was no exaggeration to say I'd saved it, and for a long time, I'd spent every moment I could there. Running it was the first thing I'd done that felt truly mine. Sunday mornings had been my one regular break.

My parents recapped what they'd done and who they'd seen in their short time back. Last night, they'd had dinner at the home of friends from the old Grace House days.

Leslie Budewitz · 73

"The McNallys were there," Mom said. "And Laura Long. You remember her."

I did. One of the younger members of the community in its later years, which probably made her fifteen years older than me. Smart but impish, with a wicked gleam in her eye when she joined us kids playing a game or putting together a puzzle. She'd worked behind the scenes, managing the community's money and getting grants for programs. I'd liked her a lot.

Mom asked how Savannah had done, working under her mother's eye. Then my dad, who loves the water, turned the conversation to Nate and fishing.

"Back to Alaska in September?" he asked, as the server arrived with our omelets and waffles and other brunchery. I was almost too busy ogling the eggs and potatoes to notice Nate shoot me a quick look. Almost. Then the server produced a coffee pot and the moment was gone.

But not my questions. I hadn't asked him about the man he and Bron had been talking with before dinner last night. It wasn't any of my business. If it even was business. Could easily have been another former crew member, or another wedding guest, newly met.

We ate, sipped, chatted, and ate and sipped some more.

"You know," I said to my parents, "I think I will go to the nursery with you. I need a pot for the lavender Liz gave me, and some decent soil. I've got some potted tulips to give you, Dad. You can pick them up when you drop me off. You take the Saab," I told Nate. In anticipation of hauling plants home, my parents had driven their SUV today, not the classic Mustang whose custody my dad had reclaimed, to my sorrow, when they returned from Costa Rica. They'd have plenty of room for me.

"No, I'll come, too," Nate said.

"I thought you had to go to the boat. Since you're leaving tomorrow."

"It can wait. This will be more fun."

A little while later, fat and happy, we headed out.

"I'm so glad you like my parents," I said as I pulled away from the curb, following my dad. Nate had gotten to know my mom last summer when she flew back to Seattle on a house hunting trip, dragging me along every chance she got. But he hadn't met my dad until

74 · *Lavender Lies Bleeding*

their Christmas visit, when they'd astonished everyone by buying back the house they'd sold years ago. The house about to get a major garden makeover.

"I like all your family. Even your sister-in-law and your aunt Izzy."

I snorted. "They have their moments. When am I going to meet your family? Besides Bron, I mean? You know I adore him. And Daria."

"She has her moments," he said and I smiled, then turned into the garden center lot.

"You need a new car," Dad said as we got out. As if to emphasize the point, the Saab's engine gave off a loud creak as it cooled.

"No time to shop," I said. Not to mention the money. But if I didn't do something soon, I'd be sad.

No chance of being sad here. Even before we crossed the threshold, my mood—already an A+ on the congeniality scale—soared. Raised wooden planters were bursting with brightly colored annuals I couldn't name. Ceramic pots and gazing balls were clustered around the planters—cobalt for this one, hot pink for the next, lime green for a third. White iris in full bloom provided continuity. Wind chimes sang softly. A red willow chair invited me to sink into its cushions, a tile-topped wrought iron table waiting for my book and coffee.

I wanted to carry it all home. Every pot and stick and plant. No matter that my veranda measured four feet by twelve.

The open doors beckoned. We entered the shop, greeted by home and garden decor, houseplants, and more. I could have browsed for hours, but instead followed my parents through the shop into a greenhouse. Lush, hot, humid, the earthy smell of rich soil, the sweet fragrance of a world in bloom.

Heaven.

Then we sauntered out to an open yard where perennials and shrubs sat on the graveled walkways and on sturdy wooden tables like the built-in tables in the Market Arcade. In flower or in waiting, every plant invited me to touch, to scratch, to sniff. In the far back, fruit trees and evergreens stood in rows like singers in a choir.

"What can I help you find?" a cheery woman asked, a long, green, bibbed apron over her T-shirt and pants.

"My dad's on a mission," I said.

"I'm redoing an old garden," he said. "Long story. I've got a list. Starting with lavender. I've never grown it, but my daughter's got me thinking about it."

"A perennial favorite," she said. "This time of year, we're pretty picked over. Let's see what we've got." We followed her to the next aisle.

If this was picked over, what did a full house look like? Or smell like?

"Hardy, with pretty blossoms and a good fragrance," my dad said, "but also good for cooking. If that's not too tall an order."

"I know exactly what you need," she said. "A grower we work with is developing a hybrid that combines the culinary qualities of *Lavender angustifolia* with the showier, more aromatic lavandins. Her greenhouse and farm are only thirty miles from here, so the plants won't even need to adjust to our climate."

"That sounds ideal," my dad said.

And it sounded familiar. Was she talking about Liz?

"Do you have it? That new varietal?" I asked. A twin to mine?

"Sadly, no. We'd hoped to have plants by mid to late summer, but the grower experienced a setback. Nothing to do with the plants," she added quickly. "They're sturdy and robust. Nursery buyers are already lining up for them. She's going to have a huge hit on her hands."

Now I was certain she was talking about Liz.

"Another grower claims he'll have something similar for us," she continued. "But I'm not sure we can count on him. For your needs right now, I'm going to suggest this classic 'Munstead.' Good for cooking, and the peduncles—the stems—are long enough for bouquets or wands. It's a good all-purpose plant, and the grass-green foliage is pretty in a garden bed or border." She ran her fingers over a nicely shaped shrub, releasing the sharp, floral scent.

"Sold. And the 'Hidcote Pink.' Those pink blossoms will be fun." Dad pointed and Nate loaded the plants onto the green metal cart he'd snared. "Now, I was also hoping to find—"

"Pepper, come inside with me. Something I want to look at." My mother grabbed my hand. I glanced over my shoulder at Nate, who didn't seem to notice.

"Aren't you interested in the landscaping?" I asked as I followed her into the retail shop, where displays held pots and soaps and kitchen accessories with garden themes. Garden sculpture. Garden furniture. Garden this and garden that. At the end of the main room, a long wall held clippers and pruners and other garden tools and gear. I love tools and gear, but right now, I was thinking about Liz and her setback, and this mysterious grower talking about a similar new varietal. "I mean, I know Dad's doing the outside work, but—"

"Male bonding time."

"What? Oh-h-h."

I sank into a willow chair like the one I'd seen out front, anchoring the garden room of my dreams. If my dreams had a garden room.

If it soothed the senses like this place did, I might never leave.

Twelve

The fragrance lingers on the hand that gives the flower.

—Chinese proverb

I WOKE MONDAY MORNING WITH A FEELING OF BLISS. SUNDAY had been the perfect day, doing things I love with people I love—and not worrying about work. When Nate and I got home, we'd rescued the dog from his own bliss—Glenn and Other Nate totally spoil him—then the three of us strolled along the waterfront. For most of my life, it had been plagued by a built landscape that separated it from the rest of downtown, divided further by its own split personality—half working waterfront, half tourist attraction. With the Viaduct gone, the city had embarked on a massive project to reconnect the waterfront to the downtown neighborhoods, including the Market. With more people living down here, like us, it made sense, and the result was worth all the noise and disruption.

Small towns like Salmon Falls weren't the only places making tradeoffs.

Back home, we'd repotted the lavender, me promising to love and cherish it, to treat it with respect, and to protect it from grasshoppers and spittle bugs. "Sounds like you're making wedding vows," Nate had said, and though I'd laughed, I did feel a sense of obligation and commitment. If not to the plant, then to Liz. She evoked that kind of loyalty, in part because she embodied it. I'd been less sure about the flowering hydrangea Nate had brought home. It was big; the veranda was small and already crowded.

"They were my grandmother's favorite flower," he'd said, "and hearing your dad reminisce about the lavender his grandmother wore made me want a plant, to honor her."

Fair enough. I'd designed and decorated the loft myself, before he came along, and did everything I could to make room for him. The nursery woman had assured us the hydrangea would do fine in a pot. If it didn't, we could always stick it in my parents' garden or give it to Kristen. The creamy white flowers with a touch of pink, an update on the classic lollipop shape, were lovely and graceful, as he said his grandmother Seward had been.

Then we'd made one of my favorite dinners, Indian butter chicken and asparagus with a goat cheese vinaigrette inspired by one of Seattle's best-loved restaurants, and topped it off with lavender crème brulée I'd picked up in the Market. I love to cook, but that didn't mean I had to make everything myself. Nate had spotted a stray bit of the caramelized sugar topping stuck to my lip and insisted on licking it off himself. That had led to other things that made me shimmer at the memory, and I reached for him now, hoping to recreate a bit of the magic. Without the lavender-infused sugar.

But he wasn't there. I sat up. He never had made it to the boat yesterday, and according to a sorry/not sorry text from Bron, neither had his brother. They'd promised to meet at the boat early to get everything shipshape for this week's trip. But I hadn't heard Nate leave, and he wouldn't have left without saying goodbye.

I slipped out of bed and tugged on an oversized T-shirt. The loft was strangely quiet. No sounds of a man in the shower or in the kitchen. And no dog—or leash.

Mystery solved.

I started the coffee. Sharing a morning cup together was a ritual I had cherished with Tag during our marriage. After we split and I bought the loft, I'd been afraid I'd miss those moments of togetherness, but I'd created my own rituals to suit the rhythms of my new life. And with Nate's presence, ever-shifting with the fishing season, those rituals had morphed yet again, smoothly and sweetly.

Leslie Budewitz · 79

After a quick shower, I dressed for the day in the shop. The coffee was ready and I poured a cup, then stepped through the window to the veranda to scope out the day's weather—always a factor in retail—and check on the plants.

"Looks like you made it through your first night," I told the lavender I'd nicknamed Lizzie and the hydrangea I secretly called Mrs. Seward. "The first of many, I hope." No clouds, the air cool but not cold. If we're going to have rain, Monday is a good day for it, when the Market is slow anyway. But no one in Seattle ever complains about a clear day, especially if the mountain is out. I couldn't see Mount Rainier from here, but judging by the sparkling view of the Olympics to the west, I was betting the old volcano would shine brightly today, its glaciers sending ripples of joy throughout the region.

I hoped a bit of that joy would touch my friends in Salmon Falls. Determined as Liz was to power through the cleanup and repairs, I knew the destruction had hit her hard. To see something you love in ruins is deeply painful, whether it's a business or a relationship or a dream. Sara, too, was troubled by the damage and what it might mean for the town. I trusted that Abby would bounce back from her disagreements with her boss, though I did wonder about the impact of Desiree's plans on the community.

The loft door opened. In came my guys, sweaty but grinning. I've heard the claim that dogs don't have feelings, that when we say a dog is happy or sad, we're projecting our human emotions on them. Fie on such clueless people. I stepped inside, set my cup on the weathered picnic table that fills my dining room, and crouched, arms open. Arf leaned against me, resting his big chin on my shoulder. Fifty-two pounds at his last vet visit, all muscle, fur, and love. I hugged him, kissed his snout, and disentangled myself to greet his second-favorite dog walker.

"Where did you two go?" I asked Nate after a kiss. "Coffee?"

"Oh, uh—just up Western a few blocks. Coffee smells great, but I'll have to grab it on the way out."

He headed for the shower, leaving me a little disappointed. But I've learned in relationships that you can't be upset when unspoken expectations aren't met. Or when work gets in the way. Mine certainly had, far too often.

80 · *Lavender Lies Bleeding*

I sat at the picnic table, a trash-day find by my former mother-in-law, in one of the pink wrought iron chairs Tag calls ice cream parlor refugees, and ran my fingers over Arf's silky ears. Having Arf in the shop with me is great, but summer can get busy, and when I get called away, I can't always take him along.

"Remember we're meeting the people at the doggy daycare today," I told him. "Be on your best behavior." He did not reply. I'd heard nothing but good about the place, and drop-ins were always welcome. I'd miss him, but he'd have fun and be well taken care of. And that's what counted.

Trade-offs.

Then Nate was ready to leave, and the three of us walked down to the parking garage beneath the building and climbed into the cab of his truck. It was almost as old and noisy as my Saab. At the corner of Western and Virginia, Nate pulled over, leaning across Arf to take me in his arms.

"Love you, Spice Girl," he said. "Miss you already."

After a long kiss, I stood on the corner, Arf beside me, waving as the truck drove away.

"Be careful," I whispered into the wind. "And come home safely to me."

AT THE NORTH end of the Market, quiet reigned. A woman I suspected lived on the streets sat on a park bench, pigeons clamoring at her feet. The shops weren't open yet. No line had formed outside Starbucks, though I could see through the front windows that it was plenty busy. The tables in the North Arcade were mostly empty, not needed on a slowish day.

A change in perspective can change everything.

I didn't need coffee, but I did need a bite. Arf and I bypassed our shop and headed into the fray. At Three Girls Bakery, the oldest shop in the Market and the first business in the city licensed to a woman, I ordered a breakfast sandwich. Caught up with Misty, the manager, who gave Arf a special treat. Waved at the Orchard Girls, sisters who sell jams from their family's orchard. Blew a kiss to Jamie, one of my favorite artists, setting up her table.

Herb the Herb Man's white van idled on the cobblestones. Maybe he could shed some light on the tensions in Salmon Falls.

Leslie Budewitz · 81

But then I saw Logan the Love Bomber, the sales agent who regularly fills in for him and other vendors, unloading buckets of herbs from the van onto a cart. Pooh.

Inside my shop, I alternated bites with morning tasks. Arf settled into his bed in my office, dreaming doggy dreams. The Monday crew arrived.

"Savannah couldn't stop talking about the shop," Kristen said. "All day yesterday, it was this spice and that customer and this other thing. Mariah started making fun of her, and I thought they were going to get in a fight."

"We've created a spice monster," I said as I counted the cash drawer. "But I'm glad she liked it."

"Everything but the sore feet."

"Oh, I hated that. But I learned." Vanessa balanced on one foot and stuck out the other to show off her black sneaker with hot pink laces. "You can have comfort and cuteness."

"I've got a recipe for a lavender sugar scrub," Cayenne said. "As good as a pedicure, and cheaper. I'll write it out for you later." She grabbed a fresh sleeve of paper cups and began unwrapping them.

"I can hardly wait to try it," Kristen said.

"Hey, Pepper," Cayenne said. "Sunday, we went to a baby shower for the woman who runs the senior housing program for the PDA. Sara Vu was there."

"Oh?" My staff had friendships in the Market that I didn't have. I like that—it makes them happier and more invested in their jobs. I like it even more when they share the gossip they pick up. Though I prefer to think of it as news.

"I told her we bought eggs from Brooke Manning. I got the idea she thinks Brooke is a younger, blander version of Liz."

"Blander, meaning not so blunt?"

"You got it. Brooke and the ex think Liz is going overboard, protesting the plans for the event center." Cayenne straightened the trash can next to the tea cart.

"What does Sara think?" It hadn't come up during our visit last week. "Anything that brings visitors to town is good, right?"

"Yeah, though she didn't sound happy about it. Apparently, there was another buyer lined up, but Desiree and her husband swept in at the last minute. Then it was time to play baby name games and I didn't get to ask her more."

82 · *Lavender Lies Bleeding*

"Ooh, baby names," Vanessa said. "Have you settled on one yet?"

"As soon as I think we're narrowing it down, one of us adds to the list. Plus, you know my family. Everyone has an opinion."

Time to open. As customers trickled in, we confined our conversation to business.

Cayenne's mention of the PDA reminded me that I'd promised Liz I'd find out the process for getting one of the pop-up farm stalls on the cobbles. Were the slots taken for this year? Or did "pop-up" mean there was always room for one more? If we hurried, I could stop and ask on our way to the doggy daycare. I grabbed Arf's leash and we hit the cobblestones.

Near the fish market, Tag, long and lean in his police uniform, stood astride his stopped bike. He pointed a gloved hand, making "this way, then that" gestures.

"Thanks," the visitor said. "Probably not part of your job, but I appreciate it."

"It's all part of the job," he said with a smile. Then he aimed his gaze, hidden by mirrored sunglasses, at me. "How can I help you, pretty lady?"

One of his standard greetings.

"Sending her to my shop, I hope."

"Actually, she was looking for the tattoo artist."

Ah. Madame Lasorda. Her work decorates many a Market merchant and vendor, though I'd never visited her studio myself. I'd been tempted a time or two, after catching sight of an intriguing design on someone else, but then I thought of the pain and the moment passed.

"Hey, I have a question. Do you know Sheriff Joe Aguilar, out in Salmon Falls?"

He stroked Arf's ear. "No, I don't think so. Want me to ask around? What kind of trouble are you poking your nose into now?"

"Thanks. No, it's not worth your time." Circumstances had forced me to ask for Tag's help a time or two since I bought the shop, despite my reluctance, and though he'd given it, his help had come wrapped in caution tape. "One of my vendors suffered major damage to her greenhouse, and she doesn't think Aguilar's taking it very seriously."

Leslie Budewitz · 83

"Hmm. If it's felony level, he should be. But you know the drill. Just because the cops don't tell the complaining witness everything they're doing every minute doesn't mean they're sitting on their hands."

"That's what I told her. Thanks anyway." I blew him a kiss and Arf and I started down the hidden stairs leading to Lower Post Alley. They aren't actually hidden, though everyone calls them that—just not readily visible from Pike Place. They are the quickest route to the PDA office, and to the Gum Wall, inexplicably one of the Market's—and the city's—biggest attractions.

In the PDA lobby, I ran into Cayenne's pregnant friend, looking as if the baby could come any minute. I told her I heard the shower had been fun and wished her well. The Market Master's assistant gave me the info I needed, and I stood outside on the curved steps, texting Liz.

Then I sent a follow-up. *Hey, I met a woman at a nursery here in town who's super excited about your new lavender. She also said another grower is working on something similar. Competition???*

I hit send, then watched for the "delivered" message and the tiny dots indicating a reply in progress.

As if. Danny couldn't compete if he tried. And that's too much bother. Somebody's here—gotta run. More later.

"What do you suppose that's about?" I asked the dog as I slipped my phone into my tote.

"Talking to yourself, Pepper?" a voice asked. Not just any voice, but Yolande Jenkins, one of the Market managers.

"Hey, Yolande. Arf and I are going to check out the doggy daycare. Taking your advice."

I'd run into her and her pup, Corker, an adorable black-and-white French bulldog, outside the daycare last winter. She'd raved about the place, and her dog had appeared happy.

"I wish you'd take my advice on this lavender festival idea," she said, and a pit formed in my stomach. "You're asking an awful lot of people, in terms of time and money. Supplies, special projects. If it doesn't fly . . ."

She didn't need to finish her sentence. She was one of those people with a talent for making their doubts and disapproval clear, even if they didn't utter a no or a nay.

84 · *Lavender Lies Bleeding*

"I know. You don't see what it will do for the Market. How it fits the mission," I said. The magic phrase that greases the bureaucratic wheels. From her perspective, and she hadn't been alone, my plan had been irritatingly nonspecific. I had identified vendors and producers who might participate, and suggested a few activities for kids and adults. I'd brought samples to the meeting—lavender lemonade and lavender shortbread. But I hadn't been able to project increased foot traffic or sales, or any of the other "measurables" so dear to strategic planners.

"It's a strain on resources," she said. "You're taking a big risk."

One risk was failure to follow through. A while back, another merchant had proposed an event, gotten approval, then dropped the proverbial ball, leaving a trail paved with confusion and disappointment, cemented by resentment. Not going to happen on my watch.

The biggest risk was festival fatigue. More likely later in the season, in my opinion. The Market got so many visitors—roughly ten million a year—that those lured by lavender would easily make up for those who stayed away. But I did take her point. There would be naysayers who blamed me if they didn't sell as many bars of lavender-scented soap or photographs of lavender fields forever as they'd hoped.

Win some, lose some? Can't please everyone all the time? The adages are as true here as anywhere else.

About the same time as I'd suggested celebrating lavender, a group of artists had submitted a proposal for a studio tour. Yolande had put her energy and support into that. The first tour, along with demonstrations in the Market, was scheduled for this fall. I thought it was a great idea. And I understood that from Yolande's perspective, it made sense to focus the Market's resources on one new event at a time.

"I just hope you know what you're doing," she said, then opened the office door and slipped inside.

"Me, too," I told my dog. "Me, too."

Thirteen

Around the time of the Market's founding in 1907, traffic watchers noted a range of vehicles at First and Pike: express wagons hauling furniture and meats; lumber wagons toting brick, gravel, sand, coal, and garbage; trucks carrying groceries, milk, and laundry; and buggies ferrying passengers, all horse-drawn.

I SHOULDN'T HAVE BEEN SURPRISED THAT MY DOG HAD friends I'd never met.

"Arf!" A thirty-ish woman in a blue hoodie reading BARK PLACE BY THE MARKET crouched beside my dog in the daycare lobby. He leaned into her with obvious memory and affection. "So good to see you again!"

"Wait. You know my dog? How do you know my dog?" I asked. "He's never been here. I talked to a man on the phone, but this is our first visit."

She rubbed Arf's head one more time, using both hands, then stood. Wiped one hand on her black leggings, obviously no more bothered by fur on her clothes than I was, and held it out. She wore no makeup, not bothering to disguise a small scar high on her cheekbone, her dark blond hair in a loose topknot.

86 · *Lavender Lies Bleeding*

"Raine McGuire. I'm the resident vet tech. I meet every new dog and check them over. Arf and I got to be friends when I volunteered at All Creatures, in Pioneer Square."

"Oh, I know that clinic," I said. "They treat pets of homeless and low-income people. Sam, his previous owner, used to take him there." I'd acquired Arf from Sam, a Market regular who'd gotten tangled up in a murder. My first case. After Sam returned to his family in Tennessee, a bunch of us who knew him made a group donation to the shelter clinic. I'd thought about volunteering, but instead, I'd gotten involved with an organization training disadvantaged people to work in food service, teaching about herbs and spices. "I'm Pepper Reece, by the way. I run the Spice Shop in the Market."

"Good to meet you. Let's take care of Arf's paperwork. Why do we still call it paperwork when it's on the computer?" She led the way to a small desk, Arf and I pausing briefly to watch the dogs at play on the other side of the glass wall. "I know some people, even vets, think that if a person can't afford to keep an animal healthy, they shouldn't have one. And I never knew if Sam was unhoused—"

"Off and on," I said.

"But that dog gave him a reason to live, when life was hard. I heard that Sam left Seattle. I hope he's doing all right."

"He is. No email, and he's not much for the phone, but I talk to his sister every couple of months, and I send her pictures of Arf to show him."

"Arf is the picture of health and happiness. He was always one of the best behaved dogs at the clinic." Raine asked me for my particulars, then we moved on to the dog. Vet, check. Vaccinations, check. Date of birth? She started to type, then stopped and looked at me, eyes inquiring, hands poised above the keyboard.

"No idea. Best guess, he's about five. No health problems. But I've always wondered how he got to be so well trained. Maybe whoever owned him before Sam? His vet thinks probably a woman, given how he responds to me. And to her. But we don't know."

We went through the rest of her checklist, and Arf and I followed her to a private room where she gave him a once-over and pronounced him "a delightful little man." Then we got a quick tour of the main playroom, where Arf sniffed and was sniffed, and the nap space. We all approved.

Leslie Budewitz · 87

I wasn't ready to set up a first day yet, let alone a regular schedule, which was all fine with Raine. I couldn't speak for Arf, but I left feeling both happy to have a safe, caring option for him, and sorry that I couldn't keep him with me all the time. Like a parent on the first day of kindergarten, I imagined.

We walked back to the Market along First Avenue so I could stop at the Italian grocer and deli to pick up staff lunch. Outside Stories, the bookshop that's anchored this block for decades, a window display of gardening books caught my attention. My eye quickly focused on a pair of titles on growing lavender. Not the two I'd found in Salmon Falls and suggested to Kristen, thank goodness. There are half a dozen bookstores in and around the Market, and we wanted to complement their selection, not compete with them.

Inside, a woman replaced a book in the display. Our eyes met and moments later, she rushed out the door toward us.

"Jenn!" I cried as the former law firm staffer greeted me with open arms. After the firm collapsed, Jenn had followed her passion and gone to work at the mystery bookshop in Pioneer Square. When I discovered a stash of Brother Cadfael books and videos in a box my parents had stored in my basement locker and plowed through them, she introduced me to other historical mysteries. It had been her idea for the Spice Shop to carry culinary cozies, as the light-hearted mysteries focused on food are called, and she gave me oodles of recommendations. Sadly, the mystery bookshop had closed. "So sorry I haven't had a chance to pop in and see you."

Not quite the truth. I knew she'd made the job move, but I hadn't come in because—well, I'm embarrassed to admit the real reason. Our jealousies and grudges always sound so petty when we say them out loud. Stories was owned by a kindhearted elderly man whose only fault that I could see was having a granddaughter who'd had an affair with my husband. Not that I blamed RD Clark for any of that. Fault lay solely with Tag and Kim. Now Officer Kim Clark, the Seattle Police Department's family liaison, but then, a lowly meter maid. (Technically a "parking enforcement officer," as if her official title made adultery any better.) When I'd almost tripped over them practically plugging each other in the back corner of a restaurant where I'd gone for drinks after work with friends, on an evening Tag had said he was working late—well, that was the end of our thirteen-year marriage. But after running smack into Kim in the Northwest history section, I hadn't returned to her grandfather's bookstore.

Now I understood that my marriage would have ended anyway, much as Tag and Kim's fling had petered out. And she and I had developed a professional relationship of sorts last fall and winter when first an old friend, and later, one of my staffers, got caught up in trouble that brought them into close contact with law enforcement.

But that didn't mean I wanted to run into her any old time.

"It's okay," Jenn said. "I keep meaning to swing by the Spice Shop, too. This is such a great bookstore. So much to learn. I hope you liked the garden books Nate picked up last week."

"Nate? Garden books?"

"Oh, no." Jenn covered her mouth with her hands. "I'm so sorry. Were they supposed to be a surprise? For your birthday? It's coming up, right? Don't tell him I told you."

"No, no. I won't say a word." Why was Nate buying garden books? Not for my birthday, I was sure. For someone else, then, because I hadn't seen them in the loft.

We promised to get together soon. Another hug, a kiss for the dog, and Arf and I trotted on.

I SPENT THE afternoon in the shop, catching up on paperwork. Raine the vet tech was right—funny to call it that, but pixelwork sounds silly.

Fabiola, our graphic designer, had created social media graphics and a logo for our minifestival. As usual, I loved her designs. This was starting to feel real.

I was on the shop floor searching for a nutmeg grinder a bride had put on our wedding registry but that our automated inventory system claimed we didn't have, when a customer stopped me.

"I've always loved to cook," she said. "But lately I've been noticing I'm not enjoying food as much as I used to. I think I need to learn to use spices better. Any suggestions?"

"We're planning some classes on cooking with herbs and spices this fall," I said, "but you probably know the basics. Smell is as much a part of our enjoyment of food as taste. It's not uncommon for taste and smell to diminish with age or from some illnesses or medication. Quite a few customers lost part of their sense of taste after Covid."

Leslie Budewitz · 89

She was approaching fifty, with short gray-brown hair and lively brown eyes that widened as she listened.

"Oh. I never thought about that. Not Covid. But I had breast cancer and chemo." At the look on my face, she put out a hand. "I'm okay now, thanks. But could that be the cause? No one ever said."

"Maybe. Talk to your doctor. Or you might have old spices. And I don't mean the men's aftershave." That got the chuckle I'd hoped for. "The more colorful herbs tend to have some of the strongest and most interesting flavors. Think cumin, turmeric, the paprikas. You up for some taste testing?"

She was, so I spread an array of spices on the nook table. I opened jars, handed them to her for a sniff, then used tiny spoons to give her samples.

"I think I need to go through my spice cabinet and do this," she said after a few rounds, usually more than enough for the average nose and tongue. "I probably haven't bought new spices since before my diagnosis."

"Good idea. You can also add some zing with blends." I showed her our trusty za'atars, our lemon seafood rub, and one of my faves, herbes de Provence.

She chose several, and when I handed her the full shopping bag, she touched my arm again. "Thank you. I was terrified at the thought of losing something I love, and you've given me hope."

"You're welcome," I said, the words catching in my throat. "Come back and tell us how it's going."

Late afternoon, Arf and I strolled up to the park, pausing at the Tree of Life sculpture that commemorates the homeless who died in King County. Too many, symbolized by the cutouts in the tree's black steel leaves. Holes in the fabric of our society. Sam had managed to avoid becoming one, and Raine hadn't been wrong when she credited much of that to the furball trotting by my side.

Then we stood at the wrought iron railing gazing out at the Sound. I have no idea what was on Arf's mind, but I was thinking of Nate. Change was on his mind, I felt sure. I had absolutely no doubt that he loved me. So why wasn't he talking about it with me? We work differently, I knew, but I still felt left out.

And that is never comfortable.

After a few minutes, we trekked to Upper Post Alley, home of the Wine Merchant. I'd been a customer long before I started working in the Market, but once I bought my shop, Vinny quickly became one of my closest friends here. Half mentor, half mentee, and total mensch.

Through the window, I saw Vinny seated at a high-top in the shop's addition, a laptop open in front of him, a dark vest over his white button-down. I looped Arf's leash to a hook outside where I could see him, and told him to be a good boy. As if he needed to be told.

"Hey, Vinny," I called. "I have wine on the brain."

"Join the club."

"Nate and I went to a wedding out at Cascade Vista over the weekend. The owner's daughter married one of his former crew members."

"Oh, Mindy. I met her at a tasting a few weeks ago. Sharp cookie. Loves the business, but unlike so many of the younger generation, it's not all about glitz and profit to her. She likes to get her hands dirty."

"She looked pretty glitzy in that wedding dress, especially when she was dancing. At dinner, they served a Columbia River red blend they called a Rhône style. We loved it. Do you carry it?"

"Sure. Far right, near the top." He pointed to the black boxes with X-shaped inserts lining the walls.

"Great. Thanks. One of the other guests was a young lawyer I used to work with, Macy Cameron. Her family has a small vineyard outside Walla Walla. Feather something."

"Featherhill Farm. Small place, limited production. Great wine. But no worries. I'll double your employee discount."

Vinny's running joke. Not that I would ever work for him in a million years, but I would never be so rude as to refuse a discount.

"Thanks. Hey, one more question. Do you know anything about a small vineyard near Salmon Falls? On an old farm? I've been talking to friends out there who say the place is being sold for an event center. Word is the buyers want to plow the vines under. Can they be transplanted or saved somehow?"

Vinny shuddered. "Ought to be a crime. Assuming they're any good. Have they done a harvest and crush? Bottled anything?"

I didn't have a clue.

"You know who you ought to talk to about that," he continued.

Leslie Budewitz · 91

I did not.

"Mindy Jarrett."

"Mindy? Seriously?" I asked. "They're honeymooning on San Juan Island. But I can call her when they get back."

The shop was quiet and Vinny had a new red blend he wanted to try, so I texted Cayenne to say I'd be a bit longer while he uncorked a bottle and poured us each a taste.

"Why can't these new owners keep the vines and host weddings or reunions or whatever?" he asked. "Agritourism, they call it. People love it."

"That's what the locals say. I suspect they're afraid the secret plan is to break it all up into a cookie cutter subdivision of McMansions or whatever." I took the glass he handed me.

"So, what do you think?"

"Of McMansions? Oh, the wine." Vinny is easy to tease. I took a sip and let it sit on my tongue. Rolled it around. Swallowed. Pondered, under the weight of Vinny's expectations. "I like it. A hint of blackberry and chocolate. And—oh-h-h. Is this one of those wines from the big smoke year? When the vintners were afraid the grapes were tainted and the vintage might be ruined?"

"Got it. And you like it. Good. I trust your palate. But it won't be for everybody."

"It would make a great appetizer wine. Serve it with green table grapes and seed crackers. A tangy goat cheese. Talk to Sandy Lynn at Say Cheese! She's great at flavor pairings. I'd serve it with Edgar's Baked Paprika Cheese any day." An appetizer one of my favorite customers had created using one of my favorite spices.

Food, friends, and flavor. What more could a girl ask for?

BACK IN THE shop, it was almost closing time. The slower pace of a Monday had given us a chance to restock the shelves, clean the hidden corners, and catch up on a few projects.

Then I turned off the lights, locked the doors, and followed the staff out as we called our goodbyes. Arf and I trotted down the Market Steps to Western and home. I had leftover butter chicken and rice in the fridge, and wine from Vinny in my bag. With Nate away, I was planning a good binge watch. I'd caught up on *Father Brown* and moved on to *Rosemary and Thyme*, getting tips for the garden I'm not going to build and reassuring

92 · *Lavender Lies Bleeding*

myself that it's perfectly normal for everyday people to snoop out crime.

I kicked off my shoes, gave Arf his dinner, and clicked on the TV. I'd stopped in the middle of an episode in which Rosemary and her partner in crime, Laura Thyme, were rehabbing a neglected vineyard at an old hotel. A famous gossip columnist had been murdered, and the pair, a former policewoman and an ex-prof turned professional gardeners, were hot on the trail. That's the kind of fun I can drink to.

Every shot of the vines and hotel grounds made me think about Liz and the damage to her greenhouse. If Orion had smashed the glass and destroyed Liz's precious plants, the sense of betrayal would haunt her long after Sheriff Aguilar wrapped up the case.

Right now, I wanted nothing more than to collapse on the couch with a glass of wine and dinner and lose myself in fictional troubles. But before I did that, I kept a promise to my mother. She'd set up a meditation space in the attic of their new-old home, and had been pestering me to finally use mine for its intended purpose. *Twenty minutes. Surely you can manage that*, I could hear her say. I paused the video, changed my clothes, and climbed the steep ladder. Arranged the pillows, including the quilted pink Hmong pillow. Got out the roll-on lavender oil I'd bought in Salmon Falls. I was about to light the lavender candle when a text came in. I know, both my mother and my yoga teacher would frown at taking the phone upstairs with me, but it's got a built-in timer.

The message was from Cayenne. *Turn on the news.*

I climbed back down and found the remote. Clicked a few buttons. On screen was the sign for Salmon Falls Lavender Farm, and next to it, the red-and-white protest sign. The camera panned to a reporter standing beside Liz's purple truck, telling us all that Lavender Liz was dead.

I clapped my hand to my mouth.

And remembered the other promise I had made.

Fourteen

Researchers at Duke University say more than 400 genes are involved in controlling the receptors that determine how we smell a particular odor, with nearly a million genetic variations. So, the person standing next to you in the garden center or at the perfume counter is literally smelling something completely different.

I CALLED CAYENNE RIGHT AWAY AND TOGETHER, IN OUR separate homes, we watched the full report. (Seattle's major TV stations seem to run the evening news on virtual repeat. If you miss it at 5:30, tune in at 6:00, or 7:00, and again at 9:30 or 10:00.)

"I should have taken her more seriously," I said.

"You took her seriously. Besides, what could you have done?" Cayenne's indignation came through loud and clear. "It's that Sheriff Aguilar who should feel badly, not you."

Some truth to that. "Listen, I know this is hard. You're off tomorrow, so I can't keep an eye on you. Promise you won't sit home and cry about it all day."

"Only if you promise you won't walk around blaming yourself all day."

"Deal." Though as the shock rippled through me, touching off anger and rage and sorrow, my teeth chattering and my hands shaking, I wasn't sure it was a promise I could keep.

94 · *Lavender Lies Bleeding*

According to reporters—and I watched every channel, as if the news might be different and she might be alive on one—Liz had been found dead among her plants, not far from the wrecked greenhouse. Sheriff Aguilar spoke briefly, saying that a neighbor had found her, and refusing to answer questions about the cause of death or virtually anything else. His voice and expression were steady, giving no hint of emotion. It might not speak well of me to say so, but like Cayenne, I hoped he did feel bad. Only the killer—and Aguilar implied that a search was in progress—was truly to blame. But a sliver of guilt over not taking the damaged greenhouse as a threat to Liz's personal safety might spur him on.

It was firing me up.

I called my staff. We'd all liked Liz. Her determination to succeed as a grower, and as a woman on her own, had been inspiring. I love men, some of them dearly, and I don't underestimate what it takes to follow your dreams, no matter who you are. But the world can be hard on ambitious women, especially those in nontraditional occupations.

"She was like you, Pepper," Vanessa said. I'd caught her on her walk to the bus after an evening accounting class.

"Like me? Why do you say that?"

"She's—she was smart, and strong. She knew what she wanted, and she followed her principles. She could be kinda scary—"

"I'm not scary."

"You are, a little, at first. Not in a bad way."

How scary could be good, I wasn't sure, but I kept mum.

Without a doubt, Liz's death would leave a hole in our Spice Shop community. Not to mention questions about our lavender supply. But that was minor, compared to the loss of a friend.

My mother saw the news and called me. I debated calling Nate. He'd never met Liz, but even so, he would worry about me and wonder if he should come home. Besides, he often moved in and out of cell range, and a dropped call or a troubling message he couldn't reply to would make us both anxious. So I sent a gooey good-night text he might or might not get, and left it at that.

Knowing what to do with myself was trickier. Real-life tragedy made the TV mystery shows seem pointless. No ball game tonight. I found a home and garden channel and stared absently at people ripping out perfectly good kitchen cabinets and perfectly terrible

Leslie Budewitz · 95

bathroom floors. I took Arf for a walk around the block and downed an extra glass of wine.

Then I tried to get some sleep. I'd never taken a sleeping pill and didn't have one but if there was ever a time, this was it. A pill, or a gummy. Had Liz ever told Aguilar that was the reason she hadn't heard anything the night her greenhouse was damaged? I didn't know how he interpreted her failure to hear the glass breaking and the other sounds. Surely he didn't take that as reason to think she was complicit.

I was going to have to tell him.

THE ALARM JOLTED me out of hard-fought sleep. I'd tossed and turned, blinking away images of Liz that my mind conjured as it tried to make sense of the senseless. I pictured her in her purple hiking skirts and lavender hoodies. Her floral-print hiking sandals. Her purple truck, and the coffee mugs decorated with sprigs of lavender.

And heaven help me, some of those pictures had been spattered with blood. Because when you don't know what happened, the imagination easily fills in the worst. Too easily.

Not quite fifty degrees out, the veranda wet. I choked back a sob at the sight of the lavender plant Liz had made me pledge to keep safe.

What would Cadfael do? Everything he could to keep the people he loved safe and bring the killer to justice. The old monk lived by the Benedictine rule, and while the code I live by differs from his in many ways, we had that in common.

I pulled on wellies and a slicker and took Arf out to pee. Not a real walk, though long enough for Arf's fur to pick up a glisten of moisture. "Later," I said. "Promise."

In the hallway outside my door, I ran into Glenn.

"'Morning, neighbors." He raised one arm, a raincoat draped over it. "We might need these today."

"We might."

He rubbed Arf's ear. "What did you think of the rooftop views, eh, little buddy?"

I was puzzled. I'd never taken Arf up to the roof.

At my expression, Glenn went on. "Saw him and Nate coming down yesterday morning."

I frowned. What was that about? Nate hadn't mentioned it. No reason he should have, I supposed, but it was odd.

Back in the loft, I showered and dressed quickly. A black shirt and black pants, a purple scarf to remind me of Liz. As if I could forget.

I stopped for flowers. No sign of Cua. I'd call Sara later. How could I reach Abby? If Liz had been murdered, Sheriff Aguilar would be questioning her and doubling down on his hunt for Orion.

Outside the shop, Arf and I shook the mist off our coats. I grabbed the morning paper from our doorstep—I like a paper-paper, plus it's a nice addition to the nook.

Inside, I set the dog loose and dumped my things in the office. Plunked the flowers into a vase, not bothering to fluff them. I was sitting in the nook, my go cup of coffee half full and cold, when Kristen arrived.

"You did everything you could," she said, sliding in across from me.

"We texted yesterday." I tapped my fingertips on my phone, beside the uninformative newspaper. "She said she had to run, someone had just come. I never heard back from her. What if it was the killer?"

"Pepper. Whatever happened, it was not your fault."

Our eyes met briefly. It's not always comfortable, when someone knows you so well.

"Have you eaten?" she continued.

"Not hungry. I wonder if they have her phone. The timing of our texts might be relevant."

"I'm sure you'll hear from Sheriff Aguilar." She stood. "Tell him then. I'll be back in ten minutes with your breakfast. And don't argue with me."

"I wouldn't dare." We'd lived in the same household from before we were born until my family moved out when we were twelve. I trust her with my life and more, and she does the same. She's two weeks older and thinks that gives her the right to boss me around. Me, I'm just bossy by nature.

Fat lot of good that did right now. I should have told Liz to keep an eye out. To make sure someone else was around at all times. Would she have listened? Would it have made a difference?

Leslie Budewitz · 97

The rest of the staff arrived, a somber crew. Kristen returned with a fat slice of quiche and a double shot latte. I wolfed down both.

Then I donned my warm, padded slicker again and ventured out. Herb the Herb Man was at his stall, the stoop of his shoulders and the bend of his neck telling me he'd heard about Liz even before I saw his expression. He always reminds me of a basset hound, bald with a long face and full jowls, and kind, droopy brown eyes.

Today, he had an end spot, and the moment he saw me, he came around the tables to wrap me in his arms. After a long moment, he kissed the top of my head and stepped back.

"Sucks," he said. "No other way to put it."

"I swung by yesterday to chat, see what you knew about problems in Salmon Falls, but you were off. Busy with the garden?"

"My wife's niece got married down in Ocean Shores and we took a few days. You've got to do that now and then."

So everyone kept telling me.

"About Salmon Falls," he continued, setting buckets of fresh herbs on the table. "Not much I can say. Tensions over development, but that's hardly new or unique. What I do remember"—he paused, digging for the details—"I think it was in Salmon Falls. A growers' co-op tried to buy a farm, but at the last minute it sold to someone else. Can't blame the sellers, I suppose—you get a better offer, you take it. But I kinda do blame them, you know?"

I nodded. "Price is not the only value."

"You got that right." He straightened the chalkboard advertising today's herbs. "I'm lucky. I own my own land, and I don't need much of it. But it's hard on renters. They can get their leases jerked out from under them any time, and moving a farm or a garden is hard work. You can lose a season, or get behind, and that costs you sales. Some of the Hmong have had a particularly rough time. But we need those small growers. I bet if you took a survey"—he swept his long arms wide—"half the growers and producers in the Market are working on five acres or less. Way less."

Of course, you could do a lot on a few acres, as the nine-acre Market proved.

98 · Lavender Lies Bleeding

"I agree. So many reasons to eat local, to know where your food comes from. What I want to know is who had a reason to kill Liz? And did it have anything to do with this farm sale you're talking about, or the clashes over preserving farmland?"

That, Herb couldn't say. There was only one place I could hope to get answers.

Salmon Falls.

Fifteen

The sixteenth-century English herbalist John Gerard cautioned against the use of lavender by "unlearned physicians... overbold apothecaries, and other foolish women," fearing that its use to treat the wrong conditions could "do very much hurt, and oftentimes bring death itself."

NOW THAT ARF WAS ALL SET UP AT THE DOGGY DAY CARE, IT was a breeze to make the call, then drop him off a few minutes later. Behind the glass wall, half a dozen dogs his size were playing with an attendant and a pair of large balls. It reminded me of the children's game "Red Rover," organized by Labs and border collies.

"I know exactly which dogs to introduce him to first," the attendant said as he took Arf's leash. No sign of Raine, the vet tech I'd met yesterday. "Some of our regulars are excellent guides for the newbies." He gave me a reassuring smile that sent a clear message: Time to go.

I kissed Arf's snout. "I'll be back in a few hours. Have fun."

But not too much fun. This really was like leaving your child on their first day at school.

The mist turned to drizzle turned to showers, and by the time I got to Salmon Falls, it was full-on rain. Under dreary skies and a steady downpour, the town had lost much of its perky charm. Even the welded moose looked sad.

100 · *Lavender Lies Bleeding*

Outside the Lavender Association and Festival office, water streamed off the edges of the brightly colored flag. I took a chance that its presence, however bedraggled, meant the office was open and Sara Vu was in.

Through the glass pane in the front door, I saw her sitting behind the reception desk. I took off my wet slicker and shook it before walking in.

"Pepper. You came." Her normally shiny black hair hung limp, her bright eyes red and dull.

"Sara, I am so sorry."

"I can't believe she's gone." Sara ran her fingers through her hair, let it fall back across her face, then shoved it out of the way. "No one worked as hard as she did for this community. I can't believe it's come to this."

So many questions.

"What happened?" The snippet in the morning paper had provided no new details, except for Aguilar's assurance that the killing appeared to be an isolated incident and there was no threat to public safety. "Who found her? Do you know?"

"Brooke, her ex's wife. They live in the old farmhouse next door."

The egg woman. The blander version of Liz.

"Sir, Liz's cat, came over and pestered her while she was getting the kids out of the car. At first, she was kind of peeved that Liz was late feeding him. The cat, I mean. It's happened before. Liz didn't answer her phone, so Brooke went over there."

"Oh, my god."

"It gets worse. Brooke didn't have any reason to think Liz was hurt. She assumed Liz had lost track of time, with all there was to do. She took the kids with her."

Sara's face paled, and she paused before continuing the story.

"Liz was lying in the dirt, between two rows of plants. She'd been stabbed in the neck with a pruning knife. Brooke said—" Her voice broke. "She said the blood was everywhere."

The carotid. Liz would have bled out in a hurry. So it was murder.

"Do you know when?" I checked my phone for the time of Liz's last text. "If Liz was like most people, she probably fed the cat when she got home, before making her own dinner."

Leslie Budewitz · 101

"Pepper, it was the middle of the afternoon. Sir didn't go to the farmhouse because he was hungry. He went to get help. They found bloody paw prints on the stone walkway."

Now I felt sick. I wrapped my arms around myself.

We sat for a long moment, the single sound the hum of the mini-fridge in the outer office.

"Sara, what did you mean when you said you couldn't believe it had come to this?"

She buried her face in her hands. A box of tissues sat on the desk and I slid it toward her.

"I keep asking myself who could do such a thing. Who could be so hard-hearted and ruthless? I know they say we're all capable of murder in the right—or wrong—circumstances. If we're pushed hard enough. But . . ."

"But it's one thing to say that, another to believe it happened."

She sniffed back a sob and jerked a tissue out of the box, tipping it over.

"Did anyone see or hear anything?" I asked.

"Not that I've heard. TJ and Brooke are the closest neighbors and they weren't home."

"Who wanted Liz out of the way? Who would benefit from her death?"

"That's what I keep asking myself, but I don't have any answers."

"You think it was Orion Fisher? I know Sheriff Aguilar thought he damaged the greenhouse, then took off. Is he back?"

"Not that I've heard, but why would he hurt Liz?"

"Liz opposed any development that would take farmland out of production. Might she and Orion have argued over that?"

"I don't think so. He was as passionate about local agriculture as she was, and I can't see him wanting to give up working the land. Unlike some people."

TJ Manning, sitting on a big spread but preferring to run a business in town instead? Every rural community needs a farm supply dealer, for seed and irrigation pipe and who knows what else. An event center wouldn't help his business. Unless he was looking to cash in.

"What about the Mannings? They run one of the biggest farms around, right?"

"Yes. TJ's brother runs it, with his kids. One's still in high school, but they're totally committed. No," she said firmly. "They are not one of those families where the next generation goes off to do its own thing and never looks back, once they sell the land and cash the check."

Was there some other gripe between TJ and Liz? I had to assume the vandalism and her death were connected.

"Who do you think might have gone after her?" *Killed* was too ugly. I couldn't say it.

"I don't know, Pepper. I mean, it's got to be connected to the tensions over development and what we want this town to be, doesn't it?"

"Oh. Desiree?" I asked. "I mean, those tensions are long running, but the current hot spot is her plan to build this wedding venue and event center, right? It would create jobs, first in construction and later in hospitality. Could Liz have stopped it? And did that create a conflict for you, since both Liz and Desiree are—were—important parts of the festival?"

Sara pooched out her lips. "I did everything I could to keep the growers and the festival out of it. I—" Behind me, the front door opened and she stopped midsentence.

A woman entered, shaking out a red umbrella behind her. Sixtyish, attractive, her gray hair in a collar-length bob. Knee-high red rubber wellies that matched both her glasses and her umbrella. I was lucky my boots matched each other, let alone anything else I happened to be wearing.

She strode into Sara's office, her sweeping glance dismissing me. Sara's tear-softened jaw went rigid. Who this woman was, I didn't know, but clearly, she was not on the top of Sara Vu's friends list.

"Sara, how are you?" the new arrival asked, her tone exuding a warmth I instinctively didn't trust. Like the saying goes—if you can fake sincerity, you can fake anything. And I had a sense that this woman was an old hand at putting on a show of whatever emotion the situation required.

Sara sidestepped the question. "Nina, this is Pepper Reece from the Spice Shop in Seattle. She's setting up a lavender festival in Pike Place Market. Pepper, this is Nina Ascension, editor of the weekly paper."

Leslie Budewitz · 103

"Editor, owner, photographer, and head janitor," Nina said, extending a red-tipped hand. I'd have to ask Kristen if there was a polish called Dragon's Blood.

"Nice to meet you," I said. I can fake on occasion, too. "Although I'm not here about the festival. Liz was a friend of mine."

"That poor girl. She put our local lavender on the map. She and Sara. And Desiree White." She shifted her focus to Sara. "I'd like to run a feature article on Liz in the next issue. Can we talk?" Her gesture dismissed me. If I were a journalist on the trail of a story about a murder in a small town, I'd want to talk with everyone who knew the victim—particularly an out-of-towner I might not get another chance to interview.

"Your group has lost an important ally," Nina told Sara. "Although the fight was doomed from the start."

Sara's brows narrowed. If Ascension meant the fight over the event center, the accusation seemed unfair. I was sure Sara had done everything she could to keep the growers' group and the festival plans above the fray. Zoning changes are never a sure thing. Other layers of regulatory approval could take time, or scuttle the project altogether.

"Nina, I know you think you can sell more papers by getting the townspeople to fling dirt at each other, but it's not going to work. Especially now. We're in mourning. I would think you, of all people, would have some respect for that." Sara stood, signifying the end of the conversation.

The older woman's eyes hardened and she raised her chin at the unexpected rebuke.

"I do understand, Sara. I understand that grief can cause us to say things we might regret." Nina hitched her bag higher on her shoulder. "I'll come back when you're feeling more like yourself." She shot me a withering glare, as if I was responsible for the mild-mannered Sara's sudden sharpness, then left, snatching up her red umbrella as if it were a sword and she of a mind to stab someone.

After a momentary silence, Sara and I looked at each other. She covered her mouth with her fingers.

"I feel like I just talked back to the school principal and got away with it."

"Who is that witch? So much for journalistic objectivity."

"Nina's late husband worked for a newspaper chain somewhere—LA, I think. On the business side, not the news side, but he'd always wanted to run a paper of his own. When the *Herald* went up for sale, they bought it. He was a good guy, but he died of a heart attack last summer. Nina took over, but I think it's her bitterness that's in control."

"She's stuck with a paper she doesn't want to run, can't sell, and can't afford to shut down," I said. "Curious, though, that she doesn't mind deliberately antagonizing a major advertiser."

"She knows we'll never pull our advertising completely. We've shifted a lot of our budget to other media, to boost regional tourism. But we need her paper and we want to support it. A community can't thrive without a newspaper."

"Hmmph," I said. "She said your group had lost an ally, and that's true of the growers. But the festival is more than that, right? The retailers, restaurant owners, innkeepers." Of which Desiree was two of three.

The guarded expression returned to Sara's face. Was there active conflict between the festival and the association? Or was it simply that their interests didn't completely overlap? How much did serving both complicate her job?

I stood. Time to head to the farm. "I stopped for flowers this morning, but I didn't see Cua. I hope she's okay."

"Tired, is all. Even a tough old bird like her has to take a day off now and then." She walked to the door with me. "Come to the festival planning meeting next week. And tell me everything you hear, about Liz and—and all this."

I agreed. Outside, the rain had stopped. I stood by my car, thinking. Down the block, Jeffrey White emerged from his office and glanced my way, then strode into Blossom. If Abby had not gone back to Blossom, there were other restaurants and bars in town; she could find a new job easily. But she'd be devastated by Liz's death, and the suspicion continuing to circle around the boyfriend she was convinced was innocent.

Maybe yes, maybe no. It was more than the clouds making it hard to see clearly in Salmon Falls.

Sixteen

The French monks at the Abbaye de Sénanque in Provence got so tired of repairing damage to the fence by photographers aiming to improve their shots of the famous lavender fields that they cut and framed a hole for future shutter bugs.

IN LESS THAN A WEEK, SALMON FALLS LAVENDER FARM HAD completely changed.

Scrubby plants had become full-sized shrubs. Small, tight buds on wand-like stems had burst into full bloom. You didn't have to run your hand over the leaves or blossoms to release the fragrance. It floated on the air.

The biggest change was the loss of their patron. Did the plants sense it? If they did, I couldn't tell.

The bees danced around one of the taller plants, the hand-painted row marker too splashed with mud to decipher the name of the variety. One bee flitted close, and I swatted it away.

"Go," I said. "Don't bother me. Bother the plants and take the pollen home." I waved him toward the bee boxes, at the edge of the field.

That's when I saw the purple Adirondack tipped onto its side, the crime scene tape strung around the photo op spot.

I grabbed my rubber boots from the car. Walked slowly down the muddy row to the place where Liz had died.

106 · *Lavender Lies Bleeding*

The nearest plants, the new ones, had been uprooted. Someone had tapped them back into place, although a couple of bare spots remained. A test patch for the new varietal?

"Liz," I said to the woman who wasn't there, but should have been. "I am so sorry. I am going to miss you."

Head bowed, I trudged back toward the cottage. On the stone walkway, Abby waited for me. Beside her stood a woman with a similar build and features.

"I am so sorry," I repeated as Abby and I released each other from a quick hug. I turned to the older woman. "Pepper Reece, one of Liz's customers. And friends."

"Maggie Delaney. I'm Abby's mother."

"Oh, you're taking over the cottage this summer," I said. "What will happen to it? To all of this? I imagine it goes to her cousin, but they weren't close."

"No idea. TJ said for now, we should carry on, until the lawyers figure things out," Abby said. She gazed out over the acreage, and Maggie and I did the same. "Nobody can replace her."

Liz had been an only child, and her father had died when she was young. When her mother died of cancer, Liz had dropped out of college, taken the small nest egg she'd been left, and come west, seeking solace working the land. That was about all I knew of her life before lavender.

"We've been trying to finish the cleanup and get the place put back together," Abby continued. "Liz had already lined up the contractors, thank goodness. The metalworker is coming tomorrow to repair the frame, so the new glass can be installed. Then the ventilation system can be replaced."

"What about the distillery? Although I guess you won't need it until later in the summer."

"I hope Orion can fix it," Abby said. "He always works with Liz on the distilling process."

Maggie gave her daughter a sharp look that I couldn't interpret, but Abby got the message.

"He'll be back, Mom. He just needed to clear his head."

Something pressed against my leg. The big gray tux. I scooped him up. "Hello, Sir. What a good, brave cat you are. I bet you miss your mom."

Leslie Budewitz · 107

"What is that boy thinking," Maggie said, "traipsing around in the woods with that dog, when there's work to be done here?"

"He didn't know, Mom. He left before the greenhouse was damaged."

"Dog?" I asked. "Is that why there's a water bowl sitting out? I assumed it was for visiting dogs."

"No, it's for Brambo," Abby said. "Orion's dog. They are inseparable." She tapped her phone screen and showed me a picture of a slender young man with light brown hair and a silly grin, sitting in a black camp chair with a reddish-brown dog sprawled across his lap. A dog who had long outgrown lap sitting, though neither of them wanted to admit it.

"What a dog! What is he?" I asked.

"A Pudelpointer. They're German, a cross between a poodle and a pointer." Abby tucked her phone away. "Orion got him as a puppy. They're hunting dogs. Orion doesn't hunt, despite his name, but they hike. And swim, and hike some more. He's a total goof and I adore him."

She was talking as much about Orion as about Brambo, I thought. And I thought a man that attached to his dog would not have left a water bowl upside down. He'd have righted it without even thinking.

Though that was hardly evidence, and hardly likely to convince Sheriff Aguilar of Orion Fisher's innocence.

"Well, Orion can't come back soon enough," Maggie said. "We need help. I don't know why you refused Danny's offer."

"Mom, you know Liz didn't trust Danny. She didn't want him anywhere near the farm. And if Orion was here, Sheriff Aguilar would throw him in jail." She sneezed. "Sorry. I'm allergic to cats."

I set Sir on the ground and wiped my hands on my pants. He moseyed off, in search of field mice.

Tires crunched the gravel as the sheriff drove slowly up the driveway.

"Speak of the devil," Maggie said, in a tone reeking of opinion.

"What does he want?" Abby muttered. "He's already raked us over the coals. Taken all the pruners and who knows what else. How are we supposed to run a farm without tools?"

108 · *Lavender Lies Bleeding*

"Hello, Maggie," Sheriff Aguilar said when we met him by the cottage. "Ms. Reece. I suppose I shouldn't be surprised to see you."

I acknowledged him with a nod.

"Abby," he continued. "You've been hard to catch up with, since your former boss's unfortunate passing."

"I've been home, here, or at Mom's house. If you haven't found me, that doesn't say much about your sheriffing skills."

"Abby," her mother chided, but Abby's face remained defiant.

"Why don't you save us both all this trouble and tell me where he is?" Aguilar asked.

"I keep telling you I don't know. He went camping north of Stehekin. I can't reach him. He had nothing to do with this. You and Desiree, you both think he's a criminal. He's not."

"Stehekin?" I'd been there once, ages ago. "On Lake Chelan? You can only get there by boat, right?"

"Right," Abby said. "He takes the ferry, then backpacks."

Meaning it wouldn't be easy to slip in and out unnoticed.

"Joe," Maggie said. "You know if Orion were anywhere near Salmon Falls, he'd have been here every waking moment since the vandalism occurred, working his tail off."

If he'd been here, would Liz still be alive? *Don't play "what if" games, Pepper,* I told myself. They never help.

Aguilar ignored Maggie and trained a steely eye on Abby. "You think you know your young man. Admirable to stand up for him, but sorely mistaken."

Abby blanched. Her mother put out a steadying hand, glancing from her daughter to the sheriff and back.

"Sheriff, that's a serious allegation," I said. "If you know something about Orion, why not tell us?"

"Fair enough. He has a pair of juvenile arrests for marijuana possession. Last winter, he picked a fight with a man in the Draught House. Threw a punch. Broke the man's nose."

"He says the other man started it," Abby said.

"And every witness in the bar disagrees. He's a hothead, capable of physical violence, even if he hasn't shown that side of himself to you," Aguilar said.

Abby flushed a deep red.

"I could overlook all that, if it weren't for another matter. Back when he was a practicing pothead, he was also arrested for vandalism. Twice. He and a couple of buddies busted up a car. Then he went after his grandfather's shoe repair shop. Smashed all the windows."

Abby's face made clear this was news. Big news.

"Seems your boy likes the sound of broken glass," Aguilar said, jerking his thumb toward the ruined greenhouse.

"Joe, stop this." Maggie put out a hand. "You're being deliberately cruel."

I wondered about the history between them. "Was he charged?"

"Juvenile court, for the car. The grandfather refused to cooperate. Said it was a family matter. Kid got off easy—no time."

"Juvenile records are sealed," Abby said. As if the sheriff couldn't know the details he'd recounted. As if he must be making it up.

"Law enforcement has access," he said, and I knew he was right. Unless a juvenile record is formally expunged, a step rarely requested or granted, those files remain available to law enforcement and prosecutors. And sometimes, to employers. I'd uncovered a few surprises over the years in running background checks on job applicants.

The possession charges and a single fight weren't particularly shocking. Did the vandalism add credence to Aguilar's theories? Liz had admitted she'd argued with Orion, though she hadn't said why. But it was a long way from smashing shop windows as a teenager to stabbing your boss in the neck.

"Is that what Desiree was referring to?" Abby directed the question to me. "But how would she know?"

"Didn't you tell me she rents to him?" I asked.

"She and Jeffrey. Her husband," Abby said. "He sells real estate and manages rental property."

"That's how she knew. From the credit check a landlord can run on a potential tenant. I learned that doing HR, in a former life."

"Ohh-kayyy," Abby said. "So, all that looks suspicious. I get it. But what about the plants? The ones that were damaged in the greenhouse and the ones uprooted when she was killed are all her new hybrid."

As I had suspected.

Aguilar looked skeptical. "What are you talking about? Plants are plants."

110 · *Lavender Lies Bleeding*

"No, they're not," I said. "My parents and I went to a nursery over the weekend. My dad was scouting the lavender. The nursery woman said some varieties are better for cooking and others for fragrance, but she knew a grower working on a hybrid that would combine both. Previous attempts weren't very vigorous, but this was a sturdy plant, grown right here in the region. She said it would be huge. Highly sought-after."

"What's your point?" Aguilar's tone said he doubted the relevance.

"She also said they'd hoped to have the plants later this summer, but there had been a setback." I pointed at the ruined greenhouse. "Like that."

"See?" Abby's voice rose in indignation. "If Orion was angry enough to damage the greenhouse and kill Liz—which I don't believe. But if he was, why would he have targeted just those plants?"

"A stabbing is usually a crime of opportunity, isn't it?" I asked. "A crime of passion."

"That's no defense," Aguilar said.

"No, but it might help us understand the crime and narrow the field of suspects."

"There is no 'us,' Ms. Reece. This is a matter for law enforcement."

I swatted his objection away, another buzzing bee. "Abby's right. Anyone acting out of anger would not have been so careful. This person was focused. He—or she—wanted us to think this was a crime of rage. The heat of the moment. But I think the killer had a plan. And he knew what plants to look for."

"Someone wanted to blame Orion?" Abby demanded. "To make him look guilty? But why?"

Always the question.

"You're saying a person or persons unknown committed murder to keep this mysterious plant off the market," Aguilar said. "That doesn't make any sense."

"If the theory doesn't explain the facts," I said, "then we need a different theory."

"Or more facts. Though I keep telling you, you're not part of this investigation."

But he was beginning to question his own thinking, even if he didn't want to admit it. That was a good start.

"I don't get what makes this lavender special," he said. "Everyone around here grows the stuff. They put it in vases and lemonade and dresser drawers. Doesn't matter what variety it is."

"We get this question in the Spice Shop," I said. "There's thyme you grow between the stones on your walkway, and thyme you grow to eat. Turkish oregano gives you one flavor profile, Mexican another. Same with bay leaves. Lavender has aromatic properties, along with culinary and medicinal uses. As you say, you can use any variety for any purpose, but some are optimal for particular uses."

"It's like apples," Maggie said. "You want a snack, you grab a Red Delicious. But you wouldn't bake a pie with them—too mushy. The mouth knows, even if the brain can't explain the differences."

Aguilar nodded, slowly. I sent Maggie mental thanks for the metaphor.

"Have you identified the weapon?" I asked.

"You ought to know I can't talk about that," Aguilar said.

"That's why you took all the pruning knives from the greenhouse, though, right?" Abby asked. He didn't answer, and she changed the subject. "Do you have Liz's phone? We need to keep the business going and it would help."

"Not ready to release it."

"If you have her phone," I said, "you know she and I were texting yesterday afternoon. That might help you determine the time of death." I pulled out my own phone and started scrolling. "She said she had to go—someone was coming. Maybe her other texts will tell you who that was."

"The killer," Abby cried.

"Or the beekeeper," Aguilar said. "The UPS guy. An insurance adjuster. People are in and out of here all the time."

"Sheriff," I said. "You know Liz had a public spat with her old friend, Desiree White, over Desiree's business plans. We know Desiree is vengeful—she fired Abby for standing up for Liz. And she may have known about Orion's juvenile vandalism. What if she went after Liz, in a way that diverted your attention to Orion?"

"Believe it or not, Ms. Reece, I have actually considered Ms. White. But she was tied up at the B&B all afternoon. Staff training."

Parsley poop. After the way Desiree spoke to Abby Saturday night at the wedding, I seriously wanted some heat and blame to scorch her.

112 · *Lavender Lies Bleeding*

I had to get going. I scribbled my cell number on a business card and handed it to Abby. "Call me anytime. Maggie, it was nice to meet you despite the circumstances."

I was about to ask Aguilar for a private word when he fell into step beside me. Wanting to make sure I left?

"I've asked around about you," he said.

Uh-oh. What he heard would depend on who he talked to. Detectives Spencer and Armstrong would vouch for me. Detective Tracy might brand me a meddler or begrudge that I'm occasionally helpful. Depended on his blood sugar.

"I know you've been useful to the Seattle Police Department a time or two. But I don't want another felony, or another victim."

"I'll be careful, I promise. Sheriff, Liz told you she didn't hear anything when the greenhouse was damaged, and you were skeptical. But she told me she'd taken a gummy for sleep and the THC knocked her out." I pointed to her house. "Her bedroom's on the far side, as far as you can get from the greenhouse. She didn't tell you because you had this theory that the vandalism was a frustrated search for pot plants, and you might connect all that and not take the damage seriously. Not look hard for the real culprit. But now . . ."

"Are you saying she knew about Fisher's record?"

"Maybe. She probably didn't run a credit check—most small employers don't, especially when they hire someone they already know. Like the Delaneys."

A look I couldn't read flickered across his face. What was his connection to that family? And was he feeling some of the same guilt that was weighing on me?

"Anyway, there could have been a lot of reasons she was having trouble sleeping. But I suspect it had to do with the struggle over the future of farmland. Which brings us back to Desiree White."

"Hmmph," was all he said. Then, when we were almost at our vehicles, he spoke again. "I know it looks to you and Abby like I'm focusing on Orion unfairly. A walkabout is not a solid alibi, especially for a man with a history like his."

Fair enough.

"But that's not all," he continued. "I have a witness who swears Orion Fisher stood right here ranting and raving the day before the greenhouse was damaged."

"Liz said they had a disagreement, but that it would blow over."

"More than that, according to my witness. And no, I will not name names." He glanced over at Abby and her mother. No doubt he didn't want me telling the girl who'd spilled the beans about her boyfriend.

Aguilar climbed into his rig. Sir had followed us and I picked him up, stroking his silky gray fur. What would happen to him?

I watched the sheriff motor down the driveway.

And what about the sheriff's question: Who would kill for lavender?

Seventeen

One thing you can count on in a small town: You may not know what you're doing, but someone else will.

IN GRACE HOUSE, THE COMMUNITY WHERE I GREW UP, THERE was always a card table in the living room, a jigsaw puzzle in progress. The men and women who came and went, young and idealistic, drawn by the community's programs or caught up in the causes of the day, would snap a piece or two into place as they passed by. The image on the box—the Swiss Alps, the Sistine Chapel, Salvador Dali's melting clocks—emerged slowly. Not until someone sat and made an effort did the picture come into focus.

I hadn't worked on a jigsaw in years—decades—but I was working on one now, in my mind, as I drove north on Mrs. Luedtke Road. If I read the tiny map on my phone right, it would swing around and take me back into town. Not from the moose end of Main Street, where I'd come out, but from the other end, where the curious garden grew.

Alas, I was working a puzzle without benefit of the picture on the box.

The time of death didn't help much, not without knowing who Liz had been expecting. Knowing the type of weapon didn't narrow things down, either. In this town, the question wasn't who had a pruning knife, but who didn't. Even then, the killer could have

Leslie Budewitz · 115

grabbed one from the greenhouse, in the corner where Liz kept her tools.

The road curved and twisted, a reflection of my thoughts. I crossed a narrow bridge, a sign warning of ice. Not today.

Thinking of the greenhouse reminded me of the copper distilling urns and pipes. When all we were dealing with was vandalism, I'd wondered if the culprits had intended to steal the copper but been spooked into running off before the deed was done. Not by Liz, deep in sleep, but a passerby or a sudden noise. A dog barking? But the murder put an end to that speculation.

Assuming the two were related. They had to be, didn't they?

The road had curved away from where I thought town lay. I was lost, in more ways than one.

"Slow down, Pepper," I said out loud.

I pulled into a farm turnout to give myself a moment to work things out. An irrigation stream wound through the fields, past the backside of a weathered gray barn, cattails signaling a nearby pond. A cluster of bushy green shrubs I couldn't identify clung to the stream bank, scaffolding for a tumble of red azaleas whose blossoms dipped into the water. An old homestead, a farm woman's prized flowering shrub now gone wild. Add a few sheep or a water wheel for an idyllic scene. Perfect for a jigsaw puzzle.

Focus, Pepper.

Aguilar had initially thought the greenhouse damage was a work of random vandalism. Thrill seeking. Destruction for the sake of destruction. Then, when he unearthed Orion Fisher's juvenile record, he'd concluded that the presence of a young man with anger issues and a history of violence—how had he put it? A love of broken glass—painted a clear picture.

Add in a recent dispute between said young man and the property owner, and the sheriff had been convinced.

Never mind that by all accounts, Orion and Liz got along great. But they'd had a disagreement. I couldn't overlook that. Liz hadn't said what it was about, and neither had Abby, if she knew. Was that why Orion had taken to the woods with his dog and his tent and left no word of his plans?

A dark pickup drove past me. Time to get a move on. Pretty as this place was, and conducive to my musings, I had places to be and people to quiz.

116 · *Lavender Lies Bleeding*

I needed to come at this from a different angle, I thought as I slipped the Saab into gear. Say the greenhouse damage had been deliberate. Why target Liz? What was the message?

That she could be stopped, or slowed down? Not likely. Anyone who knew Liz knew a roadblock only made her work harder.

I checked the road and my mirrors and hit the gas.

Then there was the stabbing. I'd wondered briefly, in our conversation among the plants, whether the uprooting of the new varietals was meant to destroy the plants or make two separate crimes appear similar. To appear linked.

Two different criminals. Two different patterns. Two different goals.

But if they were linked, was the goal to get rid of Liz or to destroy the seedlings? Which was the target, which the collateral damage?

Well, pooh. Mrs. Luedtke Road hit a dead end. Kind of like my thoughts. Without warning, it teed into an unnamed crossroad. A small sign pointed right, to the state park, home of the actual falls. I didn't bother checking GPS, and took a chance on left.

Detective Michael Tracy of the Seattle Police Department Major Crimes Unit, aka homicide and other dastardly deeds, would cringe to hear that I considered him a mentor. I was an amateur in his mind, a meddler who'd gotten lucky a time or two—or more—identifying clues and stopping a killer without getting seriously hurt, or worse, in the process.

Reflexively, I rubbed the knee that had been scraped raw a few weeks ago when a killer tried to drown me in the city's Ship Canal.

But Tracy had taught me a few useful lessons. One is that when two incidents happen in close proximity, or in the proximity of the same person, there's a strong likelihood that they are connected. Logical, and I'd seen how often it was true.

This time, I wasn't so sure.

The road straightened. I passed a small subdivision of family homes on large lots with lush, green lawns and sturdy fruit trees. An old orchard, maybe? Pretty and inviting, and the very fate Liz and other farm advocates hoped the event center property could avoid.

I'd also learned that some crime truly is random. Wrong place at the wrong time. Coincidence, much as cops like Tracy and Aguilar dislike the thought. But even random crimes have their logic. The perpetrator wants something. It could be as simple as a rush, as stupid as a dare. As purposeful as a desire to make someone who'd hurt them suffer in the same way. What had the vandal wanted? What had the killer wanted?

I had no idea. As Aguilar had said, we needed more facts.

The road made another turn, curving back into Salmon Falls. I breathed a sigh of relief.

Near the garden, I slowed. An unexpected splash of beauty, like the wild azalea or this garden, stirs the soul. A man hoed between the rows. A blue bike leaned against the side of the garage turned potting shed. A shepherd lay next to it. The same man, bike, and dog Cayenne and I had seen last week on our drive out of town.

I parked and climbed out. Opened the metal gate. At the squeal of the hinge, the gardener stopped and straightened. Hmong like Sara, with the same olive skin and dark eyes. He took off his hat and black hair flopped across his forehead. He shoved it back, like she had.

"What a fabulous garden! And what a great location."

"Thanks. Glad for the rain, glad it stopped." At the sound of the man's voice, the shepherd pushed himself up and ambled over. The man stroked the dog's ear.

A small sign sprouted amid the zinnias. 'Community Alliance of Salmon Falls,' it read.

He followed my gaze. "We want people to know who we are. Our plans may have been blocked this time, but we're not going away."

"I'm not sure what you mean."

"There are people in Salmon Falls," he continued, "who call gardens like ours eyesores. They'd rather see some fancy event center than snap peas and sweet peas. I want them to see how beautiful a garden patch in the middle of town can be. When I'm here working, every single person who walks or drives by stops. And they buy."

Gardens like ours, he'd said. Who were the others he was referring to?

"I take it the Community Alliance is a group of growers?"

He snapped a fat pod off a vine. Handed it to me. Before I could bite into the ripe sugar pea, a thought struck me.

"Oh," I said. "Is the Alliance the group that tried to buy the farm that ultimately sold to Desiree White? Are you all Hmong?"

118 · *Lavender Lies Bleeding*

And then another thought hit me, but I kept it to myself. Was the Alliance the group Nina Ascension had been referring to, when she told Sara that Liz's death would harm her group's efforts? When Liz spoke up for the small farms, had she been advocating for the Alliance? Now I remembered that she'd mentioned a meeting.

"Roughly half." He leaned on the handle of his hoe, gazing up the street. "And they are not going to stop us."

They? I turned to see what he saw. No one. The sidewalk in front of Lavender House and Blossom was empty.

Oh. He meant the Whites.

I didn't need flowers or vegetables. But I needed facts, and this might be the place to dig up a few.

"Pepper Reece," I said. "I am—was—a friend of Liz Giacometti. And of Sara Vu."

"My cousin and co-conspirator." His wary look gave way to playfulness, now that I'd identified myself as friend, not foe. "Preston Vu."

I bit into the pea. Crisp and green and so tasty. "Can I get some of these? Is it U-Pick?"

"If no one is here," Preston said. "Right now, let's call it Help-U-Pick." He grabbed a tin bucket from an upside-down stack at the end of the row, and we dropped the pea pods in. "Baby carrots? Rainbow colors. Fresh spinach and chard."

"How about the carrots and zinnias?" I watched him pull a pair of clippers out of a bulging pocket. Was there a pruning knife in there, too?

But why would this friendly man have gone after Liz or her greenhouse? She'd been on his side.

"Was Liz part of the Alliance?" I asked as I watched him snip zinnias and strip off the bottom leaves.

"Not formally." He unwrapped a length of twine from a roll stuck on a post, snipped it off, and tied it around the stems. "She had land. She wanted to help us get ours, through purchase or a long-term lease. She tried to act as go-between, but it didn't pan out."

"What happens now that she's gone?"

"We keep trying, reaping what we sowed." He gestured to the rows of raspberries and blackberries, strung on wires like grapevines, the raised bed filled with strawberries, and the other bounty in waiting. But I didn't think that was all he meant.

Leslie Budewitz · 119

One more question. "Who owns this property? The Alliance?" If the Alliance couldn't match the bid for the farm, how could they have bought a piece of prime real estate in the heart of town?

"The squash blossoms are really coming on," he said, pointing at a deep green plant filled with pale yellow flowers. "You can sauté them or stuff them."

I was about to press him on the property ownership when his pocket buzzed. "Gotta take this," he said, pulling out his phone. "Nice to meet you." We shook on it, and he retreated to the garage, the dog at his heels.

I slipped cash into the metal box and tucked my finds in the car. Stood on the sidewalk, wondering what to do. Lavender House Bed and Breakfast was right next door. Dare I?

Before I could make up my mind, a side door opened and a man in a brown uniform emerged. Walked briskly along a stone path beside the house, and through a gap in the hedge to a parking area behind the B&B.

Sheriff Joe Aguilar.

Decision made. Next stop: Lavender House. If Preston Vu was watching me, I didn't mind.

Aguilar had said he understood my suspicions, but that Desiree was not who Liz had been waiting for at the farm yesterday afternoon. The restaurateur, caterer, and innkeeper had been tied up at the B&B, training new staff for the busy season ahead. Had he come back to probe deeper?

What was that old line about alibis—only the guilty need them? Not that I was that cynical. But it wouldn't hurt to ask a few questions.

The grand old house would have been right at home in the uphill, upscale neighborhoods of Seattle. Deep flower beds curved around the front porch, filled with white azaleas, tall butterfly bushes, and golden lilies. Stone urns of rosemary, lavender, and other herbs stood guard at the foot of the steps. A pair of tasteful pots held the plant Sara had introduced me to, amaranth or love-lies-bleeding. I admired the gracious style of the place all while knowing what a lot of work—and money—maintaining it must take. Wicker chairs and small, round tables waited patiently for guests to sit and enjoy the view of town and the foothills. They made me want a mint julep, and I don't even know what's in a mint julep. Besides mint.

Ooh. We should do a class on herbal cocktails. I made a mental note.

I opened the door—golden oak, with polished brass hardware and an oval window—and stepped inside.

It was like stepping back in time. Wood floors gleamed, giving off a faint scent of orange oil. Dark beams matched the wainscoting and the staircase. The furniture was a timeless mix of leather sofas and Mission-style tables and chairs. Twin wingbacks, beautifully upholstered in a pink and green fabric, reminded me of the sweeter aspects of my recent misadventures. Even the lighting was perfect, straight from a Tiffany copycat showroom.

If this had once been a family home, as I surmised, it must have belonged to a wealthy family. The town banker, or the manager of the power company out at the falls. Had it belonged to Desiree's family? No—Daria had said she and Jeffrey bought out here after Desiree had burned her bridges in Seattle.

Every town has its haves and have-nots. And its hardworking people in the middle, like Liz. Or me.

"Can I help you?" a female voice called. I put on my pleasant retail expression. The voice, smooth and polished, belonged to a woman in her late fifties, a salon blonde with an inviting expression. She stood behind a reception counter that was obviously not original but built to match.

"I hope so. Your place would make a terrific getaway, when my honey gets home. We live in Seattle, and he's been away for work, and well, you know."

"I know just what you mean." She gave me a sly wink. "We specialize in romantic getaways. Champagne and chocolates when you arrive. Breakfast any time you like, at Blossom, our restaurant next door. And the rooms are luscious. We have a couple of vacancies right now, so I can show you one or two."

"Oh, great! If you're not busy."

"Oh, no. Afternoons are always quiet around here. When are you thinking? Summer dates are filling up."

"Hmm. Early June? We could come midweek."

"Let me check." She studied a screen I couldn't see.

"The place is beautiful."

"Thanks. I can't take credit—I'm just the front desk manager." She clicked away. "We've all worked here for years."

Leslie Budewitz · 121

"That speaks well of the owner." If the crew was experienced, who was Desiree training? My guess, she'd given Aguilar the lie, not expecting him to check. Until a few minutes ago.

"She likes to say the place practically runs itself." The desk manager raised her head. "First two weeks of June, we could do a Tuesday check-in and a Thursday or Friday departure."

"That could work," I said.

She grabbed a set of keys and came out from behind the desk. "The two of you, no kids or pets?"

Did Bark Place do overnights? I didn't think so. But Arf loves Glenn, and Kristen's girls are always begging to take him. "No kids and the dog has his own getaway."

I followed her up the polished stairs, running my hand along the satiny-smooth railing. As promised, the rooms were elegant but comfortable, with all the right touches. Including, I noticed, large vases filled with roses and lilies and other blooms I had not seen outside or in the Alliance garden next door.

In the second guest room, where the wallpaper was an ode to the peony, I walked to the window.

"How wonderful to have that beautiful garden so handy. I bet the owner is thrilled."

"Ye-e-s," she said, not meaning it.

They weren't buying flowers and produce from the Alliance, I was sure. Too soon, the conflict too fresh.

I followed my guide down the stairs. "Do you hold weddings here? Perfect setting."

"Small ones. We hope to have another location soon, for bigger events."

I thanked her and left. A romantic weekend away might be just the ticket for Nate and me. But not here.

I strolled up the street, past Blossom and Jeffrey White's office. Tonight was movie night, the weekly gathering of my Flick Chicks pals. We were meeting at Laurel's houseboat, and I could not remember the name of the movie. Dinner is potluck, except when Laurel hosts. She runs a fabulous deli in downtown Seattle and brings home our favorites. Seetha and Aimee, neither enthusiastic cooks, would bring the wine. If I remembered right, Cayenne and I had walked past a gift shop, closed at the time, that carried locally made fudge. Always in good taste.

122 · *Lavender Lies Bleeding*

The shop was open, the sweet tinkle of the bells that hung on the door summoning a woman from the back room.

"Welcome to Calico," she said. "Our shop is an arts collective, carrying work by a wide range of local artists. Just browsing, or is there something I can help you find?"

"My kind of place. I need a treat for movie night, and I hear raves about your fudge." What I'd heard was "killer" and "to die for," but those were words for a different day.

"All well-earned." She pointed to a glass-front case. "The six varieties on the bottom are the classics, always in stock. The six on top are a rotating cast of flavors. Care for a sample?"

Chocolate with hazelnuts and cherries. White chocolate lemon. Peanut butter fudge. How could I possibly choose?

The sample—dark chocolate raspberry—clinched the deal. I chose two each of six varieties, leaving the rest for next time. "Hmm. I need a bite for the drive back to Seattle. Oh." I pointed at a tray of creamy white and purple squares. "Are those violets on top?"

"Lavender fudge, made with honey and white chocolate, topped with candied forget-me-nots."

A stabbing pain pierced my chest and I caught my breath.

I will not forget you, Liz, or my promise.

As the woman packed the fudge, I walked around the shop. I admit being a bit jaded, after working for years now beside some of the best artists and crafts people in the region, but most of what I saw compared nicely. A beaded leather bracelet called my name, and I was sorely tempted by a pair of swirling copper earrings. The children's corner held wooden tops, trucks, trains, wooly lambs, and other snugglies.

"Those are done with alcohol ink," the woman called when I paused in front of a wall of ethereal paintings. Then I came to a display of framed photographs. Mount Rainier, Mount Baker, a field of poppies. Breathtaking images of iris and lavender. And half a dozen different shots of the barn I'd seen this afternoon, including one with the barn in the background and the red azaleas tumbling into the stream. The vision that had quite literally stopped me.

I plucked it off the wall. "What is this place?"

"Oh," she said, sealing my box with a gold sticker. "That's Salter Farm. So picturesque. I hope it doesn't get ruined in the pursuit of progress."

Leslie Budewitz · 123

Salter Farm. Monica's family place? "What do you mean?"

"I mean, I know our economy needs diversification. But it was a highly productive farm for generations, and it could be again, with the right hands behind the plow." She set the box and a small white bag next to the cash register. "No charge for the lavender squares."

"Thanks. I'll take this picture, too."

Next to the register was a display of stickers and buttons. 'Eat Local.' 'Don't Complain About Food Prices with Your Mouth Full.' And 'Farms are for Farming.'

"All proceeds from the stickers and buttons go to the Community Alliance," the woman said. "The group that tried to buy Salter Farm but got priced out. Raw deal, if you ask me."

"I gather that sparked a bit of a debate in the community."

"Shouldn't have, but it did. Art is essential. Celebrations and gatherings make us human. But first, we need to eat."

"In other words, farms are for farming." I added a button proclaiming the motto to my purchases.

Minutes later, I stashed my shopping bag in the Saab. Salter Farm. So fertile that landless growers were willing to band together to sink their roots into it. So enticing that a local entrepreneur wanted to turn it into an event center. So picturesque that photographs of it filled a gift shop wall.

I'd been handed a critical piece of the puzzle. But where did it fit? What was the picture taking shape?

Every metaphor has its limitations, and I'd run smack into the limits of this one.

Eighteen

The first automobile drove across the Lake Washington Floating Bridge, connecting Seattle to Mercer Island, in 1940, after eighteen months of construction by 3,000 workers using floats on concrete pontoons. In November 1990, after a week of high winds and rain, the bridge sank.

ONE MORE STOP BEFORE I GOT BACK ON THE ROAD.

"Stainless steel blade," the sixty-ish man in the ag supply said, plucking a shiny tool off a wall full of shiny tools. "Beveled on both sides. You want a folding knife, or your gardening pants will all look like mine." He pointed at the leg of his canvas work pants, the fabric scuffed and scarred where he'd missed the hammer loop and cargo pocket with his tools.

"Isn't that how gardening pants are supposed to look?" The blade on the knife he handed me was three or four inches long, gently curved, the point as deadly as the blade itself. "It's for my dad. Now that they have a house again, he's all in on gardening. He wants to make sure his new lavender plants keep their shape."

"Father's Day is coming up. Lavender, you say? Then you want—" He broke off. Turned away, a reddened fist to his lips. "Sorry about that. You're not from here, you wouldn't know, but—"

Leslie Budewitz · 125

"No apology needed. I own the Spice Shop in Pike Place Market. Liz grows—grew—all our culinary lavender. I'm as shocked by her death as you are. It's why I came out to Salmon Falls today."

"Heck of a girl," he said. "I told the boss he was a fool not to hang on to her, but you never know what's going on between people. Then he goes and marries a girl who could be her kid sister." He shook his head at the ways of men. And women. "Plenty of folks around here grow lavender and some are pretty good at it. But Liz had a special touch. And plans."

"Connected to the new varietal she was working on?" I asked. "She gave me a seedling."

His eyes were wide and damp as they met mine. "Guard it, young lady. You might be one of the lucky few."

I nodded, my own eyes and throat swelling. I had been lucky to know Liz, and to call her a friend.

I gestured at the shelf full of pruners, both clippers and knives. "I'm guessing you sell a lot of these."

"We do. Out here, everyone's a grower, whether they're tending a single heritage lilac or acres of cherries and apricots. Some folks prefer pruning shears, but if you want a knife, the one you're holding is a good all-around option." He pointed to an empty spot. "I'm partial to that one. Handle has a nice feel to it—good balance." He closed his fingers lightly around an imaginary pruner, as if testing the heft.

"Looks like plenty of other people agree with you."

"Joe Aguilar took the last one, first thing this morning. Took one of each." He pressed his lips together. "I didn't have to ask why."

Neither did I. "I'm sure my dad will get a lot of use out of this. Thanks for your help."

I paid for my purchase and headed back to my car. Such a good visitor I was today, coming to town and leaving plenty of money behind.

My guess, and you didn't have to be educated in the ways of law enforcement to make it, was that the medical examiner's initial observation of the wounds that killed Mary Elizabeth Giacometti suggested a short-bladed knife. Possibly one with a round hilt between blade and handle, like the one I'd just bought. Could the autopsy show whether the blade had been curved or beveled? That was beyond my amateur speculation.

126 · *Lavender Lies Bleeding*

Amateur. *Amo, amas, amat.* Latin hadn't been part of the Mass or the Catholic school curriculum by the time I came along, but who hasn't heard the familiar conjugation of the verb "to love"? Amateurs are often dismissed as untrained and therefore unqualified, but I knew better. Amateur cooks and amateur homicide investigators are both driven by the same irresistible force: Love.

THE CLOSER I got to Seattle, the happier I was to be driving against commuter traffic, not with it.

I'd learned a lot today, though I had more questions than answers.

I slid the Saab into the middle lane. What would happen to the farm? Liz's cousin back east might be the heir, but from what I'd heard, she couldn't be less interested. Who would buy it? TJ and the Manning family? Their property surrounded hers. I couldn't imagine them wanting to operate a five-acre lavender farm. Growing the stuff was just the start. Then came the harvesting, distilling, packaging, and marketing, not to mention making the products. Plenty of retailers and commercial producers relied on her for culinary buds and essential oil. She'd been the heart of a thriving business. How could it survive without her?

And the seedlings. Was Abby right in thinking their damage a significant clue? Easier to understand if they'd been stolen, either for resale or for study.

Did we need another supplier? Too soon to tell. Abby loved the farm, but running it, with or without Orion, was a big job. Liz had managed, but she was a force.

Had someone wanted to keep Liz from expanding? Who, and why?

And what had they done to stop her?

I'd reached the I-90 bridge over Lake Washington, aka the floating bridge. Instinctively, I glanced to the right and then to the left. Clear skies and a two-mountain day—Mount Baker to the north, Mount Rainier to the south. Guaranteed to make even the grumpiest commuter smile.

Seattle's drawbridges are charmers, but the two long spans crossing Lake Washington can be daunting, especially for those of us who don't drive them often. And now I'd been on both in less than a week.

Leslie Budewitz · 127

That thought reminded me of going to Mindy and Javier's wedding a few nights ago.

Mindy's family was fortunate—not every family can keep a business going, one generation to the next. TJ Manning's family was doubly lucky, with one son running the farm and the other taking over the ag supply. I understood Monica Salter's sadness at watching her husband's family sell off their homestead. But her boys were urban teenagers. They spent their time on school and soccer and chasing each other through the neighborhood, not digging into the intricacies of soil composition and soaking up wisdom about irrigation methods. I couldn't blame them for selling—how long should a family hold on to a farm, on the chance that the next generation might take it over in a few years? Especially if, as Monica had said, they'd gotten an excellent offer.

But I also understood the resentment nagging Sara, Preston, and other members and supporters of the Alliance. They'd been outbid. Those who had, got more; those who had little got shut out.

At the island, traffic plunged into the tunnel. Into the dark. Fitting metaphor.

After a few more miles, I traded one freeway for another, then took the Madison Street exit. Left, right, and left again. I parked next to a sign reading 'Reserved for Puppy Parents.' Inside Bark Place, in the glassed-in playroom for the larger and midsized dogs, Arf and a fluffy white thing were nosing a ball back and forth. Like little kids passing a soccer ball, missing occasionally, twirling with joy all the while. The playroom attendant spotted me and called to Arf. Moments later, man and dog emerged, and I crouched, arms open. Was Arf as happy to see me as I was to see him? I hoped so.

"He is such a good boy," the attendant said. "He follows commands and makes friends easily. You saw how well he played with Polo."

"I bet you say that to all the dog parents." I rubbed Arf's face and ears between my hands, and he waggled his head, eager for more. "Especially the daycare rookies."

"Oh, I wish," Arf's new friend said. "Some dogs are not nearly as well behaved as their owners think they are. I don't think I heard him bark once all afternoon."

"I can't take credit for Arf's good behavior. He came to me fully trained." I took his leash and stood, my knee creaky after the drive.

128 · Lavender Lies Bleeding

"I'm grateful you could take him today, though I don't know when we'll be back."

"We'll always be happy to see Arf."

And that made me happy. Back in the car, we drove the short distance to the Market. I've been known to grumble about shopkeepers who take up the few valuable parking spaces on Pike Place. But it was late in the day and when I saw a spot open in front of the shop, I grabbed it.

Arf greeted the staff enthusiastically. They all love him, but his afternoon at Bark Place had been good for all of us.

After closing, Arf and I hopped in the Saab.

The Lake Union houseboat community is one of my favorite things about Seattle. We say houseboats, though most are technically floating homes. Some are modern architectural marvels; others, like Laurel's, are cozy retreats. I wasn't out of the car yet when a white Suburban parked beside me. I did a double take. Kristen's rig, but she was in the passenger seat. She mimed a scared face, and I saw Savannah at the wheel. The girls often join us when the Flick Chicks meet at Kristen's, but Savannah hadn't come to movie night at another house before. The lure of the chance to drive, no doubt.

"We lived," Kristen said as she opened the door and climbed out. "Happily, no freeway driving required. She's not up to that yet. But soon."

Savannah came around the front of the SUV, dropped the keys into her mother's outstretched hand, and bent to greet Arf.

"It's a day for new things," I said. "He spent his first afternoon at doggy daycare."

"I bet you were everybody's favorite," Savannah said, giving him a big smooch. We headed for the docks, passing under the giant weeping willow. Savannah unlatched the gate, and we stepped onto the long dock, greeted by the musky, fishy smells that should have been unpleasant but weren't. A pair of young cats watched us from the door mat at the first houseboat, one black with white paws and a white face, the other tortoise shell with a white stripe running down her face and chest.

A man with a watering can in his hand greeted us with a hearty hello. Was this the neighbor Laurel insisted she wasn't dating, despite their occasional dinners out and sails on the lake?

"Oh, pretty kitties!" Savannah cried.

Leslie Budewitz · 129

"Dot and Dash," the man said. "Rescues I couldn't resist."

Cute, and clearly skeptical about Arf, so we didn't stop to visit.

As we neared Laurel's boat, Aimee waved to us from the rooftop deck. Then Seetha popped into view, raising a champagne flute in greeting. Both single thirtysomethings, they live in the same building a few blocks away on Eastlake Avenue and mosey down the hill together when we meet at Laurel's.

The front door was open. Kristen called a greeting and we walked in. A large white ball of cat fur streaked past us and up the narrow steps to hide in Gabe's old bedroom. Snowball had adopted Laurel and her son, now away at college, when they moved to the dock a few years ago. The cat's history was as much a mystery as Arf's, but it must have involved a bad encounter with a dog—she hissed and fled the moment he arrived.

We found Laurel in the compact kitchen, putting the finishing touches on a charcuterie tray, a bowl of lavender goat cheese in the center. A meaty whiff caught Arf's attention and he sat, nose in the air.

"Oh, good boy," Laurel said, and held up a roll of salami. The dog remained perfectly still, but for a twitch of the nose, then she lowered her hand and the treat. He gobbled it up.

"He's better trained than you are," I said, and gave her a quick hug. She's a tall woman in her late fifties, with long, gray-brown curls. We met when I worked in the building that houses Ripe, her downtown deli.

Kristen took a bottle of Spanish cava out of her Italian leather tote bag and set it on the built-in teak table. A wooden bowl of green salad with feta, peaches, and blueberries waited for us.

"There's sparkling cider for you, Savannah," Laurel said. "In the fridge."

I set my jute tote on the bench and got out the box of fudge, the clear plastic window on top putting their beauty on full display. I hadn't managed to eat a piece on the drive home after all, and was sorely tempted now.

"I know that place," Savannah said, cider bottle in hand.

"The fudge shop?"

"No. Salter Farm." She was looking at the photo I'd bought in the gift shop, poking out of my bag. "We went there on a school field trip."

I stopped fiddling with the fudge and retrieved the photo.

"Oh, right," Kristen said, peering over her daughter's shoulder. "Aren't they selling it?"

I dropped onto the cushioned bench. "Yes. Monica told me about it when I drove up to their house to trade lavender plants. I think she said her husband's brother has been running the place. Not very well, from the impression I got."

"The barn is kinda spooky," Savannah said. "Cool, though. It's got a hay loft, and the Salter twins tried to dare us to jump out of it, but Mrs. Salter stopped them. They are total goofs."

"It's the half brother, I think," Kristen said. "He's quite a bit younger than Scott. Or maybe he's Monica's brother. I forget. One of those men who's always into something new. He must be close to forty. Monica wasn't happy about the sale, I know that, but the farm was losing money hand over fist. And it wasn't her decision to make."

"She's terrified the boys will turn out to be like Uncle Danny," Savannah said. She watched the cider bubbles subside in her glass. "I'm in drivers ed with them, and one was talking about driving his uncle's rad truck out on the farm roads. Our teacher splits them up, but no one wants to be in the back seat with either of them at the wheel."

The mysterious Danny?

"They're good kids," Kristen said. "Smart. They act like clowns but they'll grow out of it. Plus, they're twins. They egg each other on. Like the Gustafsons," she said to me.

The neighborhood terrors when we were kids. One twin had stayed in Seattle and become a neurologist. The other was a reporter I sometimes saw on TV, in the world's latest war zones.

"Do the boys want to farm?" I asked.

"I don't think so," Savannah said. "I mean, we're sixteen. Who knows?"

True enough. I couldn't remember what I'd wanted to be at sixteen, but it hadn't been a spice shop owner. Or an HR manager. Although after reading my way through Trixie Belden and Encyclopedia Brown, I might have had dreams of being an amateur sleuth.

I stared at the photo, suddenly so much more than a simple reminder that beauty lies in unexpected places.

Was Salter Farm the key to the puzzle of Liz's death?

Nineteen

A piperatorium, or pepper pot, was used in Roman times to store and serve peppercorns. Often made of silver and elaborately decorated, the pots also showed off the owner's wealth.

"OH, MY GOSH. THESE ARE FABULOUS." SANDRA BRUSHED a crumb of lavender buttermilk scone off her face. "Just the right amount of lavender. Where did you find the recipe?"

"I developed it myself," Cayenne said. "I bake my emotions."

"I eat mine," I said and plucked a scone off the tray.

The Wednesday morning staff meeting is the highlight of my work week. I love seeing the employees gathered in the nook, sipping coffee and tea over conversation and a bite, usually homemade. That's one of the advantages of hiring people who love food. It's important for the shop and warehouse staff to connect regularly, to develop trust and a good working relationship. Each crew benefits by hearing perspectives from the other side of the business.

But we were a solemn group this morning. Not everyone had known Liz, but they all felt the loss, the rip in the fabric of our community.

Liz had not been a close friend—not like Laurel, and certainly not like Kristen. But she had been a friend, and where I'd once taken her presence for granted, now her absence was everywhere.

132 · *Lavender Lies Bleeding*

We never had gotten around to watching the movie last night. Instead, we'd sat on Laurel's rooftop deck, five women and a teenage girl, working through our grief. Seetha and Aimee hadn't known Liz, and Savannah only knew of her, but it had been Laurel who'd told Liz about me when I first bought the shop. The previous owner, Jane, had not carried lavender, and Liz brought in samples to pitch me. I'd been sold on the first sniff.

We reminisced as we ate and drank, watching the sky and the lake change color. We talked and teared up and watched as the sun set behind the Olympics, as the stars came out and the lights of the Space Needle pierced the night. I worried briefly if it was too maudlin for a sixteen-year-old, but Savannah sat quietly, taking it all in, Arf by her side, and I knew if Kristen had thought it too much, she'd have steered the conversation in another direction or made an early night of it.

Grief and loss are part of life, and I remembered how my own parents had helped us learn to navigate it. Though those waters are never smooth.

"Besides the scones," Cayenne said now, "I made a blend I want you all to try." She unscrewed the lid of a Mason jar and passed it around for the sniff test.

"Girl," Sandra said. "You know we sell salt cellars and pepper pots."

Cayenne rolled her eyes. "So, try it. Tell me what you think."

I scooped up a few grains, jiggling the spoon to separate the ingredients. "Lavender, black pepper, kosher salt. Is that dried lemon zest, finely ground?" I touched the tip of my tongue to the spoon, careful to get some of everything. "Minced garlic. I like it."

So did the others. We debated leaving out the salt—requests for low-salt blends are common. Cayenne argued for it, as a balance to the pepper, and after she passed around a salt-free version, we all agreed.

"Last week, I worked with a customer who has an allium sensitivity," she said, "so that made me think I should try a version without the garlic. But it seems bland." She produced a third jar. We took more spoons and tried again.

"I can't decide," Vanessa said. "I think my tongue is tired."

"By the time my husband came home," Cayenne said, "I could not have eaten one more bite of anything lavender. Although I did manage to nibble on some lavender shortbread." She patted her belly. "For the baby. I went kinda crazy, I know. It was my way of honoring Liz and easing my own grief."

"Nothing crazy about that," I said. "I bought two pieces of lavender white chocolate fudge, and I ate them both." After I got home from movie night, too tired for the sugar to keep me awake.

"What?" Reed said in mock indignation. "You didn't bring us any?"

"Next time," I promised.

"I hate to ask," Hayden said, "but do we have another supplier? We're fully stocked for now, but Liz's stuff was the best."

"There are other growers, if we need to make a change, but let's see what happens with the farm."

"You bet," he said. "Remember the ventilation contractor is coming by this afternoon. You wanted to be there."

"Right. Two o'clock." I set the alarm on my phone as a reminder.

We went over a few other work issues—promotions, our fall blends, and scheduling changes prompted by Reed's upcoming graduation and departure. Then the warehouse staff left and the retail crew prepared to open.

I stayed in the nook with my tablet and another scone. Last night, the cellular gods had been smiling, and I'd talked with Nate for nearly an hour. I told him about Liz's death, and what I'd learned about Salter Farm and the Community Alliance.

Cayenne had finished washing the tasting spoons and set a clean jar of them on the table.

"These scones are terrific," I said. "Can we serve them as part of our lavender festival, and share the recipe?"

"Oh, gosh, yes." Her leopard print scarf complemented the beads in her hair. "Tonight, I'm going to try a lavender fondue I saw on a menu online. Sounds weird enough to be good."

"Give it a shot," I said, even though the combination did not sound great to me. "Hey, sit a moment."

She sat, her eyes questioning.

"You and Sara are friends," I said. "Has she told you anything about what's going on in Salmon Falls?"

"Not much. We first met when she came to the Market, checking the Hmong vendors. The flower ladies are the most visible, but there are others. She gives them business advice, translation if they need it, that sort of thing."

134 · *Lavender Lies Bleeding*

When Nina Ascension had flung her accusation about a conflict of interest at Sara, I'd thought she meant a conflict between the lavender growers, who wanted to preserve the area's farmland, and the festival, since Desiree, who wanted to convert a farm to another use, was a key participant. But now I wondered if she'd been implying that Sara's interest in seeing the Community Alliance, which included her cousin and other Hmong growers, buy Salter Farm was at odds with her professional obligations.

"Hang on a sec." I slid out of the booth and dashed to the office. I was back in a flash, the photograph I'd bought yesterday in hand. "Have you ever heard her mention Salter Farm?"

"Is that the farm they were trying to buy?"

"I think so."

"I don't know much. The younger generation was pushing the effort. Sara and Preston, and a few others."

"I met Preston," I said. "Her cousin. He runs the garden downtown."

"He teaches agricultural economics at a community college. He's the one who put together the bid for the farm. I didn't know that when you and I saw the garden—Sara told me at the baby shower. It's a demonstration project. To show the townspeople how direct-to-consumer sales can benefit the town, as well as the growers. He wants people to see and think about agriculture every day."

And if the Alliance had been competing with the Whites, as I was now sure, the project's proximity to Blossom, the B&B, and the real estate office was also a subtle, green middle finger.

Maybe not so subtle.

No wonder the front desk manager of the B&B had not known how to respond when I'd raved about the garden next door.

"None of this had anything to do with the vandalism, or with Liz's death, did it?" Cayenne asked.

"I don't see how." But the possibility was bugging me.

I looked at the photograph again. What was I missing?

What was I not seeing?

LIVING SO CLOSE to the shop is a plus when I need to make a delivery or run an errand outside downtown. The downside is that I don't draw many lines between my work and my life.

Leslie Budewitz · 135

I still follow the trends in HR. We used to talk about work-life balance. Now we talk about work-life fit, and aim to give employees the tools to create their own personalized integration of work and life—a flexible schedule, changes in duties, regular conversations about their goals, priorities, and aspirations.

Not so easy when you're the boss.

I left Arf in the staff's care and walked down to my building, to the garage on the lower level. The car spat and sputtered. Alternator trouble? Finally, the engine caught and settled into a decent rhythm. I crossed my fingers and drove down First to the warehouse district.

We rent space in a commercial food prep facility that serves more than a dozen different producers: ghost kitchens that prepare takeout meals for groceries and delis; a syrup maker; a pickler; and more. It's a symbiotic relationship—the pickler and the takeout guys buy spices from me, and the syrups are some of my bestsellers. Management makes sure this is a modern, food-safe facility. But a recent glitch in the ventilation system had messed with both air quality and temperature control, and I wanted to be there when the tech came by, in case he had questions or anticipated a delay in repairs that might affect us.

I parked next to the ventilation company truck. Glanced at my watch—the Saab's clock hadn't worked in years. I wasn't late. He was early. How rare is that?

Inside, I went straight to the mechanical room, where the manager stood beside a ladder, staring up at the lower half of a man dressed in sturdy Carhartts and work boots. The vent tech, I assumed.

A minute or two later, he climbed down, using one hand. Not the safest idea, even for an experienced ladder user. When both feet hit the floor, he held out his hand. Opened it to show us a collection of sticks and grasses, glued together with pale brown mud.

"I thought you got everything the last time you were here," the manager said. "That was supposed to be a thorough inspection of the entire system."

"A bird's nest?" I asked. "But—how? Aren't all the ducts screened?"

"Double screened," the vent tech said. "To keep the ducts clear even if there's a tear and debris blows in. Or flies in. No idea how we missed this. I'll take care of it right now. No charge."

136 · *Lavender Lies Bleeding*

I could tell the manager wanted to be irritated, but it's hard to be mad when a service pro acts like a pro, admits the mistake, and offers to fix it on the spot at no cost. And it's even harder to be mad at a bird, trying to make a warm, safe home for her brood.

"Well, that's a relief," I said. "I'm Pepper Reece, one of the tenants."

"Oh, I know you," the tech said. "Well, not personally. But Liz told me—" He stopped, briefly overcome, before swallowing hard and continuing. "I went out last week to size up what we need to rebuild the ventilation system. And now—"

"Liz Giacometti," I told the manager. "Lavender grower in Salmon Falls. Her greenhouse was destroyed last week, and now she's been killed."

He made the sign of the cross. "I saw that on the news."

"She mentioned you," the tech told me. "Said you were a friend she could always count on."

The compliment nearly took my breath away.

"Did she tell you who she thought was responsible for the damage?" I asked when I could speak.

"Only that she thought people were looking in the wrong direction."

Meaning Orion. But if she'd thought Desiree White was the vandal, wouldn't she have said so?

"Some people thought she was—what's the word?" he added. "Not pushy, exactly. Brusque. But I liked her."

"So did I." And I was not at all sure that Sheriff Aguilar could be made to look in the right direction.

THE WAREHOUSE CREW were all new since the first of the year. Hayden clicked off the heavy metal soundtrack the moment I walked in. I gave them a hand getting the day's special orders ready in time for the afternoon UPS pickup.

On my way back to the Market, I made a detour.

I'd never been to All Creatures, the shelter veterinary clinic, but I'm a sucker for neon and the lighted silhouette of a dog and cat tugged sharply at my heart strings. As if they weren't tender enough.

Inside, the place smelled vaguely of Lysol and wet fur. A thirty-ish man cradled a Chihuahua mix against his broad chest. The woman sitting beside him made soothing noises as she stroked

Leslie Budewitz · 137

the dog's back. Next to them, an older woman wearing several layers of clothing, despite the pleasant day, wrapped both arms around the cat carrier in her lap. I caught a glimpse of a Siamese, green-gold eyes flashing.

Despite being a place for homeless and low-income people to bring sick pets, despite the anxiety the waiting owners might feel on any number of levels, despite the hard plastic chairs, the atmosphere was warm and welcoming.

I chalked a large part of that up to the woman behind the reception counter, a full-figured Black woman with close-cropped hair and an electric smile. Her scrubs-style top was printed with the outlines of dogs and cats, a trail of paw prints running between them.

"How can I help you, dear?" she asked.

I introduced myself. "I've got a sweet Airedale, about five years old. I met a woman who used to volunteer here, and she and Arf recognized each other immediately, from when he came here with his former owner. He's perfectly healthy, but that got me thinking about his background."

"Our records are by name of owner," the receptionist said, turning to her screen. "I don't suppose you know—"

"I do. Sam. Well, that was his nickname. Winfield Scott Robinson the Third, he'd be happy to tell you. He left Seattle two years ago this fall, and entrusted Arf to me. Though he wasn't Arf's original owner. After talking with Raine—Raine McGuire, the vet tech—I thought you might be able to fill in a few details. If that's not too much to ask."

The woman's eyes darted toward me, and her manner shifted from warm to wary. What rules of confidentiality might apply, I had no idea. Did HIPAA privacy laws cover critters?

"I remember Sam," she said, her tone softening as she clicked a few keys. "One of those souls who's too gentle for this world."

"Good description. He's back in Memphis with his family, doing well."

"He and that dog had a special bond. But I don't know what I can tell you." She pressed her lips together and studied her screen, then gave a slight shake of the head. "Tell you what, dear. You leave me your name and number. I'll check into this and give you a call."

138 · *Lavender Lies Bleeding*

I gave her my card and my thanks. A side door opened and a woman wearing scrubs in the same animal print called out a name. The anxious couple with the Chihuahua stood.

"We're going to figure out what's going on with Tiny, and get him back to health," she said, her voice as warm and reassuring as the receptionist's.

I may not have known Arf's history, but it was clear that he, too, had been well treated here, and I sent the Universe a silent thank you for this special place.

Twenty

A pepperpot is a thick, spicy soup or stew of root vegetables, beans, and peppercorns, often flavored with bacon rind or tripe. Called "the soup that won the war" when a Revolutionary Army cook scrounged what he could to feed hungry troops, other versions have West Indian roots, brought to the colonies through the slave trade.

I PARKED THE SAAB IN THE LOFT GARAGE AND TOOK THE Market elevator from Western up to street level. That delivered me straight into the clutches of the flower ladies. I didn't understand a word of Hmong, but I made out my name. And there was no mistaking the looks and gestures aimed my way. If they'd been wilted by the long day, the sight of me perked them up.

"Miss Pepper," Cua called. "You were in Salmon Falls yesterday. You see my silly niece."

Sara? Silly? Hardly. "Yes," I said. A few bouquets remained, the empty buckets stacked behind the table. "The tragedy has hit her hard."

Cua dipped her head. I didn't know the details of Cua's story but I knew that, like many immigrants, the older generation of Hmong had seen a lot of tragedy.

"Sara and her cousin worked hard to help us put down roots. That Liz, she helped, too. She argued with her friend. She rallied other farmers. She talked to—who are those people?" Cua made a pulling motion with one hand, as if to drag the word she wanted out of my mouth. "People who make decisions."

"Zoning," another of the ladies said. "Planning and zoning."

"That," Cua said, chopping the air with her hand. "Yes. She talk, they listen. What will they say? We not know. But, too late."

Too late for Liz, but I didn't think that was what Cua meant. Too late to persuade the committee to reject Desiree's request for a zoning change so she could throw fancy parties? Too late to prevent working farmland from becoming mere scenery?

But even if they said no, it was too late for the Alliance to buy Salter Farm.

"That dumb kid messed things up," Cua continued.

Who did she mean? Not Sara or Preston, surely. Orion? Abby?

"We—" She thumped her chest with one sturdy finger. "We know who we can trust. Some of you—" She stopped short of pointing at me. "You give up what matters. Land. Loyalty. Family."

She didn't mean me personally. I understood that. She meant what I represented. White people, with education and access to money. Even though I hadn't finished my degree and my mother had cosigned the loan I'd taken out to buy the Spice Shop. I'd paid her off before my first anniversary in the Market. Cua meant that some of us had the option, the privilege, of valuing our individual desires over the needs of the community.

"Help Sara," Cua said to me, then turned to a woman inspecting the remaining bouquets.

I had been dismissed. I walked to my shop, wondering what Cua wanted me to do.

First things first. I dropped off the supplies I'd brought back from the warehouse, then Arf and I took a quick walk. The glorious clear sky had the visitors in a good mood, among them cruise shippers with their telltale wristbands. Most carried shopping bags, some from the Spice Shop. That always boosts my mood.

Back in the shop, a quartet of customers was visiting with Cayenne.

"Pepper," she called. "We have students who wanted to say hello."

A small woman with short white hair in a stylish cut held out her hand. "We were just telling Cayenne how much we enjoyed the class last month. We didn't know you or your shop, but we adore Speziato. So, when Edgar said come, learn about herbs and spices, try making some of his dishes, how could we say no?"

"That's why you look familiar. I'm glad you enjoyed the evening. When it comes to food, doing what Edgar says is always a good idea." I'd known the Salvadoran chef well before he got his own restaurant, an Italian place he'd made into a city-wide draw while keeping the neighborhood vibe. He was one of my best customers, and I tried to be a customer of his as often as I could. He had been a fabulous partner for our first class.

"Our friends are visiting, so we brought them to the Market," she said. Introductions were made and purchases approved. Both couples had stocked up on our seafood blends and smoked paprika, the star of Edgar's Baked Paprika Cheese. The visitors had scored bags of spice tea and gift sets for their friends and family back home, and plenty of tasty treats for themselves.

"In fact, we're going to Speziato tonight," the white-haired woman said. "We'll tell Edgar we saw you. And we can hardly wait for the next class."

They left, smiling.

Cayenne grinned at me. "Told you spice school would be a hit."

"You were absolutely right." No reason to remind her it had been my idea.

I stayed after closing to reply to a few emails and finalize our next customer newsletter. The shop's original owner, Jane, had thought marketing unnecessary. "Good products sell themselves," she'd told me. Her staff had known otherwise, urging me to create a mailing list and social media accounts as soon as I took over. And if there's one thing I'd learned managing staff HR in a giant law firm, it was the importance of listening to the staff. The idea of a weekly missive to customers had been daunting at first, but I quickly got the hang of it, and now I enjoy writing it. We tell them what's new in the shop—spices, blends, books. We share a recipe or two, highlighting new finds and old favorites. It's also a great way to advertise our spice club and other specials, and when we finalized the schedule for our fall tastings and classes, subscribers would get first crack.

If the customers I'd chatted with this afternoon were any indication, we had a good thing going.

142 · *Lavender Lies Bleeding*

Arf and I locked up and headed home. I fed him, then opened the fridge. Laurel had given me some of last night's lavender whipped goat cheese, along with a bowl of blueberry peach salad. I sliced up some grilled salmon from earlier in the week and found pita chips for the cheese.

Not quite like dining with Edgar, but not bad. Not bad at all.

The Mariners were leading three to one in the top of the third. I carried my plate and a glass of wine outside, and Arf joined me. It was the perfect evening for dining al fresco, and I thanked the stars for this life, this loft, this dog.

I didn't know precisely what Cua Vang meant when she criticized others for not being loyal to their families, or what she wanted me to do. But she had been right about one thing. I truly was a lucky woman.

ALL DAY THURSDAY, between the sun and the rain and the gray in between, the shop kept me busy. But my brain buzzed with thoughts of Liz and what was going on in Salmon Falls. What was I missing? What was I not seeing?

I'd sat on the veranda under the night sky texting with Nate—the connection was better than voice—and had come up with nothing. I drank two cups of morning coffee and came up with nothing. I chatted and sold spice and answered customers' questions, but could not answer my own.

Midmorning, I texted Sara to ask if she knew anything yet about plans for a memorial for Liz.

Her cousin isn't making plans. But we want to do something. I'll let you know.

Had Cua been talking about Liz's own family, when she said others didn't understand its importance? I'd never experienced family estrangement or betrayal firsthand, unless you count Tag's infidelity, but I'd certainly witnessed it. And it had always been unmeasurably painful. "No one loves you like your family," a coworker deep in the throes had told me once, "and no one hurts you like them, either."

"You gonna be ready for another day working with your offspring?" I asked Kristen, busy unpacking a shipment of books. A pair of new foodie mysteries from Emmeline Duncan and Cleo Coyle caught my eye. Festival goers would love *Lavender Blue*

Murder, an older entry in Laura Childs' Charleston tea shop series, a perennial favorite. Plus books on cooking with lavender.

"Actually," she said, "I wanted to talk with you about that. What if I took the day off? I know you like a full staff on Saturdays, especially as business picks up. But I think it might be better for Savannah if she got a chance to work without feeling like I was watching every move she made."

"Which you were."

"I know." She crinkled up her face. "I just couldn't stay out of her way. And that's no good for anybody."

"Fine with me," I said. "Hey, you rake any more intel about the Salters out of the recesses of your brain?"

"Oh, thanks for reminding me. I was telling Eric about the rift in Salmon Falls over the sale of the Salters' farm, and he said he's sure it's Scott's brother, not Monica's, who's run the place into the ground. So to speak. He and Scott work out at the same gym and Scott was asking him about liens and foreclosures. Not his expertise, so he couldn't help. But the guy was pretty anxious."

Liens and foreclosures? That meant mortgages. On inherited property? I hoped it wasn't the house they were behind on. It had looked like a pleasant family home, and Monica clearly loved it.

Talking about Salmon Falls reminded me of Preston Vu's pop-up garden. When I'd asked who owned it, he hadn't answered, changing the subject to squash blossoms. I texted Jenn at the bookstore and asked her to use her legal research skills to find out who owned the property.

On my way to pick up staff lunch, I ran into the beekeeper, another daystaller.

"Pepper, I have to admit, I'm a little concerned about this lavender thing you're doing."

"Tell me why." I hadn't asked her to participate, even though she occasionally carried tiny, pricy jars of exquisite lavender-creamed honey. I'd focused on merchants and vendors who could marshal an array of themed products. And, to be honest, on the ones I thought would be enthusiastic and easy to work with.

"This entire thing is new and untested. It's not even an official sponsored event," she said. "I'm afraid it's going to draw attention away from the rest of us."

144 · *Lavender Lies Bleeding*

"I wouldn't worry too much about that. I'm betting you don't lose business during the Flower Festival or the Pumpkin Party, even though you don't sell flowers or pumpkins."

"Well, I hope you know what you're doing." She stalked off.

New and untested. Of course it was new and untested. Everything is, the first time around.

Not to say that I didn't understand what was at stake. I'd asked people to commit time and money to the idea in the hopes that it would entice new customers, expand our sales, and be fun. What could be wrong with that?

As for whether I knew what I was doing, heck no. Not that I ever let that stop me.

Twenty-One

Tastes and smells live on in our memories, like personalized time travel.

I FELT THE EXCITEMENT BEFORE MY FEET HIT THE BEDROOM floor. Friday. The day Nate would be home.

We were coming up on a year together and we hadn't talked about how to celebrate. Maybe we could make a few plans this weekend.

Then I got his text. Engine trouble had grounded them in Hoquiam, far down the Washington coast. They needed a part, and Bron had driven south three hours to Vancouver with a friend to get it. Fingers crossed, they hoped to make it home Saturday.

Even lavender-creamed honey on my toast couldn't dispel that downer.

When I got to the shop, I called Sheriff Aguilar for an update.

"You can read about it in the paper, like everyone else."

"If there had been anything in the paper, I wouldn't have had to call you." This was one of those times when I wished for one of those old phones you could slam. The man was seriously annoying. To be fair, he probably felt the same about me.

Then I called the warm-voiced woman at the shelter clinic, to ask if she'd found any trace of Arf's records.

"Hon, I'm so sorry I didn't get back to you," she said. "We've been as busy as ants at a picnic, and our files, to be honest, are not as organized as I'd like them to be. I hunted all over, high and low, up and down, but there was not one scrap of anything about your sweet boy. I know—" Her words rose in a rush, as if to forestall a protest. "I know he was here. Sam brought him in like clockwork. Good to hear that Sam is doing well. Thank you for that update. Everyone thanks you. I told them all you'd been in and what you told me and everyone was so happy to hear that both Arf and Sam are doing well."

She was going on way too long, as if covering up what she wasn't saying by saying anything she could think of.

"We've had so many computer changes," she continued. "Why is it that a company you haven't shopped with in years can track you down even if you move halfway across the country and change your email and your phone number, but when there's something you need to find, it's nowhere. Vanished. I swear. I'll keep digging, hon, and let you know what I find. You give that sweet pup a big old kiss from me, now, you hear?" And she hung up.

A computer change. A reasonable explanation, though Arf's last visit to the clinic couldn't have been much more than two years ago. What was she hiding?

And why was I so paranoid?

Then there were the showroomers. I was taking a turn out front when I noticed two women with trendy handbags and expensive hair. One held my favorite spice grinder.

I was about to extol its virtues and ask if they'd like a demonstration when the other woman said, "You can find it cheaper online."

"Yes," I said, the interruption startling them. "You probably can. But here, you can see it and touch it. You can tell by the heft how well-made it is. We can show you how to use it, and how it compares to other grinders. What you're holding is the best all-around spice grinder on the market. It's got two blades, for an even grind, and it's adjustable, so you can grind delicate dried leaves or rock-hard peppercorns. It comes with an extra grinding bowl and a storage lid. It will transform your cooking and it won't take up more than a few inches of cabinet space."

I paused for breath. Their attention was locked on me. "Sure," I went on. "You can treat my shop as a showroom and buy it online. But what guarantee do you have that it will be in stock or show up when you expect it? What if it's damaged or you don't like it? Yes, you'll spend more here, but you'll never have to buy another spice grinder in your life. And it's forty-four dollars. You're going to spend more than that on lunch, aren't you?" I was wound up, almost not caring if they bought it or flounced out the door aiming unpleasant words in my direction.

"Boss," Sandra said, taking my arm, then she spoke to the customers. "Excuse me. I need to borrow her for a moment."

She dragged me to the nook and fixed me with a glare. "What are you doing? Where is your head?"

I glanced at the two women. Not only were they still here, they appeared to be seriously considering the grinder. I watched as they debated, then the woman holding the display model put it back and took one in a box. Her friend did the same.

"Let me handle this," Sandra said.

"Give them extra free samples. Peppercorns and cumin seed, so they can try some of the harder textures."

"Already on it."

Some days aren't meant to go smoothly. Two minutes after the spice grinder fiasco led to a surprisingly nice sale, Hayden called. The driver we use for in-town deliveries outside the Market and environs had ghosted us, again. Hayden had texted, then called. No answer. Our commercial clients needed their orders for the weekend. Kitchen prep would start in a few hours.

Sometimes, the best cure for a bad mood is a change of pace.

Arf and I trotted to the loft, then drove to the warehouse. While Hayden loaded the deliveries into my car, I fiddled with the route map on my phone. Matt and Reed had created the app one rainy afternoon last fall. It was genius, and I couldn't make heads or tails of it. Matt didn't work for me anymore and Reed was in finals this week. Finally, Hayden pushed the right buttons on the phone and off I went.

My mood lifted with each stop. It was early enough that traffic behaved, and I barely had to use the freeway. I adore Seattle's neighborhoods, full of quirk and history. And I adore my customers. Most of them, anyway. I missed the frequent brief interactions that kept us connected. When we upgraded our online ordering, long overdue, then hired a delivery service, I'd vowed to make up for the lost face time with regular visits to keep in touch, but it wasn't so

148 · *Lavender Lies Bleeding*

easy. (My mother says, "just call them," but who wants to talk on the phone anymore? Especially a chef who's more concerned with making sure he's got enough beef and bartenders for the weekend than chatting up a supplier.)

Finally, I hit the home stretch. It had taken a few hours and a few gallons of gas, but the Saab and I had covered a good chunk of the city without either of us falling apart. The Saab did overheat briefly outside a Turkish restaurant in the north end, but the owner had seen me waiting and brought me a glass of hibiscus rose tea with a mint sprig he plucked on his way to the parking lot. Tangy and refreshing, the perfect example of how good florals can be in food and drink.

Other customers had given me go-boxes of pad thai and bags of scones. We'd even scored a bone for Arf, happily chewing in the back seat.

Food, friends, and flavor. How can you not be happy surrounded by bounty like that?

While I was waiting for the sous chef at a seafood restaurant in Green Lake, I checked my phone. A text from Jenn left me scratching my head.

Farm you asked about belongs to Salmon Falls Acres, LLC. Tried to find out who owns the corp, but the site was down and I didn't have time to check it again. Cruise ships are in!!!

I sent a thumbs-up emoji, then texted Sandra to let her know I'd be back within the hour. Thank goodness for a capable staff.

My last stop was a tiny pizzeria in Interbay, not far from Fishermen's Terminal. I'd started doing business with Emerald City Wood-fired Pizza a few months ago, after Daria hooked up with Bron. Most of her picks were the usual suspects—thyme, oregano, India red chile pepper flakes—but she likes to mix things up. I adore any kind of pizza, but the best ever is her fennel, honey, fig, and feta pizza, with fresh fronds and my fennel seeds, lightly crushed. Chef's kiss.

The front door was locked—they open at three and close when they run out of pizza dough, no matter how long the line—but her second-in-command let me in.

"Thanks. I come bearing herbs and spices for the pizza lovers of the Emerald City." I handed him the heavy canvas tote, and a minute later, Daria emerged from the back, the empty tote from the last delivery in hand.

"Pepper, hi. I'm surprised to see you in person."

"I was surprised to see you on the delivery list. I thought you were closing on weekends."

"Not until after graduation party season. We're even taking phone orders, for three pizzas or more." She led the way to one of the picnic tables she'd added to the side yard when the weather warmed. Her building had started life as a service station, still clad in the white stucco and green trim of a 1930s Texaco, though over the decades, it had housed half a dozen different businesses. The shed out back was crammed with old marine equipment found on the property. "It's extra work, but it's also extra profit, and it will help make up for Saturday closures. Besides, Bron's not home this weekend after all."

"Nate always says Bron's the best diesel engine mechanic he knows," I said. "But that boat has been nothing but trouble lately."

"He's had job offers. Aaron from the crew mentioned it the last time he stopped in for pizza. I didn't let on that it was news to me. Then there was that guy at Mindy and Javier's wedding."

"You saw him, too? All I could tell was he had some kind of business in mind, but what, I have no idea."

"Rats. I was hoping you could tell me."

The Seward brothers were peas in a pod, sharing the same build, the same walk, the same green eyes and brown hair. And, apparently, the same tight lips.

"It's the one thing that's ever caused a problem between us," Daria said. "I know, we've only been together five months. But would it kill him to tell me what he's thinking?"

I didn't know Daria or Bron well, but she was clearly distressed, so I risked a guess. "I've learned that Nate likes to work things out on his own before telling me. Not that he makes executive decisions and springs them on me—'this is the way it's going to be.' More like, he wants to narrow down the options, then say 'I'm thinking about this. What do you think?'"

"Yes, yes. That's it exactly. Me, I'm all over the place." She waved her hands. "I'm saying 'I could do this, or this, or what would you think about this?'"

150 · *Lavender Lies Bleeding*

"If Bron's like Nate," I said, "he listens and takes it all in, then lays it all out, pro and con, risks and benefits. Pretty helpful, to tell the truth."

"When you put it like that," Daria said, "it sounds like a lot of work, being with us."

"I think they like us." I grinned. "Interesting, isn't it? They both picked women who think very differently than they do. And we're not going to change them."

"I get that." She sighed. "But I wish I knew what was going on in those heads of theirs."

"You mean, like changing jobs, so they're in Seattle more often?"

"Yeah. Do you think . . ."

"Maybe. We just have to trust that they'll tell us when they're ready," I said. "And we'll be waiting. Because we like them."

Twenty-Two

In France, the entree is the first course of a meal; in American English, it's the main course. According to linguist Dan Jurafsky, writing in The Language of Food, *both uses arose from the complicated evolution of the modern three- or four-course menu, each retaining different aspects of the original meaning.*

I WAS IN MY OFFICE EARLY SATURDAY MORNING, WORKING on the accounts, when I heard pounding on the front door.

I stepped into the dark, quiet shop. The pounding continued.

"Okay, okay, I'm coming," I muttered as I passed the nook and wound between the bookshelves and an oak table that had once anchored someone's dining room. Not until I neared the counter could I see who was summoning me so urgently. True to form, Arf stood at the glass door, watching, not making a sound.

I snicked the lock and opened the door.

Cua Vang bustled in. She shooed Arf away, though the gesture was unnecessary. He'd stayed quiet, and now he stepped back, letting her pass, because he knew her. Those gentlemen's manners.

"Come. You must come."

"What? Why? Has something happened?"

"Sara. You must talk to her."

152 · *Lavender Lies Bleeding*

It took several tangled exchanges before I was certain that Sara was not injured and in need of emergency assistance requiring higher powers than mine. Put simply, she was helping with the flower stall today and Cua wanted me to come talk with her. About what wasn't completely clear.

Sandra hadn't arrived yet, so I texted to let her know where I'd gone. *Back before opening, I'm sure,* I said, hoping I wasn't jinxing myself. *Arf is in charge.* I followed Cua down the cobbles.

"So that's where you went, Auntie," Sara said. "You sneaky old woman, you."

"Talk to her. Tell her. She will help," Cua said, all but shoving Sara away from the table.

Or at least that's what I got out of the mix of English and Hmong the two women exchanged.

Finally, Sara let out an exasperated sigh that needed no translation and joined me on the street.

"Where can we talk? Away from prying ears?" She jerked a thumb over her shoulder at Cua and the other flower ladies.

Lots of places for coffee and a bite, not so many places to sit for a private conversation. Not the shop; the staff would be arriving soon, customers on their heels. Nothing said in the nook stays in the nook.

"Up." I pointed to the second-floor coffee shop that overlooks Pike Place. Minutes later, Sara and I were sitting at the same table where I'd sat with Liz a week ago.

"Cua insisted she needed my help today. She was feeling under the weather and one of the other ladies couldn't make it—blah-blah. All lies to trick me into coming to the Market with her so she could force me to sit down with you." She spread her arms, gesturing. "It worked."

"I never complain when someone buys me coffee," I said. "But what does she really want?"

The runner arrived with Sara's macchiato and my cappuccino, sweeping the little number tent away.

"She thinks you can step into Liz's shoes and help us."

"How? I'm an outsider. And who's 'us'? You mean the Community Alliance?"

She'd been about to take her first sip when her hand froze. Slowly, she set the cup down, then raised her gaze to mine.

Leslie Budewitz • 153

"I'm sorry, Pepper. I wasn't completely honest with you."

That much I'd figured out.

"When the small growers in Salmon Falls heard about Salter Farm coming up for sale, some of them wanted to buy it. But it's too much acreage for any of them to manage, let alone buy, on their own. So, they approached the Hmong growers."

"Through you."

"Through me. You have to understand the Hmong community. We aren't like other Asian groups. We didn't come here voluntarily, for economic opportunity or a better life. We came here because we had to. Other Americans think of the Vietnam War as only about Vietnam. But the war in Southeast Asia was much bigger than that. And it didn't leave us with many choices."

I was the daughter of a Vietnam vet turned history teacher. I knew some of this, but the personal impact was a whole other story.

"No small-scale grower in Salmon Falls, Hmong or white or Hispanic, could make an offer," she continued. "No one has the capital, or the credit history. And bankers don't always see farming as a reliable investment. But what we lack in cash, we make up for with hard work. With family and community support."

That I could understand. It's what Cua had been talking about.

"The Hmong work together," Sara continued. "Take the flower ladies. They talk trash like cutthroat rivals, but they don't see it that way, even when they bark and snipe and try to outdo each other for customers."

"They put on a pretty good show."

"They do. But behind the scenes, they're in it together." She took a slow sip, as if seeking strength from the sweet coffee.

"Where does the Alliance come in?"

"That was Preston's brainchild. He wanted to bring together the Hmong growers with others, to form a collective that could buy the farm. It was a bit uneasy at first."

"And your role?"

"Since I live there and know so many people, I tried to bridge the gaps. Help the growers get acquainted. Learn to trust each other. Liz was a major asset. I stayed in the background—I didn't want anyone to think I was using my role as director of the festival and the growers' association to exert undue influence."

As Nina Ascencion from the newspaper had implied. "But the Alliance was able to make an offer, right?"

"We formed a legal entity, which could take out a loan. We had the bank's tentative commitment, although the terms weren't firm, so there was some fear of losing that. But it was chicken and egg." She waggled her hands back and forth. "While we were working on all those details . . ."

"Desiree swooped in."

"I couldn't believe she would undermine us. Doesn't she have her hands full, with Blossom and the B&B, and all she does for the festival? Although this year, she hasn't been as active. Too busy hatching this event center plan and pulling the rug out from under us."

"Wait. Go back. If you had a deal to buy the farm, how could she interfere with that?"

"We had a handshake. They got to contract before we did. At a much higher price."

"But they"—I paused, thinking this through—"they need a condition met. Their plan is to convert the farm into an event center, which requires official approval. If they don't get it, is the deal off?"

"I think so."

"Okay." I sipped the last of my capp, bits of foam still stuck in the cup. I resisted the temptation to wipe them out with my finger and lick it. "Back to Liz. She wasn't a member of the Alliance, but she supported you, right, and not her good friend Desiree?"

"Which caused a major rift between them."

"You think Desiree damaged Liz's greenhouse and attacked her to stop her? Surely there are other people in town who oppose her plan, in addition to the Alliance. Besides, she has an alibi for the murder." I didn't mention the teeny tiny pinhole I'd popped in it.

"No, no. She wouldn't—well, I don't know if she would or wouldn't. I don't have any idea why this event center is so important to her. She's got a successful business—two of them. Three, if you count the catering company. And Jeffrey has two—the real estate office and the property management firm. Why do they want more? Why do they need so much, when the growers just want a piece of land to call their own?"

That was the heart of the matter, wasn't it? A piece of land to call their own, yearning tied up with resentment of those who had plenty and weren't satisfied.

Leslie Budewitz · 155

An ugly thought crossed my mind. If Desiree wasn't the vandal and the culprit, and if Sara's frankness ruled her out, what about Preston? But how would that have gotten him what the Alliance wanted?

"Why does Cua think I can do anything to help?" I asked. "I'm an outsider. I can't go to the planning board and argue against an event center. You locals can make that case better than anyone."

"Because you know these people. The sellers. She saw you with Monica Salter. And because of everything you've done in the Market. Your first year here, you identified the real killer when everyone pointed their fingers at the homeless people. You helped Sam reconnect with his family. Because of you, Hot Dog stayed clean and finished the food service program, and now he runs his own food cart. You took down the killer in Vinny's shop. Heck, you even got the traffic committee to see eye to eye."

"Whoa." I put out both hands. "You're giving me way too much credit. I barely know Monica Salter. Besides, it's her husband's family farm. She told me it was their decision, not hers."

"Yes, but—" Sara's phone buzzed and she grabbed it. "Gotta go. Auntie insisted I talk to you, and now she's insisting I come back and help her. I swear." She gathered up her things and slid out of the booth. "Pepper, thanks for letting me dump all this on you. You come up with any brilliant ideas, you'll have free flowers for life."

"Ha. Like Cua would ever go for that."

Though my cup was empty, I stayed put after Sara left, thinking about what she'd said. The Alliance had gone forward to arrange financing and the legalities of ownership without a contract to buy the farm. Not quite chicken and egg, but I knew what she meant. More like getting their ducks in a row, to stretch the poultry metaphor. But meanwhile, the Whites had made the Salters a better offer. Legally, the Salters had been free to take it, conditional as it was. I was starting to think Liz's death had nothing to do with the whole mess. Hers was one voice in a sea of opposition to the Whites' proposal. Though without question one of the clearest and most adamant. Had she made herself an easy target? But even if Desiree was furious with her friend's interference, even if she was through-the-glass-roof angry, how would busting up Liz's greenhouse have helped her? It would only have made Liz more determined.

156 · *Lavender Lies Bleeding*

Liz herself had not thought Desiree was involved in the vandalism. And before I accused the woman of murder, I needed more than a suspicion that she'd lied to Aguilar about her alibi.

I thought again about Preston and the Alliance. No one on that side of the property dispute had anything to gain from Liz's death. Unless there was some complicated scheme to cast suspicion on the Whites and influence the planning board decision. Pretty cynical. Pretty complicated. But not impossible.

Still, I couldn't quite wrap my head around it. Which didn't mean it wasn't true—only that I needed more facts. More pieces of the puzzle.

Bottom line, the dispute over the future of Salter Farm might not have anything to do with the vandalism and murder. And much as I might want the Alliance to prevail, to get a piece of land to call their own, a piece of land with a picturesque old barn and a red azalea tumbling into a stream, that wasn't my fight. I'd promised Liz that if anything happened to her, I'd help make sure justice was done.

If only I had a clue what to do next.

Twenty-Three

Lord, make me the person my dog thinks I am.
—The Dog Owner's Prayer

BACK AT THE SHOP, I WAS AS NERVOUS AS THE CAT ON THE proverbial hot tin roof, and it wasn't all the extra caffeine. Or not just the caffeine.

I had to focus on business and on the festival. Anticipating a bump in sales, I checked our inventory of the most popular herbs and spices, and made a note to double the batch next time we blended our signature spice tea. I checked with Joy of Joy Juice to order more of her Blueberry Lavender Syrup, and connected with a couple of other nearby growers.

Shop locally, eat globally.

Out front, I rearranged Kristen's book display to include a poster advertising the upcoming festivities. We'd listed each participating shop and vendor, and the poster promised special treats, discounts, and prizes.

"Oh, lavender!" a customer exclaimed. "We saw the most beautiful lavender fields at an old monastery in Provence. Abbaye de Sénanque, it's called. It was founded in, I don't know, the eleventh century? The twelfth? The monks still run it. We took a tour, and there they were, in their robes, praying in the sanctuary. You have to go."

158 · *Lavender Lies Bleeding*

"Bucket list," I said. Not that I had a bucket list. But forty-four was rapidly approaching. Maybe it was time.

"Maybe you know," another customer said. "My sister loves Earl Grey tea."

"One of my favorites."

"I'd like to take her some. She wanted to come ashore with us, but her knee's been acting up, so she stayed on board. I spotted a tea shop earlier and looked, but there were so many varieties, I got overwhelmed and I didn't know which one to pick."

I led her to the red Chinese apothecary a neighbor had given me ages ago. Long before I ever imagined that I'd own a spice shop and turn the heirloom into a tea display. "There are several theories about how the tea came about, and even whether Lord Grey, a British earl, had anything to do with it. It's a black tea—ours is Assam, from northeastern India—flavored with oil of bergamot, an Italian citrus fruit."

"Ahh, that's what gives it that spark," she said, reaching for a box. Customers love to pick up things and hold them while you talk. That's why our displays are so important.

"Exactly. Now you may have seen it with lavender." I pointed to another box. "That's a more recent addition, giving it a floral touch. I like it, too. These days, Earl Grey is also used as a flavoring in cakes and chocolates. There's a chocolatier Down Under who makes Earl Grey truffles, and they are so good."

"I'll take both. Then tell me where to find this chocolatier."

On our way to the cash register, I scooped a dirty napkin off the floor. Most customers are good about the trash, but things do get dropped now and then.

I let Savannah ring up the sale, for practice.

"You're so lucky," the tea drinker's sister told her, "to be able to work so well with your mother."

The blushing teenager opened her mouth to explain, then simply said, "Thank you."

"Was that okay?" Savannah asked after the customers left. "I didn't want to correct her."

"Perfect."

"I hate to say this, but it is easier to work with you than my mom," Savannah said, her face scrunched, her tone apologetic.

Leslie Budewitz · 159

"I know. It's because she's cranky and old," I said, and Savannah covered her mouth to hide her snort of laughter. "What are you making for her birthday dinner?"

"I was thinking about your Indian Butter Chicken. And the Five Spice Apple Cake. She says it's her favorite." We made sure she had all the right spices, then I put her to work attaching price labels to a new stack of handmade aprons. Me, I was having trouble focusing, thinking about Sara and Cua and Liz and Salmon Falls. Kristen had been wise to take the day off, but I missed bouncing ideas around with her.

The day continued in its unpredictable, delicious way. The staff agreed the new girl should choose lunch. When she returned with the sandwich tray, she handed me a small white paper bag.

"When I walked by the cheesecake shop, the baker called me over," she said. "Samples, for the festival. He wants your opinion."

"Taste testing is part of the job," I said. "You up for it?"

Who says no to cheesecake? No one I trust, that's for sure, and Savannah's eyes lit up.

"Best part of the best job ever," she said a few minutes later, as we sat in the nook nibbling tiny squares of creamy, lavender-truffle cheesecake with a chocolate crust. In my role as mother for the day, I dabbed at the side of my mouth with one finger. She did the same, coming away with a spot of filling. She licked it off.

"Now that hits the sweet spot." Don't ever let it be said that I don't take my job seriously.

I finally let out my breath, figuratively speaking, midafternoon when Nate texted that they were coming into Shilshole Bay. Then the locks, Salmon Bay, and home.

Home. Talk about the sweet spot.

I DON'T KNOW who was more excited that the pack was reunited, Arf, Nate, or me. I can say, tails were wagging all around.

"I gotta tell you," Nate said, leaning back in the bistro chair on the veranda. His foot grazed the pot holding the hydrangea. "One more trip like that and I might just toss a match on that rust bucket of a boat and send the whole thing up in flames."

"Don't. If the fire spreads, you could be guilty of arson. They'd throw you in prison and I'd never see you again." I slipped onto his

160 · *Lavender Lies Bleeding*

lap and kissed him in a way I hoped would show him what he'd miss if he spent the rest of his days behind bars. Away from me.

"Well," he said when we finally pulled apart. "That'll keep me in line."

"It better, or I might need to resort to more extreme measures." I stood and stepped through the window. Came back with the wine bottle and a plate of appetizers. Topped off our glasses. Nate plucked up a wonton. I'd made the rounds of some of his favorite spots in the Market. Not coincidentally, they were also my favorites. We're in sync gastronomically, with a few exceptions. Like sweet potatoes.

"So, what about the boat?" I asked. "Are you thinking about selling it?"

"What makes you ask that?"

"A hunch? Your threat to burn it? Your conversation with the man at the wedding?"

He leaned forward, forearms on his knees, hands on his elbows. "I didn't know you'd heard that."

"Saw, not heard. I was hoping you'd tell me what it was about."

"Fair enough." He sat up. "Bron and I've been talking. We've been fishing a long time. We like the life, but it's hard. We're not getting any younger, and we both—" He broke off and sipped his wine. Thirsty or buying time? "We've missed out on things. And it might be time for a change."

I held my tongue.

"The man you saw at the wedding is a friend of Mindy's father. He's a boat broker. Javier knew him from the sale of a boat he'd worked on, so he talked to him—"

"You told Javier but you didn't tell me?" I heard the edge in my voice and swallowed hard to keep it down.

"I'm telling you now." Nate's words were as steady as his gaze. "Bron asked Javier if he could put us in touch, to see if the broker would look at the big boat and give us an idea what we might get for it. And our Alaska permits—they're worth a good chunk."

The big boat was *The Kenai Princess*, currently in Dutch Harbor, waiting for its owners to make a new plan.

"I was going to wait to tell you until after we heard back from the broker," he said.

But I remembered how Bron looked at Daria at the wedding, and I thought his mind was made up. I'd told Daria I thought the

Leslie Budewitz · 161

Seward brothers' minds worked the same way. Had I been right? At this very moment, I couldn't tell.

"So if you sell the *Princess*, what will you do?"

"Good question. So much is still in the air. The broker hasn't even seen the boat. It could take a while to sell, and we've got to run it while we own it, to cover the costs. One season, two—I don't know. After that—" He shrugged. "With the parts we found in the salvage yard, we can fish down here a while longer without having to replace the smaller boat. But after that? Who knows? I don't have the same job skills Bron does."

"You have other skills. You know fish."

"Can you see me in rubber overalls hawking halibut to tourists?"

"You'd be cute. But there must be other jobs for retired fishermen. Wholesale fish sales. Boat sales. Other boat business stuff."

"Yeah. I might even go back to school. Your dad mentioned an accelerated program that trains adults retired from other careers to be teachers. And no, I never said anything to him about changing careers. I think he was trying to nudge me, without coming out and saying so."

"That would be my dad," I said.

Nate took my hand, and it was a long time before I thought about anything else.

Twenty-Four

Lavender is best harvested early in the morning, before the heat of the day dries out the oils in the leaves and flowers.

IT WASN'T UNTIL TUESDAY THAT I GOT BACK OUT TO SALMON Falls. Sara had invited me to the next festival committee meeting, and the way Cua glared at me that morning when I stopped for flowers, I knew I had to go. Thank goodness Nate had the dog for the day. I called my mother and left the shop in Sandra's hands.

"This will be fun," Mom said half an hour later as I merged into traffic on the 520 toll bridge. Fun for her, since I was doing the driving. "I haven't been out this way in years. I feel like I'm getting to know my home ground all over again."

The skies were as clear, the water as sparkling, as when we'd driven to Cascade Vista for the wedding, but the mood was different. Mine was, anyway. My mother was all in for a girlfriend-tourist jaunt, but me, I carried the burden of my unfulfilled promise to Liz. It wasn't like I sensed her haunting me, hovering in the ether as a spectral reminder, but yeah, I sort of did.

Today, I told myself and the spirit of my dead friend. *Today I'll find out what happened to you.*

At the entrance to Salmon Falls, my mother exclaimed over the welded moose grazing in the field of flowers. I drove down Main Street slowly, giving her a chance to eye the town.

Leslie Budewitz · 163

"Oh, the garden!" she said, charmed.

We had plenty of time to eat before the meeting, and Blossom was the spot. Ordinarily, I would pick a place I hadn't been to yet, but I was on a mission. I'd dressed for tourist season in a black T-shirt and grass-green cropped linen overalls scattered with peace signs. White tennies. Dangly earrings from the Market, made of metal cut from the wreckage of a vintage VW bug. Funky and fun, the perfect disguise for an amateur sleuth.

"My goodness," Mom said as we followed the hostess. "Look at those photos. Those must be from tea rooms in downtown Seattle."

She pointed to a section of wall I hadn't paid attention to on my last visit.

"Good guess," the hostess said. "The menus, too. Desiree, our owner—her mother collected them. She wanted to recreate some of that feel here."

No question Desiree had a gift for design. Despite their objections to her plans for the farm, no one could seriously doubt that the finished project would be beautiful.

Mom pointed to a photo of the tearoom at the Frederick and Nelson department store, long closed.

"My mother took me there once, for my tenth birthday. I had a pale pink dress embroidered with deep pink roses and black patent leather Mary Janes. We ate tiny sandwiches and cream puffs, and she even let me drink tea, from a porcelain cup the waitress chose because the flowers matched my dress. Afterwards, my mother bought the cup and saucer. It was a day I'll never forget."

I was astonished. I'd never heard that story. In my memory, my Hungarian grandmother was a penny-pincher—kind and loving, and generous in other ways, but with no patience for expensive frivolity. "The teacup that used to sit on the oak dresser in the front entry?"

"The one your brother broke." Mom shrugged and we took our seats.

"I was here a couple of weeks ago," I told the hostess, "and our server had a long blond braid. Abby, I think. Is she working today?"

I was fishing, knowing we'd see her later at the lavender farm. Hoping to find out what Desiree had told the staff.

164 · *Lavender Lies Bleeding*

"She left. Quit. Short notice—no notice, but under the circumstances, what could Desiree say?" The woman looked genuinely distraught. "She's taking over the lavender farm outside of town. The owner . . ."

"Oh, the woman who died," my mother said. "We heard. We're so sorry. Was she a friend of yours?"

"She—Liz—was a force of nature. I don't know what town will do without her. Desiree was her best friend, and she's so upset. She's hardly been in since it happened, though she's got a lot going on, with the season, and all the plans for the new place." The hostess wiped a damp spot on her cheek. "Coffee? Tea? We have a delicious Ceylon iced tea flavored with lemon balm and lavender."

"The iced tea," my mother said. "Pepper, you should try it. It sounds very calming."

"Sold." When your mother directs you to have a calming drink, you do as you're told.

"This Desiree," my mother said when we were alone. "She was Liz's best friend, and they fell out over her plan to buy Salter Farm and convert it to an event center?"

"That's the size of it."

"And you think that might be connected to Liz's death?"

"Has to be. I just can't see how."

We ordered and ate, chatting about the new house, Dad's garden plans, and my brother's kids. I did not fool myself—Charlie and Lizzie were the magnets tugging my parents home. Carl and I ran a distant second.

"So glad Nate got home safely," Mom said. "I know boats are those boys' business, but they are so much trouble."

I told her about last night's conversation.

"Hmm," she said when I'd finished. "He's at a crossroads. He's lucky to have you as an anchor."

"Nice way to put it, despite the mixed metaphor."

"While you're busy," Mom said as the server cleared our plates, "I'll be shopping. I'd like to find a painting or a photograph of the flower fields, for the wall behind that darling little wingback you gave me."

Ah, the wingback. A chair full of stories.

"You should go to Calico, the co-op gallery," the server said.

Leslie Budewitz · 165

"Is that the place that sells the fudge?" Mom asked.

"Among other things. There's also a terrific arts and antique shop down the block. The owner is a painter, and I think you'll love his work."

We found the place a few minutes later. "Looks dangerous," I said. "Remember, we're driving a small car."

My mother made a shooing motion and ducked inside. I made my way to the festival office.

There's a moment, when a stranger walks into a room full of people who know each other, of surprise. Of curiosity and questions. Of discomfort and doubt.

I felt that now, as ten pairs of eyes studied me. Some faces were welcoming, some neutral, one or two skeptical. A single reaction can set the tone.

"Pepper!" Sara called, arms open as she swept toward me for a hug. The mood in the room shifted.

Introductions began, my brain reaching for the memory tricks I'd learned in HR. People are always more willing to talk when you've made an effort to connect. I met growers, artists and crafters, shopkeepers, and community volunteers. And the fudge maker, who gave me a toothy smile when I told her how much my friends had enjoyed her creations.

"The lavender oil is working, I can tell," the gift shop owner Cayenne and I had met said. Willow, her palms soft from lavender-scented shea butter, her gray hair tinged with light purple. "Your aura is much brighter."

"I'll take that as a good sign. My mother will love your shop." I turned to the antique dealer, the one man in the room. "And yours, which is where I last saw her. It could be scary."

"Mothers are some of our best customers," he replied. "My assistant will help her find just what she's looking for."

"Liz told us all about you," another woman said. If I had the names and faces straight, she owned Poppy, the B&B on a farm outside town. One of the places Sara had recommended to the visitor who dropped in when Cayenne and I were here.

"I hope not," I said, and she laughed.

We moved into the conference room and found seats around a rectangle formed by battered folding tables.

166 · *Lavender Lies Bleeding*

"No Desiree?" I asked Sara.

"Nobody's seen much of her lately," she said. "Nursing her grief, I think."

"Or her guilt," the antique dealer said. "Stoking the fires, fanning the flames. She had to have known someone would take her threats seriously."

"Oh, no one really believed her," Willow the aura reader said. "Town won't shrivel up and die if she can't hold weddings and reunions at the old farm."

"You're not defending her?" he said. "After all that's happened?"

What had Desiree said? I was dying to know, but the festival committee chair, the fudge maker, took charge before the exchange could continue. Each member updated the group on progress. The street closure plan, the parking plan, the teenagers who would tack up 'No Parking' signs the night before, were all in place. The tow truck driver was on notice. All details I didn't have to deal with.

Why had Liz and Desiree let competing visions of the town's future tear their friendship apart?

Why did this event center mean so much to Desiree? Did Liz honestly expect someone else to shelve business plans because she disapproved? Of course, Liz hadn't been the only person in town who believed farms were for farming. By the same token, I was sure a few of the friendly folks gathered around the table thought the event center would boost town's fortunes.

I couldn't help thinking about what Cua had said. When did the desires of the individual outweigh the needs of the community? Who decided? It was more than a question of property rights—"this is my land, and I can do what I want with it." It was a question of responsibility.

Liz had supported the Alliance because she believed in its goals, but she hadn't joined it. She hadn't needed more land. I thought of the patch of bare ground behind the greenhouse. The loan she'd applied for. The eagerness of the nursery woman we'd met for the new varietal. I was increasingly convinced that Liz had meant to expand into the wholesale nursery business, while continuing to nurture what she'd already built.

Committee talk had moved to a workshop track. Wreaths. Flower arranging. Aromatherapy. Designing and planting a polli-

Leslie Budewitz · 167

nator garden. Too bad I hadn't brought Cayenne, our new events coordinator, but it was her day off.

"Abby Delaney will run the Lavender Cottage booth," one of the volunteers reported. "They'll be selling bundles of fresh lavender and the cottage products. Her mother and sister will run the cottage and the tours. The farm tour is the same weekend as the festival," she said to me, cluing in the outsider.

"What about Salter Farm?" another member asked.

"Not on the route this year. We thought it best, with the sale pending."

"Not that we're taking sides on how the planning board should rule," came the reply.

"We are not," Sara snapped. "Everyone involved agreed. Salter Farm isn't in any shape for visitors."

I thought of that weathered barn and those gorgeous red azaleas. I said nothing, watching the faces around me. The spark of tension hung in the air, but unfanned, it sputtered and died.

The next item on the agenda was advertising and publicity.

"You've got to get TV coverage," the antique dealer said to me. "In the future, they can replay footage from the previous year, but since your festival is new, get the TV crew there the first day. Even a thirty-second segment will bring out the hordes."

"Good point." I made a note.

"Long as the publicity isn't about murder," the B&B owner said.

"It's all this growth and change," one of the volunteers said. "We used to be a quiet country town. But all these newcomers . . ."

Who did she mean? Of the people close to Liz, only Orion was new to town, as far as I knew. How long the Whites had been here, I didn't know.

"Don't be naive," Willow said. "Every town has its problems, and we're no exception."

"True," came the reply. "But until now, the worst thing that happened in years was a bunch of rowdy kids toppling the moose."

Not for the first time, I thought about how funny it is—funny strange—that we humans, whose very lives depend on change and adaptation, spend so much energy resisting it. I was guilty, too, more often than I cared to admit.

168 · *Lavender Lies Bleeding*

But I got it. In the city, change is a constant. You scarcely notice. In a small town, change has a bigger impact.

The discussion of when and where to put signs for the festival wrapped up. The next topic was activities for kids, and I took tons of notes.

"What do you do about rain?" I asked. Our daystall tables are covered and the Atrium offers indoor activity space, but rain would dampen foot traffic.

"Pray it doesn't happen," the orchardist said. "Heresy to a farmer, I know, but the reality is we need this festival to be a success. Some of our artists and makers depend on a few shows a year to make their living."

They talked about tents, and keeping the school available on standby. Trash cans and recycling bins. Security.

I listened closely, aware that I liked these people. I liked their energy and enthusiasm, their determination to make this event a success. No doubt they disagreed on a whole range of topics, and yet, they put that aside for the good of their town.

But somewhere, amid all this camaraderie and lavender joy, lay the roots of a deadly clash.

"Before you go," Willow said, as committee members gathered their notes and closed their files and laptops. "The memorial service for Liz. Sara and I thought it would be good to do something in conjunction with the festival, since she was one of the founders."

"Almost got through this meeting without crying," the fudge maker said, touching a knuckle to the corner of her eye.

The antique dealer put a hand on her shoulder.

"Our plan is to gather after the booths and shops close up on Friday, the first day of the festival," Willow said. "In the park next to the school. Anyone can come, say a few words. I'll arrange for music and a blessing."

"Not too woo-woo," the antique dealer said. "Or Liz will haunt you."

"She was a practical girl, wasn't she? And I just don't know—" Willow's voice broke. "How this town, how any of us will ever be the same."

Twenty-Five

The word lavender comes from the Latin lavare, to wash, highlighting its use in the ancient world to perfume bathwater. Use too much in cooking, or serve it to someone with an adversity, and you may hear that it tastes soapy. Coincidence? You decide.

THE MEETING CAME TO A CLOSE AND THE GROUP DISPERSED. I waited until I was alone with Sara.

"Good meeting," I said. "Thanks for letting me sit in."

"Everyone's happy to help. Pike Place is a mecca for locally grown food and art. Anything you do there boosts growers and producers all over the region."

"Change of subject. Who knew Liz's plans? To take her new hybrid into the commercial market. Who wanted to stop her?"

"How do you know about the hybrid?" Her eyes narrowed, wary.

"She gave me a seedling. Raved about how it combined the best attributes of the existing varieties. Perfect for the home gardener, she said, and hobby growers in search of a multipurpose plant."

"Then you know as much as anyone," she said. "At least, anyone alive."

ON THE SIDEWALK, I checked my texts. All was well in the shop. Nate had sent a picture of Arf on the boat, as he often did. The dog

170 · *Lavender Lies Bleeding*

didn't care that the boat was old and creaky and held together with wire and luck. He adored it, and he adored Nate.

And I adored them both.

My mother was waiting outside the co-op gallery. One hand held a bulging canvas tote, the other a white paper shopping bag.

"How much fudge did you buy?" I asked.

"Oh, my gosh, it is so good. I got lavender soap and lotions. I found a handmade kaleidoscope for Charlie and a beaded bracelet for Lizzie. And this." She pulled out a plush purple teddy bear, like the one Cayenne had bought. "For BarBar's new granddaughter. A sweet dreams bear, stuffed with lavender."

My youngest cousin's adorable, but fussy, new baby. "I'm sure they'll love anything that helps her sleep."

"We have to go back to the antique shop for the painting I found."

Inside the shop, a large, flat package wrapped in brown paper leaned against the front counter. The dealer I'd met at the committee meeting greeted us like old friends, his eyes gleaming.

"It's—big," I said. "Are you sure it will fit that wall space behind the wingback?"

"I called your father and had him measure."

That was my mother, one step ahead.

The dealer unwrapped a corner to give me a peek. Rows of lavender, a faded red barn, mountains in the distance. A patch of deep orange poppies, and a rusty old farm truck.

"Your work? Painted plein air, at Liz's farm?" I asked. He nodded, and I swallowed the tears welling in my throat.

While he was wrestling the painting into the Saab's back seat, a forty-ish man in a lightweight flannel shirt—they're trendy again—and those equally trendy leather sneakers with the white sidewalls approached. He paused briefly as if sizing up the situation, then moved on. I was sure I'd seen him before, but where? Salmon Falls was a small town, and I had not met more than a couple dozen residents.

The dealer noticed me eyeing the man.

"Heilman," he said. "One of those guys who thinks the world owes him everything. Entitled."

Too funny. The dealer had refused my help, but thought another man ought to offer, unasked. That's men.

Leslie Budewitz • 171

"So much lavender! So much purple!" my mother exclaimed a few minutes later as we drove out of town. "I almost understand the people who think this lavender stuff has gone too far."

"What did you hear?"

"The potter said—oh, wait until you see the beautiful bowl I bought you. Sprigs of lavender painted over a white salt glaze." At my wide-eyed glance, she continued. "You have to pay for information, you know."

She could have been quoting me.

"I must have been in six or seven shops. Several had those 'Farms are for Farming' signs or stickers for the Alliance. I mentioned Liz, said you knew her. I hope that was all right. Everyone seemed to like her. And they like Desiree, too, but while everyone agreed her event center would be top-notch, half the people worried about traffic and noise, and the impact on farming. I lost track of how many times I heard that every bride wants the picturesque setting, but none of them wants their guests dodging cow pies as they stroll to dinner after the ceremony."

"Truth to that."

"And then there were concerns about the work force and housing. The potter in particular was worried about a possible subdivision, if the event center doesn't pan out. So pretty out here," she said as I made a left at the moose and headed for Mrs. Luedtke Road. A sheriff's rig passed us going the other way, Joe Aguilar at the wheel.

Sir the cat greeted us at Liz's farm, and I was glad I hadn't brought Arf.

"Mom, do you want a cat?"

She shot me a look that suggested I'd gone bonkers.

"Darling, have you forgotten? We're leaving in November. We can't take a cat to Costa Rica."

"Just asking. You two have been full of surprises lately." Moving back, for starters, then buying the very same house they'd sold a few years ago.

Abby and Maggie were stocking the cottage shelves with everything from lavender oil to candles, soaps, and lotions. I made introductions.

"Maggie," my mother said. "Show me around the farm." It was spooky how good she was at this sidekick business.

172 · *Lavender Lies Bleeding*

"The place is looking up," I said when Abby and I were alone. "But you're looking down. That have anything to do with the visit from Sheriff Aguilar?"

"He had more questions about Orion. Questions I couldn't answer. Didn't help that my mother was here." She gave a quick shake of the head. "After my dad died, Mom and Joe dated for a while. It didn't end well—she says she realized too late that she wasn't ready for a relationship, and Joe had trouble accepting that."

"That's rough. I'm sorry about your dad."

"Thanks. Small towns. Sometimes I think I need to get out of here for a few years."

"What about Orion? You two long term?"

"I thought so. But now I wonder." Her phone buzzed. She read the text. "Glass guy is on his way. Insurance okayed the repairs, though I don't know yet what's going to happen with all this." She picked up a basket filled with lavender wands, then put it back down. "I wish Orion was here. I can deal with the cottage or the farm, but both is too much. For me, anyway. I'm not Liz."

As the server at Blossom had said, Liz had been a force. "That reminds me. I wanted to ask, if you don't mind. If you know. Why is Desiree so set on turning Salter Farm into an event center? Is there a need?"

"Good question. She holds tons of events at the B&B, but she doesn't have a lot of space there. She's kind of a workaholic. She likes creating new things—menus, events. Liz didn't understand that. Which is funny, because that's how she is. Was. They both thought they knew what ought to happen, and they weren't about to let anyone stand in their way."

Even a good friend.

"They both knew Danny was a lost cause," Abby continued.

"I keep hearing that name. Who is he?"

"The reason Liz moved to Salmon Falls. They met when she first came to Washington, working at an organic orchard that hired kids and taught them about agriculture. She loved it. His family had an old farm, so they moved here together. She worked her butt off, but he couldn't be bothered. Then she discovered lavender, and rented this patch from TJ's family."

"What happened after that?"

Leslie Budewitz · 173

"Danny took off. He was always going off chasing the next thing." She met my gaze, her face serious. "Orion isn't like that. No matter what Joe Aguilar thinks. He just went camping with his dog. He'll be back."

"I'm sure he will," I said. "My boyfriend comes and goes. He's a commercial fisherman. It's part of the job. But I know I can trust him, like you trust Orion."

She blinked several times, restraining her emotion. "Then Liz connected with TJ, and they were together for a few years, until they weren't. But they stayed friends."

"Were Liz and Danny still friends?"

"No. I mean, she told me that when he came back last year and planted the grape vines, then built the greenhouse, she thought he'd finally grown up. They hooked up a couple of times last winter, but she said it was a mistake, and she wasn't going to do that again."

That last part of the story I knew. And as a woman who'd been tempted to repeat my own mistakes more than once, I understood.

"Then he decided to sell the farm to Desiree," I said. "What brought that about?"

"I don't know. Liz was furious. Like he did it out of spite, because she refused to give him credit for the hybrid." Abby poked the air with her finger. "But that plant was all Liz's doing. He may have had the idea, ten years ago, or more. But I was here. I saw it. She did all the work. Taking cuttings, rooting them, all the plant biology stuff. Danny had nothing to do with it."

"Wait. We were talking about Salter Farm. I thought his name is Danny Heilman." The man who'd watched us loading the Saab without offering to help. Entitled, according to the antique dealer. Just as Abby had described.

"Yeah. I don't know the details. Everybody calls the place Salter Farm."

Salter Farm. Scott and Monica Salter. His brother, with a different last name. The hybrid. My head was spinning.

Had Danny Heilman killed Liz?

"LET'S GO SEE this farm everyone keeps talking about," my mother said when we got back in the car.

I was game, but not sure how to find the property. At least, not on purpose. We drove up Mrs. Luedtke Road, me still wondering

174 · *Lavender Lies Bleeding*

who she'd been but grateful that she'd left her name behind. I slowed as we neared the stream and the azaleas.

"Oh," my mother said. "Isn't that sweet? Pretty as a picture."

I hadn't showed her the photo I'd bought. Later. Right now, I was searching for the road that would lead us to the barn. And a farmhouse, if there was one. Did Danny Heilman live on the place? No matter how enticing the view, if we saw a 'No Trespassing' sign, I was outta there. I had no desire to be greeted by a shotgun.

"Maggie Delaney is very nice," my mother said as we drove on. "Worried about Abby, waiting for that boyfriend of hers to show up and defend himself."

"Why does she think he needs defending? Orion, the boyfriend."

"You mean, does she think he vandalized that greenhouse or killed Liz? Not for a minute. But Joe Aguilar has him in his sights."

"So, is Aguilar targeting the kid to make things hard on the Delaneys, because Maggie broke off their relationship?" I passed a turnoff into a gravel road and backed up.

"No. She thinks he's trying to protect Abby from getting hurt. Seems Abby and Orion had a big fight over their relationship, and Orion took off. Maggie let that slip to Joe."

"Holy marjoroly. And Orion fought with Liz, too, though I didn't know why." One more reason for Aguilar to distrust him.

"What a pretty little lane," Mom said.

The barn stood to the right, beyond a small vineyard. Very small. Not more than an acre or two, out of several hundred. Even from a distance, the vines looked punk. Clumps of alfalfa and weedy grasses filled the fields. When had they last been cultivated?

"Maggie thinks Abby will do a good job running the lavender farm," Mom continued, "thanks to all she learned from Liz. But she'll need help."

"I agree. I don't see a farmhouse. Do you?" Just the barn, a large, empty greenhouse, and a shiny new Airstream. A pair of sturdy wooden Adirondacks sat next to a fire pit surrounded by river rock. The scene stabbed me in the gut, immediately painting a mental picture of a sight I hadn't seen—Liz's body on the ground, the purple Adirondack knocked over in a struggle, her beloved plants silent witnesses.

"No," Mom said. "No vehicles. No signs of anyone at home or at work."

Leslie Budewitz · 175

We parked the Saab in plain sight and climbed out. A row of fading red tulips bordered a weedy patch, a stone step and a brick chimney all that remained of a long-gone farmhouse. A large rhubarb plant, already sending up seed stalks, looked to be all that was left of a kitchen garden. Beyond lay a swath of golden willows and a series of small ponds, linked by the stream we'd crossed earlier. The Cascade foothills rose in the distance. Lovely or spooky? Salter Farm teetered between the two.

The vines, though, were more than symbols of neglect. The rows were set up like others I'd seen, with sturdy wooden T-shaped braces at each end, heavy-duty wires strung between them. But the vines barely reached the wire, the leaves a pale, sickly yellow, unlike the lush green vines at Cascade Vista. Clumps of grass had invaded the rows. If there was an irrigation system, I couldn't see it.

"It's an honest building," my mother said as we neared the barn, the expression puzzling me. "It isn't fancy. It wasn't built to impress anyone. It was built to do a job, one it did well for a century or more. But it wants to be used."

"What do you know about old barns, Mom? You're a city girl."

"You'd be surprised what I know," she said and swept past me. The barn doors were open a foot or two and I followed her in.

"We probably shouldn't be in here."

"No," she agreed, but kept walking.

My eyes began to adjust to the shadows. The rafters and beams looked sturdy, though stained by water and time. A sagging wooden ladder led to the hayloft Savannah had mentioned, and the scent of horses and hay clung to the air, though I saw no evidence of recent use.

A shaft of light streamed through an opening high up, setting the dust motes in motion. I suppressed a sneeze.

A straw hat lay on the barn floor. I picked it up. A woman's gardening hat, a purple ribbon tied around the crown.

We heard the rush of wings and air before we saw the bird. A speckled gray-and-white owl swooped down from the rafters, passing within a few feet of us, yellow eyes gleaming. Instinctively I ducked, but the owl wasn't after me. It snatched up a mouse, and with a powerful flap of its broad wings, flew out the open door.

"Owls symbolize wisdom and intuition," my mother said, the hand on her heart the only sign of disquiet. Not for nothing had I been raised among women who lit incense and studied astrology and read tarot cards. Women raised in the Catholic church who'd left it behind and found or created other rituals to take its place.

And they symbolize death, I thought, with a shudder I hoped the shadows hid.

"It has potential," my mother said with a forced cheeriness as we walked out into the sunshine.

"Ha," I said. "Anyone who's ever read a real estate ad knows that 'potential' is code for 'put your contractor on speed dial.'"

My mother sighed. "Too bad it has to be sold. It's a piece of family history."

Monica had not said why Salter Farm was being sold. Was it better for the place to go to a well-financed couple who would update the barn and show the property off? Or to a group of farmers who would cultivate the land and use it to feed people?

We drifted toward the pond behind the barn. Cattails marked its marshy edges, red-winged blackbirds perched among them, their song a caw and a trill, a call and repeat. A duck paddled on the surface, a cluster of ducklings in her wake. They were past the fuzzy stage, but not by much. My mother slipped her phone from her pocket and snapped a picture.

Then, in silent agreement, we left the postcard scene behind. Despite the sunshine and bird song, I was a hair spooked, and I thought my mother was, too.

We drove away with more questions than answers. No one had arrived while we were prowling where we shouldn't have been. Back on the road, I followed its twists and turns, as confusing as they'd been the other day.

"Do you know where you're going?" my mother asked.

"Not exactly." After another mile or so, I sped up to pass a tractor puttering along, taking up the shoulder and more than half our lane. I returned the driver's wave and drove on, the rattled feeling I'd had since the encounter with the owl not yet dissipated, despite the clear skies and comforting scenery.

I glanced in the rearview mirror. A big truck was approaching. A duck flew in front of us, low above the road, and I gripped the wheel tightly, prepared to swerve or brake. Mom stiffened beside me.

Then came the rasp of metal on metal. The squeal of tires and the screech of brakes.

And my mother's scream.

Twenty-Six

> *Adrenaline is part of the body's defense mechanism, the fight-or-flight hormone released when the nervous system detects danger and summons all the senses into action.*

"ARE YOU OKAY?" I ASKED, MY BREATH RAGGED.

"I—I think so. Just—shocked. What happened?"

"We got hit."

"That, I know," came my mother's testy reply. "But why? And what do we do now?"

Good questions. The impact had spun us around, facing the direction we'd come. The back end of the car tipped toward the ditch that ran inches from the narrow shoulder.

The irrigation ditch, filled with water.

"Don't move, Mom. Not yet." I took a deep, calming breath, grateful to have some experience of yoga even if I didn't get to the studio nearly enough. *I'll go three times next week*, I promised the Universe, *and every week for the rest of the summer if you get us out of here safely.*

"Right," she said. "Breathe. Then call for help."

What had happened? It was broad daylight. I'd been back in my own lane after passing the tractor. I'd seen a big, dark pickup in my rearview mirror, not giving it a second thought. Big, dark pickups were as common here as SUVs in the city or sports cars in

178 · *Lavender Lies Bleeding*

the upscale suburbs. I hadn't gotten a close look, intent on the road and on not hitting the duck. Then the truck hit me, on the driver's side. We'd gone spinning across the road, the pickup speeding past as if nothing had happened. Had it been black or blue or gray? I couldn't tell. All my mind's eye could see was dark metal, spattered with mud.

I closed my eyes. Could I picture the driver's face? The silhouette? No.

"Okay, so here's what we're going to do," I said. "I don't think the car will slide into the ditch, but we can't be sure. Do you have your phone?" Mine was in my bag, in back, but she'd had hers in hand at the farm and I hoped she had it close now. "Give it to me. Then undo your seat belt, slowly and carefully, and climb over the console. I'll open the door and slide out, then you follow me. When we're both on solid ground, we'll call for help."

She handed me her phone and I slipped it in my pocket. Thank goodness she's a small woman who makes it to yoga and Pilates more often than I do. I held my breath as I watched her push herself up and sit on the console. I unlatched the seat belt and inched my way toward the open door.

Slowly, gently, I told myself. My feet hit the pavement and I turned, holding out my hands, in case the car shifted and I needed to grab her. She drew up her legs and lowered herself into the driver's seat. A moment later, she stumbled onto the road. The car gave a small shudder, as if it were as relieved as we were. Was that gasoline I smelled, or my own fear?

We stood beside the car, arms around each other, catching our breath. Recovering from danger requires a lot of air. Not a single vehicle had passed us. The tractor hadn't caught up to us. Had it turned off, eager to be safe in its own barn?

Everything behind the driver's door was smashed. The force had shattered the rear window, but it had stayed put. Gotta love safety glass. The car perched at a precarious angle, as though it could slip sideways into the ditch with the touch of a finger.

"I could have sworn we were being followed," my mother said. "As soon as we left the farm."

"Why didn't you say something?"

"Because you're almost as skeptical about that kind of thing as your father." She had a point. "I chalked it up to the spooki-

Leslie Budewitz · 179

ness of the barn, and not knowing whether we were trespassing or not."

"Oh, we were trespassing. I didn't think anybody saw us. But now . . ."

Now I wondered. Was it crazy to think the owl hadn't just been hunting? That he'd been warning us?

THE TOW TRUCK driver had almost finished hooking up the Saab when Sheriff Aguilar drove us into town.

"You sure you don't need to go to the ER?" Aguilar asked us again, and again, we said no. Mom had called Dad, and I'd called Nate, and they'd both asked the same thing. We'd assured them, as we had the sheriff, that we were okay.

"Okay" being a relative term. We were not physically injured, but we were shaken to the core. I could still feel the adrenaline rushing through me. It does its job, getting you through the crisis, then it sits in your bloodstream, reminding you of every terrifying second. It's hot and prickly and annoying as heck, but all that's a small price to pay for being out of danger. For being safe.

"Nothing fancy, I'm afraid." Aguilar pushed open the door to his office, in the lower level of the courthouse, the single window high up on the cement wall covered with bars. Not to keep us in, but to keep the bad guys out.

We both declined coffee. I didn't need to give my nerves another jolt.

"Go over it one more time," Aguilar said. "Every detail."

We told him about going to Liz's farm—he'd guessed that's where we were headed when we passed him on Mrs. Luedtke Road—then on to Salter Farm.

"Why?"

"Because it's at the center of this whole puzzler, isn't it?" I ignored his look of exasperation and described what had happened on the road.

He grunted, reminding me of Detective Tracy back in Seattle. "Sounds like a PIT maneuver."

"A what?"

"Precision immobilization technique, also called pursuit intervention technique. It's used by law enforcement in chases to stop a car without causing injury. You've got to match the other car's speed and deliberately hit it on the rear quarter panel. It spins out, stalls, and comes to a stop." He lined up his hands like two vehicles, demonstrating. "You maintain your own speed and drive on through. We're trained to use it only when there's no other means to stop a vehicle and the risk is low. Big truck, small car—big no-no."

"Who would even know such a thing?" I asked. "Let alone use it against me?"

Aguilar pressed his lips together. If he had a theory, he was not going to share it. "We're talking about criminal recklessness. It takes a lot of nerve."

Nerve, or desperation.

"Kudos to you for keeping your car at least partly on the road," he continued. "It could easily have flipped."

And crushed us, or left us to drown. "Thanks. What does Orion Fisher drive?"

"A funky old pickup that looks like a toy. You wonder how it's still on the road, let alone getting a guy around the back country."

"What color?"

"White," he said. "Not your man."

Thank heavens. "It was a threat, wasn't it?" I asked.

"The painting," my mother blurted.

"I'm sure it's fine," I said. The tow truck driver had managed to get it out, despite the damage to the door. One corner of the package was badly crunched. It had been well wrapped—too well, I'd thought when the antique dealer wrangled it into the car, but I was grateful now. "Even if the frame is damaged, we know the artist. He'll be able to fix it."

"My deputies will go door-to-door—or farm-to-farm—to track down that tractor driver. Any luck, he can ID the pickup," Aguilar said, rising. "But I'll tell you two things. One, there's a lot of dark, mud-spattered pickups out here."

That, I knew. "Now that I think about it, it could have been the same truck that passed me earlier this week. It was going pretty fast, but I'm almost certain."

He made a note of the day and time, as best I could recall. "Second thing. While I'm not convinced that this was a threat, as you say, or even a warning, I hope you'll take a lesson from it. Back off, and leave the investigation to the professionals."

Leslie Budewitz · 181

I said nothing. I try not to make promises I don't intend to keep.

I MIGHT LIVE in the city, but I knew cities and small towns have at least two things in common: Coffee shops and bars are both prime spots for talk. Too late for one, just right for the other.

Aguilar had offered us a ride, but the business district was close by.

"The walk will help cleanse the chakras," Mom had said. Metabolize the adrenaline, I'd thought.

The Draught House was lively for a Tuesday night. A man with a scruffy beard and an acoustic guitar sat on a stool in the corner. Mom led the way to a high-top near a window.

She glanced at the beer list, on a chalkboard behind the bar.

"Order the lavender ale," she said, "and I'll disown you."

"No worries."

She ordered a stout and I ordered a lager and cheesy fries. I took a moment to text Kristen that I wouldn't make Flick Chicks—hard to believe it had been a week since we last got together—then gave our surroundings a closer look. The decor was old farm and orchard, fittingly, with a smattering of vintage gas station. Signs for feed, Valvoline, and John Deere tractors that were either authentic or very convincing reproductions hung on the planked walls. A row of metal oil cans, their colors recalling a bygone era, sat atop the backbar, picking up a glint from the lights. Wildflowers stuck in beer bottles sat on classic oak tables. The place gave off an aroma of hops and humans, with a hint of kitchen grease.

Honest, as my mother had said of the barn.

Our beers came and I had to force myself to sip slowly.

"Your father should be here soon," Mom said. It had been agreed that he, not Nate, would make the trip, having the only reliable vehicle with enough room for us and our stuff. Mom's shopping bags and the painting filled the extra chairs.

A young woman drifted by, a beer glass in hand, swaying to the music.

"Abby?" I asked.

She spun around. Her face lit up. "Pepper! Lena!"

182 · *Lavender Lies Bleeding*

"Look at you," I said, taking in the flowing, calf-length dress and lace-up boots, the bracelets stacked on both wrists. Rhinestone-studded barrettes pinned a thick strand of hair above each ear. "Modern witch, if I'm reading the look right."

"My signature, when I'm not working."

A whole different girl than the one we'd seen at the farm a few hours ago.

"Your outfit's cute, too," she said, nodding at my overalls, now stained and wrinkled. "You staying for dinner? The tomato bisque is so-o-o good. The guitar player's girlfriend is my bestie." She waved vaguely toward the bar, where a redhead sat watching the musician, an empty seat beside her.

Mom and I exchanged glances. "We had a little accident," Mom said. "We're waiting for my husband, Pepper's father, to come get us."

"Oh, no. What happened?"

For some reason I could not articulate, I did not want to explain. Because I didn't want to wipe the pretty smile off the face of this young woman who was going through so much, or because I didn't want to admit that my questions had put us in danger? "Nothing to worry about. But my car is old, and it was safer to have it towed than try to drive back to Seattle at night." With one headlight and no brake lights, Aguilar would never have let us get on the road.

"Well, this is a good place to rest up while you wait. And drink up." She tipped her glass toward ours and drained it. Not her first beer of the evening, though maybe it should be her last. "Me, I'm so relieved. Oops! Time to go relieve myself."

She burped. Wobbled. Set her empty glass on our table.

"Good idea," Mom said. "I'll go with you." She slid off her tall chair and looped her arm through Abby's, steadying the girl on their way to the restroom.

Relieved? That we were okay? It struck me as an odd thing to say, and I wondered if I'd misunderstood her.

My fries came and I dove in, suddenly ravenous. If we were being warned, as I suspected, or threatened, as I feared, why? Did someone think I was coming too close to the truth about the vandalism and the murder? Who? And what was this slippery truth?

A few minutes later, Mom and Abby emerged from the back hall. Mom parked Abby on the bar stool next to the musician's girlfriend.

Leslie Budewitz · 183

"She'll be fine," Mom said as she slid onto her seat. "A touch tipsy—her friend will get her home safely." She took a fry. "But now we know why she's out celebrating."

I waited.

"That boyfriend of hers checked in."

"He's back? Does Aguilar know?"

"No, and yes. Orion came down from the backcountry with an injured hiker he met on the trail, and called Abby from the hospital in Wenatchee. She told him what happened and that he had to call Aguilar. Smart boy. He did."

"Is he on his way home?"

"He had to go back and break camp. Should be here tomorrow."

So, Orion had been out hiking, just as Abby had said. Alone, except for the dog. He might not have run us off the road, but it wasn't a solid alibi for the vandalism or the murder. Not solid enough for Aguilar. Who hadn't mentioned a thing.

"Chuck!" my mother cried and slid off her seat. My father rushed toward her and swept her in his arms, much as when they first met, decades ago.

I stood, ready for a hug. Instead, I got the glare of a father too angry to trust himself to speak.

"Chuck, no." Mom put a hand on his arm. "We're fine, and that's what matters."

He didn't shake her off, but he didn't take his eyes off me.

"What were you doing?" he asked, in the parental tone that doesn't actually want an answer. "We raised you to use your power for good, and I'm proud of what you've done for the community, especially in the Market, revitalizing a dying business, giving people good, solid jobs, helping them out of trouble. But tonight . . ."

He broke off. "Where are your things?" he asked my mother, and for a nanosecond, until she held out her hand, I thought my father was going to take her home and leave me here in the Salmon Falls Draught House, surrounded by mementos of a past that had nothing to do with me.

Because he was right. I'd been out chasing theories, chasing ghosts and trouble. And I'd put my mother in danger.

What was I doing?

Twenty-Seven

Dog is my copilot.
—bumper sticker

MY FATHER DIDN'T SAY A WORD TO ME ON THE DRIVE BACK to Seattle. He didn't say a word as he wound his way through downtown to Western and pulled up across from the loft. He didn't say a word as I slid out of the back seat, my head almost literally in my hands, or as my mother climbed out to give me a hug.

"Don't worry about him," she said. "He'll come around. We're not hurt, and we learned quite a bit. I found it all rather exciting."

I could not match her excitement as I kissed her cheek. "Thanks, Mom. For your support and your spunk."

"That's me, a spunky old broad," she said, and in the fading evening light, I saw her wink.

Given his mood, it counted as a win that my father did not pull away from the curb until I had unlocked the front door of my building, stepped inside, and waved. Though he did not wave back.

I heard the door to the loft open before my foot hit the first step. Arf raced down the two flights and I crouched and wrapped my arms around him, my face buried in his fur. Then he broke free and bounded back up. I followed slowly, shaking with dread.

In the open doorway, Nate held out his arms and I fell into them, not quite sobbing, not quite steady.

Leslie Budewitz · 185

"I love," I said after a very long moment, "that when we hug, you never let go first."

"I love," he said, "that I never want to."

And with that, we went inside. I sat at the counter and drank a long, cold glass of water as I told Nate all about what had happened. Including my dad's fury.

"He'll come around," Nate said, echoing my mother. "For a lot of men, worry looks like anger, and it feels that way in our bodies. He just needs time for it to run its course."

"Maybe. I suppose. But he's right. I did put her in danger. And my car is wrecked."

"Pepper, listen." Nate set both hands flat on the kitchen counter, leaning forward. "You did not put your mother in danger. You didn't do anything. The other driver is one hundred thousand percent responsible, and if this Sheriff Aguilar doesn't rip him a new one, I will. Sorry. Now I'm letting my worry and anger get to me."

"I know it's his—or whoever's—fault, not mine, but I am ninety-nine percent certain he came after us because I'm asking questions. I made a promise to Liz, and I'm getting close to something."

"Maybe. Or some guy decided to get his kicks and you happened to get in the way."

That theory reminded me of the criminal hijinks of Orion Fisher's youth. "At least we know it wasn't Orion. We ran into Abby, his girlfriend, at the pub, and he's back. Or on his way." I explained.

"So his alibi for the vandalism and Liz's murder isn't confirmed." Nate held up a bottle of wine, in question.

"Not yet, thanks," I said to the offer. "No, but we do know he went camping, as Abby's been saying. I hope now, Aguilar will admit the possibility that Orion told Abby the truth and that he wasn't involved. And that he'll try to track down other campers to back up the kid's story. From what I hear, even if you didn't remember him, you'd remember his dog."

After a shower and a change into fresh clothes—adrenaline rushes stink in more ways than one—I felt like a new woman. Or at least one not doomed to lose the love and respect of the people closest to me for something I hadn't done. But the shower hadn't changed my mind about one thing: The driver had meant to send me a message. That I got, even if I didn't know who was sending it.

186 · *Lavender Lies Bleeding*

Or what fear of discovery had led to a reckless crime that put both me and my mother in danger.

Talk about anger mingling with worry.

Half an order of cheesy fries does not dinner make, so I dug around in the fridge for leftovers, and sat on the couch with my plate and a glass of red wine. A book lay open on the packing crate coffee table.

A garden book.

Arf lay on the floor next to the couch and I rubbed his back with my bare foot. Animals seem to know when we most need their comfort. I hope we return the favor.

"I didn't tell you about the farm." I filled Nate in on what we'd seen: The old barn and the new Airstream. The empty greenhouse. The vines withering a stone's throw from an irrigation stream and storage ponds. "Desiree claims she's going to remodel the barn. But after seeing the place, I'm afraid—everyone's afraid—that at some point, she'll subdivide."

"Turn all that lush farmland into houses with big lawns that are great for kids and dogs, but don't produce anything." Nate settled in next to me.

"Exactly." I sipped my wine and picked up the subject I couldn't let drop. "Orion's alibi will be hard to prove, unless the right witnesses surface. Stehekin's a trek by boat, but Lake Chelan isn't that far away."

"Meaning he could have gone camping, come home, killed Liz, and gone back to the woods."

"Right. Not that I believe it, but it is possible. It's equally possible that someone who knew his history of vandalism wanted to make it look like he'd damaged the greenhouse. The Whites knew his history from the background check they did before renting to him. But who else?"

"Who stood to gain from damaging the greenhouse?" Nate asked. "And then, when that didn't stop Liz, kill her?"

"Desiree, to keep Liz from interfering with her plans for the event center? But she has an alibi for the murder."

"What about her husband?"

"I don't know. I hardly know anything about him." I'd seen him in town, scowling outside his real estate office. "Everyone else I've met was on the same side as Liz. Well, almost everybody. So why target her? Do we have two different culprits, a vandal and a killer? Mike Tracy would roll his eyes—it goes against his theory that when bad things happen near or around the same group of people, they're probably connected."

"They could be connected, even if two different people carried them out."

"True." I took another bite.

"When you first told me about Orion," Nate said, "I figured he was one of those guys who takes a while to grow up, and things with Abby got to the point that he had to decide."

"Peter Pan," I said, though my mouth was full and it came out "peerpaa."

"Right. Growing up doesn't necessarily look like it used to. The milestones have changed. I've seen it with crew. Some guys settle into the routine, even if they get married and have a kid or two. Others give up fishing. Bron was a bit of a party guy for a while, until he decided to buy into the boat with me and share responsibility." Nate set his wine glass on the table. "I talked to Javier today. They're back from the San Juans—they had a great time."

"We should go up there," I said, then immediately hoped he didn't think I was suggesting a honeymoon. You had to get married first.

"Yeah. He's got a new project in the pipeline, rehabbing an old warehouse Mindy and her folks bought. It's going to be their new barrel aging facility. He wants me to work on it."

"Seriously? You haven't done construction since summers in college."

"More finish carpentry than construction. Like some of the stuff he and I did on the boats. I told him I'd think about it. I'm not afraid of the physical work. It'll keep me in shape."

"I like your shape."

"And I like yours," he said, a lift in his voice. "The main thing is that it's a chance to work closer to home. Try something new and see how it goes."

"Change," I said, and sipped my wine. This was the conversation I'd been hoping for, but every eager cell in my body told me not to rush it.

"Change," he agreed, then reached for the garden book. "I've been thinking about your rooftop garden idea. Maybe it's time.

188 · *Lavender Lies Bleeding*

I know—" He put up a hand. "You're going into your busy season, and Glenn says they're too exhausted from their remodel to do one more thing. I talked to your dad about it, and he's willing to help."

"That was before I put the love of his life in mortal danger."

"He'll get over it. Let me show you what I'm thinking."

I took the book from his hands and set it on the packing crate, then cupped his cheek with my hand. "Later. Right now, let me show you what I'm thinking."

Twenty-Eight

The name Post Alley traces back to the hills and regrades of early Seattle, when many buildings were supported by posts—not, as legend would have it, from hitching posts.

SOMETIMES, WHEN SOMETHING GOES WELL, I FORGET FOR a moment that other things are still messed up. That was Wednesday morning in a nutshell. Nate and I were on the same page. He'd let me in on his thinking about the boat and future work. And the garden. And all that made me ridiculously happy.

But I had no car. I was no closer to figuring out what had happened to Liz than I had been yesterday. And my dad wasn't speaking to me.

Fortunately, my mother was. The phone had pinged so madly while I was in the shower that Nate had finally peeked at it, certain it was news of the impending end of the world. No. Lena, that spunky old broad, on a texting tear. Cooking up a family gathering. Innocent sounding, but I knew her. That was her way of trying to mend the breach.

"You could just tell him you're sorry," Nate said when he came out of the bathroom, a towel wrapped around his waist, and saw me, half dressed, sitting on the edge of the bed rapidly replying to my mother.

190 · *Lavender Lies Bleeding*

"I did. At the pub, and on the way to the car with all Mom's stuff. He wouldn't even look at me. I texted him last night, and crickets."

Nate kissed the top of my head and left the room. Before I knew it, the aroma of coffee brewing snapped me out of my funk. Nothing eases heartache like a cup of coffee someone else makes for you.

"You going out to Javier's job site this morning?" I asked.

"Yep. Scope it out, see what he's got in mind. Sorry. That means I need my truck."

"Mom said I could borrow the SUV until I figure out what to do. I need to see what the insurance company says." The tow truck driver had shaken his head in a way that gave me no hope, before hauling my busted car to the body shop.

Then we went our separate ways, Nate to meet up with Javier, Arf and me to the Spice Shop. How was I going to afford a new car, if the Saab was beyond saving? The shop was doing well, but I'd plowed all the profits back into it, expanding our online business and our commercial customer base. That had meant investing in more production staff and equipment. My cash cushion was about as flat as the proverbial pancake.

A few weeks ago, I had literally been sitting on a cash cushion. If I hadn't been so determined to find its rightful owner, I'd have no trouble buying a new car. Instead, a man had died, several people were in jail awaiting trial on a pile of charges, and the fate of the money rested on an investigation that my good friends Detectives Spencer and Tracy told me was nowhere near the finish line. Though I had the satisfaction of knowing I'd done the right thing, I had no expectation of ever seeing a penny.

Life is like that sometimes.

The morning paper lay in the tiny alcove outside the shop's front door. Inside, after I made sure Arf had a chew bone to work on, I spread it open on the front counter. Searched for news about the murder investigation. Nothing.

But another piece caught my eye. I carried the paper to the nook.

The article described a popular program at the state women's prison that taught inmates to work with dogs. To train them, groom them, and handle their basic medical needs. Some inmates trained future service dogs. Others ran a doggy daycare for prison staffers.

The goal was to give the women purpose and train them to work in the field after their release.

I sat back, letting the possibilities percolate.

A few minutes later, I bounced up and grabbed my keys and wallet and Arf's leash. I'd almost forgotten I was on snack duty today. We were overdue for a Market staple from the Daily Dozen, a doughnut stand in the Economy Arcade. I bought three dozen mixed minis and was licking maple frosting off my fingers when I spotted Tag on foot, steadying his bike with one hand, talking to a delivery truck driver. I waited until the conversation—from the sounds and gestures, not a pleasant one—had ended.

"Care for a doughnut, Officer?" I held out the open bag. "I hear they're a favorite in your line of work."

Tag drew out a glazed mini and bit in.

"Guy nearly hit another truck, then he nearly hit me and claimed it was my fault. I gave him a lecture about yielding and keeping his speed down, but I can't say it will do much good. So be alert."

"Thanks. Speaking of getting hit." I told him about the Saab. We'd bought it together, eons ago. When we split up, he'd insisted I take it, for its safety and reliability. It had not been so reliable the last few months, and as for safety . . .

"But you're okay? Lena's okay?"

"Yeah. I think the car's totaled. My dad is so mad he won't talk to me."

"He'll get over it." Tag took another doughnut. "Dang, these are addictive."

"I hope you're right. About my dad, I mean. I know you're right about the doughnuts."

He gave me a sugary kiss on the cheek, then gave the dog a quick pat, and we both got back to work.

After the staff meeting, I retreated to my office to catch up on details I'd missed yesterday. Among the many emails was one from the Merchants' Association saying that Jerry, the longtime Market butcher who'd been seriously injured in a fall down the old cattle ramp a few weeks ago, was now out of the hospital and in a rehab facility on First Hill. And he craved visitors. That, I understood. After decades of greeting Market visitors and enticing them to buy sausage or a juicy steak—"money back if your mouth doesn't

192 · *Lavender Lies Bleeding*

water"—the relative solitude of a lengthy hospital stay was probably harder on him than the broken bones.

I noted the address. A visit might mesh nicely with another idea taking shape.

The rest of the morning, I alternated between business details and working with customers. A few minutes before noon, a call came in on my cell and I excused myself to take it in the office. As I'd expected, the claims adjuster had declared the Saab a complete loss. In addition to the body damage, the rear axle had bent when the car slipped into the ditch. I could accept their valuation and say goodbye to the only car I'd ever loved, or if I wanted to try to repair it myself, I could keep it and the cash, less the salvage value. Normally, they would give me three days to decide, but the sheriff's office had put a hold on the vehicle pending the results of their criminal investigation, so I had a little longer to figure things out.

I hung up and folded my arms on top of my desk. Rested my head and choked back tears.

"I'm sorry, Liz," I told the ghost of my dead friend. "I effed up. I wrecked my car, I scared my mother, and ticked off my dad. Scared myself, too. And I'm no closer to figuring out what happened than I was before. I know I promised—"

"Hey, no sniveling on the job."

I broke off. Vinny stood in the open doorway.

"Good garlic oil, Vinny. Give a girl a heart attack." I told him what had happened.

"Listen up, missy. You are one of the best things about this old fire trap." Vinny waved a finger in the air, meaning the Market. "You got ideas, you make 'em happen. You bring people together, like Matt and me. You keep your promises. But you don't have to solve every crime all by yourself. Give the cops a chance."

I stuck out my tongue.

"Now look what you've done, blubbering about your troubles. Almost made me forget why I came here in the first place," Vinny said. "You want to go up and see old Jerry with me? You know how he talks. I figure the only way to get out of there in less than a whole afternoon is to take reinforcements."

I suppressed a smile. The same could be said about Vinny.

We settled on a time. Vinny left and I turned back to my troubles, as he'd called them. First things first. I texted my dad the

Leslie Budewitz · 193

figure the adjuster had given me. *Here's what they're offering. What do you think? Love you.* Then I forwarded the text to Nate, and forced myself to focus on my shop so I wouldn't obsess about whether my normally calm, even-tempered father would ever forgive me.

Midafternoon, Vinny and I met at the bus stop on First for the ride up the hill. When I'd worked among the tall office buildings of the business district, I'd known how to get from First up to Sixth without sweating, dipping in and out of air-conditioned lobbies to ride the escalators. The air on the bus was *eau d'human*, though happily, it wasn't a hot day.

The bus crossed over I-5 and I glanced out the window. I could make my side trip after our visit. If Vinny wanted to stay longer—his fears of Jerry's loquacity aside—I could plead the need to speed out sooner on some urgent errand. If Vinny saw through me, he'd wink and wave me along.

We entered the facility through a courtyard where begonias and peace lilies surrounded a bubbling fountain. Inside, we found Jerry in the physical therapy room, wrapping up a session of balancing exercises and eager for company, despite the visible effects of exertion. He refused a wheelchair, and we followed as he shuffled back to his room. It was hard not to cringe, watching this once-vital older man now so changed, but his determination was undeniable. And enviable.

"Pepper," he called over his shoulder. "I left my water bottle in the physical torture chamber. Be a doll and run and grab it."

I did as bid. On my way back, bottle in hand, I stopped and frowned. That had to be Desiree White, pushing an older woman down the hall. I ducked out of sight. Moments later, I peeked around the corner. They were gone. I sped back to Jerry's room, relieved that it was down another hall.

Twenty minutes later, I excused myself to find the restroom. When I came out, a woman waited beside the door, arms crossed.

"Are you following me?" Desiree asked.

"I was about to ask you the same thing."

"We need to talk." She led the way to an alcove that held a small couch and a pair of matching upholstered chairs, designed to make an uncomfortable place feel more like home. It almost worked.

"I didn't kill Liz Giacometti," she said.

194 · *Lavender Lies Bleeding*

"I'm listening." At the wedding, she'd been every inch the professional caterer, the woman in charge. Now, she had second-day hair and wrinkled clothes, and dark circles under her eyes.

"She was my friend. I know—" She held up a hand. "Polar opposites. I love manicures, though I'm overdue, and she loved dirt. I'm tall and wear heels. She's—she was short and wore sport sandals. But when it came to Salmon Falls, we were always on the same page."

"Until you got the idea to convert Salter Farm into a fancy event center. That meant taking it out of agriculture and putting a burden on the community not everyone was sure it could handle."

"It hadn't been a working farm in ages. Not a successful one, anyway. They practically begged us. We ran the numbers. We couldn't see how to make the place work any other way."

"What? Who? The Salters? Did you talk to Liz about it?"

"Of course I did. We even suggested she take over the farm, but it was way too big. There are lavender farms that size, but then you need managers and systems and staff."

"Or monks," I said, thinking of the famous French abbey. "No, you're right. She would have wanted to work alone, as much as possible. No other buyers? Why wasn't the Alliance a viable option?"

"They couldn't get the money together in time, so the family came to us." She exhaled heavily. "Well, not Scott. Not at first. It was Danny. Scott wanted to sell to the Alliance, even if the price had to be lower and they had to carry the paper, but when he saw the full extent of the debt Danny had taken on, there was no real choice."

"So, Danny Heilman is Scott Salter's brother? Or half brother? And he used to date Liz?" I couldn't picture her with the man we'd seen on the sidewalk outside the antique shop. Too bougie.

"Yes. Half brothers. Different fathers, but they inherited the farm equally. Scott's hardworking and solid and reliable."

"You make him sound like a good used car." I waved a hand. "Sorry. I have cars on the brain."

"It's not a bad analogy. Danny drove like a race car driver. Another of his failed careers. He could never get it together."

"Someone else described him as entitled. Wanting the payoff without putting in the work."

"That's him. He borrowed money against the farm for one scheme after another. Alpacas. Bees. Hops. The vineyard was the

Leslie Budewitz · 195

last straw. Great idea, but there wasn't enough equity left to cover any more debt. And you can't grow a business without money. He didn't have enough cash to fix the irrigation system, and Scott couldn't cover it anymore. Not that he could ever stop Danny from spending money to look the part."

Hence the withering vines and the shiny new Airstream. The sale of the property made more sense now, but what did it have to do with the vandalism or Liz's death? For which Desiree apparently had an alibi—if Sheriff Aguilar was right and her desk manager was wrong.

"I came up to visit a friend in the rehab unit," I said. "Looks like you know your way around this place pretty well. The older woman you were pushing in the wheelchair?"

"My mother. She's on the nursing wing. She was forty-five when I was born, and I'm forty now. A surprise only child, though a welcome one. She's twice widowed, and I'm all she has. I've been coming in to spend the afternoon with her three days a week, plus Sundays when Jeffrey comes with me. She's got bone cancer. It won't be long. What about your friend? I'm keeping you from him."

"I'm so sorry about your mother. Our friend had a bad fall, in the Market. Slipped on a steep ramp he had no business being on. Half a dozen surgeries later, here he is. And no worries about keeping me from him. You're keeping me from hearing the same stories over and over."

She gave me a wry smile. "I hope he's back on his feet soon. Honestly, I wish we weren't buying Salter Farm. The financing wasn't as easy as we expected—Jeffrey's spent hours meeting with lenders. Plus, the consultants who work on planning and zoning applications. It's a long, messy process."

Had one of those meetings been the tense conversation Cayenne and I witnessed in Blossom, on our first trip to Salmon Falls?

"I don't have the time or energy to deal with the county, or the public opposition," she continued, "let alone design the building, put together a business plan, and actually create the business."

"But you will. Later," I said. "It will help you keep your mind off all this, when your mother . . ."

"When she dies," Desiree said. "No. I just want to focus on the life I have, instead of always reaching for the next thing. Instead of growing my business just to grow it. It's one thing to lose my mother,

196 · *Lavender Lies Bleeding*

who's had a long, full life. But Liz was barely thirty-eight. Losing her is putting everything I've worked for in a different light."

We let that sit, until I broke the silence. "I gather you told Sheriff Aguilar where you'd been Monday when Liz was killed, but asked him to keep the real reason to himself. To keep it from your staff?"

Tears welled in her eyes and she bit her lower lip. "I just—I need to keep it private. All this, then the fight with Liz, and now she's gone. I'm not sure I could handle talking about my mom."

"Give it a try," I said. "People can surprise you."

She grabbed my hand. Her touch was unexpectedly warm, considering her ice queen routine at the wedding and the way she'd spoken to Daria and Abby. "Yes. They can."

Before we parted ways, I had a pressing question. "Who do you think damaged the greenhouse? And who killed Liz? Was it the same person?"

"I don't know, Pepper. I can't stop thinking about it, but I'm not coming up with any answers."

"If you do, call me."

We walked back to the fork in the hallway, and I watched Desiree hurry down the hall. As we'd said, people can surprise you.

Back in Jerry's room, I glanced at my watch. "Vinny, you ready to head back to the Market?"

"I'm having so much fun jawing with Jerry, I think I'll stay," he said.

So much for needing me as an excuse to make his excuses when Jerry went on too long. But it worked for me. Jerry reached out a hand, still strong and calloused after decades of hard work.

"Thanks for coming, Pepper. You've been a sight for sore eyes."

"I'll be back." I kissed him on the cheek and walked out into the Seattle sunshine, those unanswered questions swirling around me.

Twenty-Nine

In the Victorian language of flowers, the long red flower clusters of the annual Amaranthus caudatus were thought to resemble drops of blood, leading to its association with hopelessness, particularly hopeless love, and the name love-lies-bleeding.

OUTSIDE, I TOOK REFUGE IN THE COURTYARD, ON A STONE bench beneath a lacy, reddish-gold Japanese maple, and called Sheriff Aguilar.

"Insurance company says you put a hold on them signing my car over for salvage," I said. "Glad to hear you took me seriously."

"Oh, I take someone running two women out sightseeing off the road seriously," he replied. "Even if I'm not sure it has anything to do with what happened to Liz Giacometti."

Sightseeing. Okay. "You sent a deputy out to inspect the car. Looking for what?"

Silence, while he decided how much to tell me. "In a hit-and-run, you get lucky, some of the paint transfers from one vehicle to the other, and you match it. Double lucky, and the damage patterns might match up."

"You cruising around town checking out the front end of every dark pickup you see?"

"We're keeping our eyes peeled."

198 · *Lavender Lies Bleeding*

"Any luck with the tractor driver?" I might be pushing my luck with the questions, but hey, it was my car that got wrecked.

And I understood, in one of those moments when something becomes so blindingly obvious that you can't imagine why you didn't see it sooner, that it wasn't just me putting my mother in danger that had so upset my father. It was me putting myself in danger.

Compared to that, asking too many questions was a piece of cake.

"Found him, but he didn't see the rig that hit you. Turned off right after you passed by."

Parsley poop. "I won't go into all the details of why I'm asking this," I said, "but what does Danny Heilman drive?"

"2024 Ford F-150."

"Must be a lot of those in your neck of the woods."

"Not the Raptor model, in metallic black. Retails at close to eighty grand."

"Yikes. You could buy a lot of irrigation equipment for that."

"You could," Aguilar said. "I always figured Danny Heilman for a guy who didn't want to get his hands dirty. Let alone mess up his truck. Could be I was wrong."

Or maybe I was. Much as I hate to admit, it has happened.

A FEW MINUTES LATER, I walked into the veterinary clinic at the edge of Freeway Park where I take Arf.

"Pepper!" the receptionist said. "I didn't see you on the schedule. Where's Arf? He okay?"

"Sorry. No appointment. Dog's fine, but I have questions. Any chance Dr. Z has a minute?"

She did. A compact, athletic woman who exudes competence and compassion, Dr. Zoe Zimorino is the kind of vet who makes me wish I was a dog.

"You may remember," I said, "that I've never known Arf's background. I don't even know how Sam got him."

"Sam took good care of him, as you do."

"I won't bother you with the details of what got me searching. But I went to All Creatures, the shelter clinic, and while they know Arf was a patient, they don't have any records. Not that they can find." Or not that they would give me, but that sounded paranoid, and paranoia rarely encourages confidence.

Leslie Budewitz · 199

"That's odd. Clinic was hand-to-mouth at first, but over the years, they've found their footing. Stable funding helps. Young as Arf is, you'd expect a complete computerized record."

"That's what I thought." I took a deep breath. My questions were about to get sensitive. "I read about a program at the women's prison that trains inmates to work with dogs."

"Yes. Excellent training. Participants learn grooming, obedience and service training, and basic veterinary skills. We had a groomer for a while who went through the program, but she moved out of town. One of our younger vets works at All Creatures a couple of days a month. If I remember right, they've got a few graduates working there—doing a supervised internship as part of their prerelease or whatever it's called."

Exactly the info I'd been hoping for. "Has that internship system been in place for a while?"

"Oh, I think so. Several years, at least." Her eyes narrowed and she tilted her head, trying to see where my questions were going.

But I couldn't tell her what I was thinking. Not yet.

BACK AT THE SHOP, I spent what was left of the afternoon on festival details. We'd asked the PDA for permission to invite extra musicians, beyond the usual busker quota, and they'd agreed. Mary Jean had taken on the task of finding musicians to play outside the participating merchants' doors. The schedule she'd created looked great. The balloon artist had gotten wind of the event and promised to stock up on purple balloons—light and dark—for the day. The face painter would set up at the Market Front, an open-air plaza. Purple is popular with the young girls who were her key demographic, and purple was the color of the day.

Heck, I might even let her paint a sprig of lavender on my face.

With festivities planned for Friday afternoon through Sunday, I followed up on the suggestion to get media attention early, to spur weekend traffic. Foot traffic. As Tag's encounter with the belligerent driver this morning demonstrated, extra wheels brought extra problems.

Then I went over my own finances. Again. Where I could squeeze out money for a monthly car payment, I wasn't sure.

200 · *Lavender Lies Bleeding*

After closing, Arf and I took a detour. I'd tried to time our walk home to coincide with last call at Bark Place, but a big part of timing is simple luck.

It was on our side. I saw fluffy white Polo before I saw his owner, Raine the vet tech, locking up. Polo bounced excitedly at the sight of us, and Arf's curved tail twitched like a bolt of electricity had been shot through it. Neither of them barked.

Raine pocketed her keys and glanced our direction.

"Hey, surprised to see you two," she said. "Headed home?"

"In a roundabout way. I'm sure some days Arf thinks the leash is for me, to make sure I don't get lost."

She and I shared a quick dog lover moment, then her smile faded. The scar on her cheek burned brightly against her pale skin.

"To be honest," I said, "I was hoping to catch you. You and Arf go way back, don't you? To when he was a puppy and you . . ."

She lowered her head, losing the fight to control the emotions crossing her face. "The receptionist at the shelter clinic knew what you were asking the moment you mentioned my name, even if you didn't know yet. She tried to stall you while they tracked me down, but I should have known you'd be—sorry. Dogged."

"One of my best traits," I said. "Sometimes."

Arf and Polo were nuzzling each other like two canine besties. They had the same gentle manners because they'd been trained by the same woman. Who'd learned her skills inside.

"I told myself I would tell you the next time you brought Arf in. And then I found myself hoping you wouldn't come in for a while, much as Polo and I both love him. Can we walk?" She gestured, and we strolled down Lower Post Alley, the dogs in the lead. She told me how, rootless and fresh out of high school, she'd gotten involved with a serious douchebag. How she'd believed every story, every lie, he'd fed her. And when he said she needed to chat up another guy in a bar, let him get too friendly, then stab him, she'd believed that, too.

I held my tongue. No point saying that had been stupid, she'd been smarter than that. She already knew it.

"Fortunately, my aim sucked. I got him in the arm, not the chest. Lots of blood, no permanent damage. Except to my life. Judge took pity on me for getting wrapped up with a bad dude, but I still had to do time. That's where I started working with dogs."

Leslie Budewitz · 201

"I saw the piece in the paper about the program, and it got me thinking."

"It's the best thing that ever happened to me. Except maybe Polo," she said, pure love on her face. "It saved my life, you know. They talk about job skills, and how it's a growing field and you can find a career or use it to support yourself while you train for something else."

We turned toward the waterfront, one of Arf's favorite places.

"But what they don't talk about," she continued, "not much anyway, is how good the dogs are for us. You get to care for something—someone—who loves you unconditionally. Who never judges you or tells you you're stupid or ugly or lucky they don't strangle you." Her voice broke. "You get to touch a living, breathing thing. In prison, you don't touch anybody. It's dangerous. Even casual contact between friends can set you up for trouble."

She touched the scar, and I didn't have to ask what kind of trouble.

"Then one day," she went on, "one of the rescue organizations brought in a litter of puppies who'd been found in an alley curled up next to their dead mother. She wasn't chipped and they couldn't find the owner. So, they brought them to us to foster."

"And one of those puppies was Arf."

"His name was Romeo then. Not my doing, I promise. The rescue people gave all the puppies names from Shakespeare. We trained them and—" She stopped. Tears rolled down her cheek, and she wiped them away with her free hand. "If I'm going to tell you this, I need to tell you the whole story. I got released the same time as the dogs were ready, so I took Romeo with me. Before I got arrested, I'd been using and drinking, but you go through rehab in prison and I thought I was okay. Then, a friend"—she made air quotes—"came back into my life and I relapsed. Violated probation and had to go back to prison. I lost the dog."

"I'm so sorry."

"It was my own fault," she said. "When I got out the second time, I searched for him, but no luck. This time, I stayed clean. I got an internship at the shelter clinic and started vet tech training. Then one day, in walked Sam and Romeo. Arf. I was afraid he wouldn't know me, but he did."

"Of course he did. You were the first person who loved him. You made him the fabulous dog he is." I dug in my tote for a tissue and handed it over. "Any idea where he'd been, before Sam got him? You must have about had a heart attack when I walked into the daycare with him."

"No. No idea." She blew her nose. "And no, I wasn't surprised when you came in. I used to see Sam regularly on the street. You know how he liked to walk, even when he was homeless. Then I saw the dog with you."

"Part of why Sam was willing to let me take Arf was that he knew I love walking, too. Oh-h-h." Dots connected in my brain. "It always struck me how clean and well groomed Arf was. Better than Sam, sometimes. That was you, wasn't it?"

"Mmm-hm. Sam did his best. But the shelter clinic has the big sinks and tables and stuff, and they let us bring our own dogs in to groom them. I'm sure they knew Arf wasn't my dog, but no one said a word."

"All for a good cause."

We stopped at Ivar's for fish and chips, my treat, and sat outside at the metal tables and benches. Polo and Arf were ecstatic in each other's company, and they were perfect gentlemen when the counterman brought them a fresh bowl of water. We talked about Bark Place, and she told me about her life now.

"It's gone to the dogs," she said with a laugh.

In the very best way. "Thank you for telling me your story. And Arf's." Now I was choking up. "You are amazing. The way you've turned your life around. The love you give these dogs. I know you've been through hell, but you came out on the right road."

After a long, sappy hug, Raine and Polo headed to the light rail. Arf and I strode up the waterfront. At a stoplight, I spotted a car. Not any old car, but a shiny, white, all-electric Mustang. I dug in my tote, praying to the car gods that I'd find my phone before the light changed. Snapped a picture and sent it to my dad with a string of question marks.

If that didn't melt the ice, nothing would.

Thirty

"Let food be thy medicine and medicine be thy food."

—Hippocrates

"I TALKED TO JAVIER," NATE SAID. "ABOUT THE JOB, AND SALTER Farm. By the way, the new plants look great."

"What?" I was in the kitchen. I'd sent my leftovers home with Raine; buying dinner had been an excuse to keep her talking. Now I washed spinach for a salad. Out on the veranda, Nate had lit the grill. Arf was still buzzing—he'd met up with old friends, strolled along the waterfront, even gotten a couple of fries and a chunk of fish. I wanted to tell Nate all this, and about the car, but it could wait. When you've been wanting someone to open up and they finally do, you have to listen. I set my knife down and gave him my full attention. "You taking the job? And what did you tell him about the farm?"

"I am going to take the job." Nate kissed the back of my neck on his way to the fridge for the halibut he'd been thawing. "We start on Monday. Two weeks, he thinks. The timing couldn't be better. Bron's flying up next week to meet the broker in Dutch Harbor and show him the boat."

"Great," I said.

"As for the farm, I was thinking." He set the fish on a cutting board and reached for the salt and pepper. "This won't solve Liz's

204 · *Lavender Lies Bleeding*

murder, but it might solve some other problems. If the ink isn't dry on the purchase and sale, there might be another solution."

Patience, Pep, I told myself.

"From what you've said, nobody wants Desiree to buy the farm," he continued. "And the county might not approve the change in use."

"Even she's not so sure anymore." My phone, on the counter near his elbow, pinged. I ignored it. "I'll tell you later. Go on."

"Sometimes the people with money are the problem, and sometimes they are the solution."

"Okay, now I'm totally lost."

"Mindy has money. Winery money. She loves the land, and unlike this Danny, she and her family know what to do with it." He seasoned the fish as he spoke. "Plus, Javier has experience rehabbing old buildings."

"You're saying they could buy that land, keep it in agriculture, and save the barn."

"It could solve everything, don't you think?"

"What about the Alliance? I think the town would much rather see a local buyer than another outsider. Oh-h-h. Would she finance their purchase? Or buy it and lease it back to them?" How long did you have to live in a place before you were no longer considered an outsider? My guess, the smaller the town, the longer it took.

My phone pinged again. Nate wiped his hand on his pants, picked it up, and handed it to me.

My dad. The thumbs-up emoji.

I grinned and held out the phone so Nate could see both the picture and the reply.

"Your new car? I told you he'd come around."

"I wish." I set the phone down and picked up the knife and cucumber. "I mean, yes, he came around and maybe on the car. I'd love it. But I'll need a loan. What they'll give me for the Saab would barely buy the tires."

"I have some cash. No, I mean it," he said. "I can help."

We had a lot to talk about, while cooking and eating and taking Arf for a quick walk before bed. We talked and we listened and it was good.

"I like this," I said as we rounded the corner on our way back to the loft, Arf leading the pack. "Figuring things out together."

He laughed. "Including for people who didn't ask us to figure things out for them."

"Well, yeah. But that's what I do."

"And here I just thought you sold spice."

THURSDAY MORNING WAS wet, wet, wet. Nate dropped Arf and me off at the north end of the Market. Tourist season was picking up, though the rain would put a damper on business. The last details for the festival needed to be nailed down. Sandra had called in sick. I had to figure out the car stuff. Why do emergencies always happen at the worst possible time?

"Pepper, you should have been there," Kristen said as she peeled off her yellow wellies and shrugged out of her dripping wet red and orange raincoat. We'd drooled over the coat in a shop window on First, and I was a teeny bit jealous that she'd bought it.

"Been where?" I said. The floor mop was going to get a workout today.

"At the parents' meeting last night. All about college prep and making sure your kid gets the right combination of grades and extracurriculars and community service."

"College prep? Savannah's a sophomore. And what about work experience?"

"The world has changed. Less than half her friends even want to work. Too busy." She slipped her feet into dry clogs. "Anyway, Monica Salter was on a tear. She went on and on about how Scott is refusing to consider his sons' future. How none of us appreciate what we have. How we don't understand that some people work their tails off and still don't have the security the rest of us take for granted. She would not shut up. Ranting like a street corner preacher."

"Drunk? Drugs?"

"I don't think so." She hung her coat in the back hall and stashed her boots and bag. "Just riled up. At first I thought she was talking about me. She's made snide comments in the past, about my fancy house and not having to work—"

"Does she work? Aside from the occasional delivery." Which was how I'd met her.

"Not anymore. They started the business together, before they had kids, but Scott runs it now, and it's thriving. He sells commercial espresso equipment in the coffee capital of the country, for Pete's sake. She thinks I inherited a fortune, because of the house. You know we bought it from Dad after Mom died, and what a wreck it was." Grace House, where we were raised, had been in Kristen's family for generations, but her parents had been more interested in causes than caulk, and decades as home to a revolving community of like-minded antiestablishment types had been hard on every board and window. "I admit, I'm fortunate. I work because I want to."

"And I'm grateful that you want to work for me." We circled through the shop, straightening and fluffing as we went. "Though if you were wearing your four-hundred-dollar raincoat, she might have had a point."

"I bought it on sale and you know it. You were with me." She mock swatted me with her duster. "I popped into the restroom after the meeting and she was in there, touching up her makeup. Cuts on her face. Said she'd been gardening and tangled with a barberry bush."

"She's definitely been gardening. Ripping out the shrubs around her house and replacing them. I think I might know what set her off." I explained the connection between Danny Heilman, the over-priced pickup that might need body work, and Scott and Monica Salter.

"Seriously? He ran you and Lena off the road because you were snooping around his farm? The farm he's selling to what's her name?"

"Desiree White. Oh, my gosh, I didn't tell you. I ran into her yesterday." I was wrapping up the story when the rest of the staff arrived. Without Sandra, we had to scurry to get ready for opening.

What was really bugging Monica Salter? I was missing too many pieces of the puzzle, and I didn't have time to hunt them down.

Minutes after opening, I was in my office when Sara Vu called. "Pepper, I just read about what happened. Are you okay? Why didn't you call me?"

"Read about it? Where?" In the day and a half since the accident, I hadn't thought to call her. My bad. Apparently, the small-town grapevine that ensures everyone knows everything almost before it happens didn't apply to out-of-towners like me.

"In the *Herald*. It comes out every Thursday."

Leslie Budewitz · 207

It took Google a nanosecond to find the Salmon Falls paper. "Where? I'm searching, but I only see last week's news."

"It's in the print edition. Online edition is subscribers only until the weekend. I could give you my login, but you know what happened." She snorted. "I guess Nina didn't bother calling you for an interview. Anyway, she says the sheriff's office has a suspect but no arrests have been made."

"What are people in town saying?"

"They're furious. After vandalism and a murder, criminal endangerment or whatever it's called is not good for town."

And in Sara's position, the good of the town meant everything.

"But the other thing that's happened is just as important," she continued.

"What? What?"

"Desiree White withdrew her bid to buy Salter Farm. She'll lose her earnest money, but she says she doesn't care. She came in this morning, right after the office opened, to tell me. She said she wants to focus on the restaurant and the inn, and not spread herself too thin."

Sara didn't mention Desiree's mother, so I didn't, either. I did hope Desiree would tell her staff and let them help her during a difficult time. But that decision wasn't up to me.

"That must be a relief," I said. "To you and the Alliance, though it's got to be hard on the Salters." Desiree's decision must have been another factor triggering Monica's verbal rampage last night.

"The Alliance is going to make a new offer, though if it's true that the farm is drowning in debt, we might not have a chance. Our luck, they'll find a developer with even scarier plans."

Ah, yes. Be careful what you wish for.

"Speaking of the Salters, do you know Monica?" I asked.

"Not personally. You know my cousin and his pals who run the pop-up garden at the edge of town? That's where Monica grew up. She had a rough upbringing—single mother, never enough money. No real stability. A few years ago, after Monica and Scott were married and living in Seattle, her mother was smoking in bed and fell asleep. Burned the house down. Except the little garage that's now the farm stand."

"Oh, that's horrible. What happened to her mother?"

208 · *Lavender Lies Bleeding*

Sara's silence told me the woman had not survived. No wonder Monica was so bitter.

"But she was willing to sell it to Preston?" Was he the LLC my friend Jenn had found?

"No, no. The Salter family owns it. Well, their corporation. The Whites have been trying to buy it for years, and so have others, but Monica absolutely refuses to sell. Scott's been letting Preston use it, rent free."

I had not seen that coming.

We wished each other luck with our festivals and said goodbye. Sara's revelation explained why Monica resented people in her circle who had both families and family money. No wonder she was determined to hold on to the farm, as well as the lot in town. They represented everything she'd lost. And here was her own brother-in-law, Danny, squandering his inheritance. Burying the land in so much debt, from one failed scheme after another, that it had to be sold—and even a sale as farmland would not cover it all.

As Liz had said, he never seemed to grasp that you only got what you wanted if you did the work.

Something about the picture was still askew.

My phone buzzed with a text. My dad. *Go see Laura Long at the bank this afternoon. 3:00. She's all set to give you a car loan you can manage.*

My family might not have money. But we knew who did.

Thirty-One

> The narrow cattle ramp is the last remaining segment of the original ramp system designed by Frank Goodwin and his nephew Arthur, early Market owners, architects, and managers, using the narrow wooden planks cut on the end-grain that were once common in factories, auto shops, and other high-traffic commercial spaces.

ONE MORE CALL, THEN I HAD TO GET BACK TO WORK. ALAS, Sheriff Joe Aguilar was not available. On the other hand, if that meant he was out tracking down my assailant, the vandal, or the killer, or confirming Orion Fisher's and Desiree White's alibis, my questions could wait.

My shop could not.

Cayenne and I went over our festival menu. We'd settled on samples of lavender shortbread, crackers with lavender goat cheese, and lavender limeade, served alongside our shop blend spice tea. The scones were too labor-intensive, but we would share the recipe. She and I would mix up a batch of her new lavender-lemon spice blend before the big weekend. I crossed my fingers that the label maker would cooperate.

Hayden had dropped off two crates of filled jars and flat gift boxes, and Vanessa and I got busy, assembling our three-blend

210 · *Lavender Lies Bleeding*

grilling spice sets in between working with customers. 'Twas the season.

"Why is it," a customer asked me, "that I can smell a spice and find myself remembering something I hadn't thought of in years? It happens so fast. I don't even have time to think 'oh, nutmeg. My grandmother used to sprinkle that on her eggnog at Christmas.'"

"Memory and smell are closely related," I replied. "They're located in the same part of the brain. The theory is that early humans relied heavily on taste and smell to tell them whether something was safe to eat, so their brains developed a memory bank of smells to guide them."

She spooned a few lavender buds into her palm from the wooden display bowl and gave them a good sniff. "I'm not getting much."

"Crush them lightly." I mimed swirling the fingertips of one hand against my other palm. "To release the oils. Some spices announce themselves. Paprika, for example. You open the jar and you know it. Others, like lavender or rose petals, work their way into your consciousness more slowly, from your nose or your tongue. But once they're there, you don't want them to leave."

Midafternoon, I stuffed a folder of financial doodah in my tote, put on my raincoat, and kissed the dog goodbye. I'd intended to call the loan officer I worked with when I bought the shop, but my dad had made an effort to help me by calling his friend. I took it as a sign that my recklessness in being in the wrong place at the wrong time was forgiven.

The rain had stopped for now, mini rainbow slicks of oil pooling between the cobbles on Pike Place. Deep inside my bag, my phone rang and I fished it out. Aguilar. I dislike talking on the phone in public, but sometimes it has to be done.

"I knew you'd want to know," the sheriff said. "We confirmed Orion Fisher's movements, best we could in an area without cell service, thanks mainly to eyewitnesses who'd seen him and his dog."

Brambo—big, friendly, and memorable.

Moral of the story: If you need an alibi, take your dog. I hadn't had to rely on Arf for that yet, but we were both young.

"It does appear he and Abby were telling the truth," the sheriff continued. "Fisher was not in Salmon Falls when the greenhouse was damaged or when Liz was killed. He and the girl had an argu-

Leslie Budewitz · 211

ment about their relationship. When Liz found out, she read him the riot act and that's when he took off. Needed time to think, he said. Get his head on straight, more like. Only an idiot would walk away from a girl like Abby Delaney."

The wash of relief was followed by a flood of questions. "So, if he didn't kill Liz, and Desiree White is off the hook—I ran into her yesterday. I know about her mother, and why you tried to keep that quiet. But then, who did kill Liz? And is that who ran my mother and me off the road?"

In an effort not just to scare me, but to kill me? I had not wanted to let the thought enter my mind, but now, it was all I could think of. *Don't be silly, Pepper. You don't know anything worth killing for.*

But someone thought I did, or that I would find out. Who and what?

What, what, what?

"Sorry," I said to a woman I accidentally bumped in my hurry. "No, Sheriff, not you. Never mind. Any luck tracking down that truck?"

"Not yet. I'm hoping someone will see the story in the *Herald* and come forward with information."

"I hope so, too. Thanks. Please keep me posted."

At the bank, I pulled open the heavy glass door. Laura waved from the open door of a glassed-in corner office. She'd hardly changed in years, though her short, straight hair had gone an attractive salt-and-pepper gray. I was working my way past a teller's line when a woman swept by me, her arm brushing mine. I was all set to apologize again—I was obviously not paying enough attention to where I was going today—when I realized two things. One, this time the near collision was not my fault. And two, the angry woman was Monica Salter.

I called out, wanting to make sure she was okay. If she'd seen me in her hurried flush, she gave no sign.

"Saying no is the hardest part of my job," Laura said a moment later. She nodded toward Monica, now barreling toward the exit. "Fortunately, I'm pretty sure I'll get to say yes to you. Come on in. How long has it been? Ten years? Twelve?"

"Sounds about right. So funny that you work here," I said as I settled into the client chair. Figurines of Piglet and Pooh sat on her

212 · *Lavender Lies Bleeding*

desk. To distract customers' fussy children, or simply to amuse herself? "I mean, at Grace House, you worked behind the scenes. You weren't out on the streets protesting corporate greed and economic inequality. But you were an important part of the work, and it's quite a leap from rabble rouser to banker."

She grinned, an impish gleam in her eye. "Ah, but as a loan officer, I get to help people by giving them money. And none of it's mine."

"Monica Salter aside," I said.

Her expression grew serious. "You know her?"

"Not well, but I gather the family's in a tight spot. Her twins are in the same class as Kristen's oldest—you remember Kristen." She did. I went on. "Catholic school tuition now, college expenses on the horizon."

"It's a lot more than that," Laura said. "I wish I could help them. Funny how different brothers can be, isn't it?"

Took me a moment to get that she was talking about Scott Salter and his half brother, not the twins.

"Let's talk about you," she continued. "Chuck says you need a new car. And he told me why. Stinks. Glad you and Lena came out unscathed."

Working out the details took longer than I expected, and then we caught up on family and other stuff. I emerged with loan approval and a light step. I checked my texts. Nate was on his way back from the job site visit with Javier. After decades of trekking to Alaska and back, this new commute would be a dream.

Especially for me.

I swung by the flower ladies' tables. Cua was busy with customers so I didn't stop. I waved to the Orchard Girls, swept past Logan the sales agent standing in for Herb, and stopped at the T-shirt vendor's table. She handed over the special outfits she'd created and assured me my order of lavender-themed towels and aprons would be ready on time.

All that and I made it back to the shop before closing.

A few minutes later, I bid the staff good night. Nate and I eat a lot of fish, for obvious reasons, but why cook every night when you work in a global culinary paradise? I ran through the takeout options and settled on Middle Eastern, from a restaurant down on

Leslie Budewitz · 213

Western. I called in an order for dolmas, eggplant stew, and a double order of fattoush, the fabulous Lebanese bread salad.

The rain had begun again. Kristen had found Arf a darling yellow slicker, reminiscent of the one the Morton Salt girl wears, and he tolerates it reasonably well. Now I knew who to credit for his excellent training and his patience with human foolishness like canine raincoats.

"We'll get you back to Bark Place soon," I said as I buttoned him up for the trek home. "So you can see Raine and your buddy Polo."

His ears perked up. I kissed his nose and out we went.

The Market is a curious, almost eerie place in the hour or so between when the shops close and the daystallers pack up, and when the bars and restaurants kick into gear. Like it's waiting for something it's not sure will arrive.

At the entrance to the narrow steps by the bakery, Arf stopped, his whole body twitching. That horsey smell? Though it made no sense, I almost thought I could smell it, too.

"Shake it off, Pep," I muttered and started down the stairs. Arf did not budge until I tugged on his leash.

Outside the restrooms at the bottom of the steps are two of my favorite pieces of public art in the Market, black-and-white tile silhouettes of male and female figures. A man emerged from one and bounded up the stairs past me.

Then I spotted a rolling cart, empty and untended, beside one of the big steel doors. I shifted Arf's leash to my left hand and started to grab it.

"It's never enough for your kind, is it? Now you're trying to interfere with my family's future."

The voice jolted me and I turned, astonished to see Monica Salter not ten feet away.

"Monica. What are you talking about? What are you doing here?"

"I come here for comfort. It's been my happy place since I was a kid. But you want to take that away from me, too, don't you?"

"Seriously, Monica. What are you talking about?"

"I saw you at the bank, with Laura Long. You called her, didn't you, and told her not to help me. Convinced her not to let me

214 · *Lavender Lies Bleeding*

renegotiate the loans so we could keep the farm. After persuading Desiree to pull out of the deal."

"What? I had nothing to do with any of that. Wait. You don't want to sell. Aren't you glad she changed her mind?"

"That farm should stay in the family, where it's always been," Monica said, stepping out of the shadows. "But selling is the only way we can get out of the mess Danny made. If we can't find a buyer willing to pay what it's worth, the bank will foreclose. Scott and I will lose everything. The business. Our house. Our boys' future."

"Surely the situation can't be that dire."

"Like you would understand. You and your friend, Kristen. You don't have a clue how the rest of us live. How we struggle."

The struggle she'd grown up with still haunted her.

"Hey, I don't know where you got that idea. I didn't grow up with money and I don't have money now. That's why I was in the bank, to get a car loan. Because your brother-in-law ran me off the road and wrecked my car."

"Yes," she said, and a chill seized me. I'd liked her. I'd thought we might be friends, at least before I'd heard about her rant at the parents' meeting last night. Had it been her, not Danny, in the big truck on the narrow road? No. I remembered seeing her pull up to her house in Madrona, late for our appointment, in a white SUV like every good upper-middle-class soccer mom. And it was Danny who'd raced cars, in one of his phases. Where he'd learned the PIT he used against my mother and me.

Nothing like danger in the form of a steel knife blade glistening in the light from vintage glass fixtures to bring a picture into focus. I could almost hear the puzzle pieces give a satisfying click into place as Monica snapped open the pruning knife and raised it high.

Now I understood that it was Monica's anger and resentment that drove her brother-in-law. "Danny ran us off the road. But you— you killed Liz. With that very knife. Did you destroy her greenhouse, too?"

"Yes, I killed her," she said. "But the greenhouse was his doing. Stupid."

She was strong. She'd killed Liz but not before Liz fought back, leaving the scratches still visible beneath the makeup on her face and neck.

But I was strong, too.

Leslie Budewitz · 215

"Oh-h-h. I get it now," I said. "Danny destroyed the greenhouse because of his gripe with Liz over the lavender. Did he go out there, to plead with her, and hear her arguing with Orion Fisher? That's what gave him the idea to frame Orion later, when he came back to smash up the place."

"I'll give him credit for that," she said. "It could have worked."

"You knew exactly what plant you were buying in my shop. You switched them on purpose, then let my employee take the blame. You didn't want it for your garden. When I was at your house, I saw that you'd already bought a replacement for the plant your kids trampled. No. You knew Liz came to the Market to see me, and when you saw that seedling, you knew it had come from her." Days earlier, which Monica couldn't have known, but it didn't matter. "You wanted it so Danny could propagate her new hybrid on his own, in that fancy greenhouse no one is using. You tried to dig up more, after you killed her, but you ran out of time. Not that you care about lavender, or about him. You looked at those plants and you saw green. You saw money. So you could keep the farm. A place to call yours, a place to pass on to your kids, to replace what you'd lost."

"That farm means everything to me. It was my second home in high school, when Scott and I started dating. My refuge. I go sit by the ponds. Feed the ducks. Do all the things my mother did before she set fire to her own house and everything we had went up in flames."

What? Had her mother's death not been an accident? This was not the time to ask.

Another image clicked into place. "That was your straw hat we found in the barn, wasn't it? The gardening hat you'd tossed on the bench on your front porch the day I came by. When you claimed you were running late. You were running scared. Hoping if you didn't show up, I'd just forget about the plant. Decide it wasn't worth the bother, and leave."

But I had made a promise. And now I had another chance to fulfill it.

"Idiot Danny. He didn't get that it wasn't enough to destroy the greenhouse." Disdain dripped from her voice. "That wouldn't stop her. He needed to take the seedlings, as many as he could. Beat her to the market with that stupid hybrid. I had to finish the job. Get

the plant back, then stop her with this. Like I'm going to stop you."
She brandished the knife.

"But he never could have managed all that, could he?" I asked.
"And you knew it. He had the greenhouse, and all the land and
water he'd have needed. But he'd squandered all his cash, all the
money your husband gave him. It was one more boondoggle, one
more expensive scheme he wouldn't follow through on."

"The hybrid was his idea." The blade flashed in the light.

"I don't know about that. I do know ideas are the easy part.
It's the late nights and early mornings that are hard. The determination to keep going when things go wrong, to try again and again
and again. That's what makes an idea into a thing. Say what you
want about Liz, she put in the work."

And she'd been willing to work even harder, expanding not the
acreage in plants, but the greenhouse. Taking the hybrid she, not
Danny, had created and putting it into production, supplying nurs-
eries and gardeners and other growers.

As if I'd touched the nerve her very existence hinged upon,
Monica Salter lunged toward me, pure venom on her face. Before
I knew what was happening, Arf leapt toward her, jerking the
leash from my hand. Monica knew the Market, from coming here
as a kid, and from the coffee equipment business. But I knew
it, too.

I dropped my bag and grabbed the stray cart. Spun it around
to come between us. Blocked, Monica stepped to one side. I moved
the opposite way, the cart in front of me like a shield.

The three of us danced back and forth, Monica waving the
knife. Arf nipped at her coat, pulling her away from me. She flailed
at him with one leg, missing, then she shimmied away, trying to skirt
around the cart and get to me. She was getting closer now, the knife
glinting.

"Oh, no you don't," I said, gripping the handle of the cart as I
tried to fend her off. Where was Arf? Where were the doors? Where
were all the people who should have been passing by? Heck of a
time for a lull in foot traffic.

Then I saw my fifty-two-pound ball of black-and-gold fur fling
himself against Monica's legs. She staggered, caught herself, and
kicked out. This time she got him in the kidney and he yelped.

Leslie Budewitz · 217

"Arf!" I screamed. Momentarily distracted, I lost my grip on the cart. Lost track of Monica. But she had not lost sight of me. She darted forward, slashing with the knife. Slashed a second time. At her satisfied look, I glanced down, feeling nothing, seeing the rip in my sleeve.

A sharp blast pierced the air and echoed off the brick walls and metal doors. A bark. And then another. My sweet, quiet, well-mannered dog was barking up a storm.

But I couldn't wait for the attention he might draw. Monica wasn't waiting. She'd resumed her side-to-side shuffle. I grabbed the cart, dancing to my own rhythm, keeping it between us until I'd steered her where I wanted her. I shoved the cart forward. Shoved it into her, pushing her toward the narrow open doorway that led to the past, sending her down the cattle ramp with a thud and a shriek. I let go and the cart rolled after her, picking up speed on the steep incline. It crashed into her as she lay in a heap on the narrow planks. She screamed again, a yowl of physical pain and mental anguish.

"Good dog, Arf," I said, as I sank to the floor beside my furry friend. "Are you okay? Good boy. Such a good boy."

I'd just finished calling 911 when a little lady in plaid pants and a flowered shirt appeared at my side.

"Miss Pepper, what happen? Such horrible noises. Barking and shouting and clattering. Oh-h-h." She peered down the ramp and saw the mangled cart. The cart someone had borrowed from the flower sellers and failed to return, leaving it right where I'd needed it.

"And this," she said, bending over to pick up the knife that had gone clattering out of Monica's hand. The knife she'd used to kill Liz.

"No!" I shouted. "Don't touch it."

Behind Cua stood another of the flower ladies. Turned out they'd been miles away when Cua remembered the missing cart and insisted they go back to hunt it down so they wouldn't be fined for leaving it out.

"She is the bad lady?" Cua said, focused on the purloined cart.

"Very bad," I said, scrolling for the number for Market security. That call made, I stood at the top of the cattle ramp, slick with

218 · *Lavender Lies Bleeding*

rain and oil from the streets. Monica lay near the bottom, though mercifully, her screams were now muffled cries.

What would Brother Cadfael do? I brushed the thought away. I didn't pick my way down to check on her. I didn't go around by the stairs to see what help and comfort I could give. She'd killed my friend and sent her brother-in-law after me and my mother. Then she'd kicked my dog. If all that she'd done came back to bite her now, I almost didn't care.

Maybe I was a bad lady, too.

Thirty-Two

Did a New York chef get creative when a Mrs. Benedict tired of his menu and asked for something new? Or did another chef stack up a customer's order for a poached egg, ham, and an English muffin, and spoon leftover hollandaise on top? Who cares? Eat up!

THE FAMILY THAT COMMITS CRIMES TOGETHER GOES TO JAIL together. The Seattle PD had first dibs on Monica for her attack on me, but Salmon Falls was next in line, following up on her murder confession. The EMTs had taken her to the ER. My insulated rain slicker had protected my arm from injury, but the coat was a goner, the sleeve sliced open, layers of fabric flapping as I gestured, demonstrating what had happened. Detectives Tracy and Spencer had interviewed me at the scene. I knew I'd be talking at length with Sheriff Aguilar tomorrow. Tonight, he was busy grilling Danny Heilman about the road rage, the vandalism, and the murder his sister-in-law had committed.

At the moment, all I cared about was food, drink, my dog, and my sweetheart. A Market security guard had picked up my order from the Middle Eastern restaurant and Nate and I sat on the couch in the loft living room with water and wine and plates of yummy food. Our hero dog, seemingly no worse for the wear, lay at our feet, working on a bone.

220 · *Lavender Lies Bleeding*

"I told Javier what we were thinking about Salter Farm," Nate said. "He called Mindy and she immediately jumped on the idea."

I froze, a half-eaten dolma in my hand. "She didn't go out there. To Salter Farm. Not with all the danger."

"No, no." He pointed to the tzatziki that had dripped onto my leg. I plopped the grape leaf into my mouth and wiped up the thick cucumber yogurt sauce with my finger. Then I licked it.

"No," he repeated. "Mindy knows Desiree from the catering business, so she called her and Jeffrey. He's the official listing agent for the property. He called Scott Salter this afternoon."

"When Monica was at the Market, stalking me."

"Sounds like Salter had no idea what his wife had done. And I have no idea what will happen now." Nate sipped his wine. Our favorite light red complemented the food beautifully. "But Mindy and her family are people who make things happen. I think she's considering making an offer."

"I hope there's room for the Alliance in the transaction."

"It's a good possibility. Last I heard, Mindy was on the trail of Preston Vu."

God bless women who make things happen. Like Liz. Like me, too, on a good day.

"If Javier takes on that old barn . . ." I left the thought unfinished, unsure whether I was being pushy or encouraging.

"Yeah," Nate said. "There could be a job in it for me. Close to home."

All I could do was nod my head. Nod, and smile, a deep, warm sense of belonging in my heart.

OVER THE NEXT few days, more puzzle pieces snapped into place. The paint and crash patterns matched, the Saab serving me one last time as a silent witness. Danny had seen me in downtown Salmon Falls—me and my distinctive car—then saw me leaving the farm and gave chase. Sheriff Aguilar wouldn't venture a guess whether he'd followed me with malice on his mind or simply saw an opportunity to execute the highly dangerous PIT maneuver and took it. Didn't matter. Either way, the law called it vehicular assault.

Fingerprints found on the copper and glass at the greenhouse, along with Monica's statements to me, established that Danny

Leslie Budewitz · 221

was in fact the vandal who destroyed the greenhouse. He'd overheard Jeffrey White telling Desiree about Orion Fisher's juvenile record, and figured a copycat crime was the best way to blame the younger man. I speculated that he thought Liz might give Orion a share of the credit—and profit—for the new plant variety, and hoped to throw an obstacle in Orion's path. I'm pretty good at twisting myself into knots to see the world from other people's point of view, but even I couldn't understand the logic in preventing someone who was willing to work for what they wanted from getting it, just because you'd once wanted it, too, but had slacked off and given up.

WITH THE CRIMES in Salmon Falls now resolved and my promise to Liz fulfilled, it was time to put my pledge to work less and play more into action, despite the busy season ahead.

In other words, it was time to party.

Kristen kicked off the festivities the next Monday, showing up for work with a giant box gift wrapped in paper that looked like a clown had lost his marbles.

"Happy birthday!" she said.

"What is this?" I asked.

"You won't know until you open it." Two weeks older than me and always bossing me around.

But she was right. Inside lay a beautiful, hooded raincoat, red with yellow and white dots. I lifted it out carefully, as if it might break.

"It's gorgeous."

"It's reversible. The inside is yellow. I hope that doesn't remind you too much of what happened with Monica. I picked it out weeks ago."

"Monica Salter took a lot from a lot of people to try to keep what wasn't even hers," I said. "I am not letting her take the love of a yellow raincoat from me. It's perfect. Absolutely perfect."

Midweek, I took Arf to the doggy daycare, where Raine and Polo greeted him like old friends. Which they sort of were. Then Mom, Cayenne, and I went out to Salmon Falls. We drove my new car, a dark blue electric Mustang, with four seats and plenty of room for hauling spices, junk store finds, and a dog.

It even sported a personalized license plate. *SPYCGRL.*

222 · *Lavender Lies Bleeding*

On Main Street, we picked up the painting that the artist and antique dealer had repaired. I'd already hung the photo of the barn and the red azalea in my office—no matter what happened to Salter Farm, the moment of sheer joy I'd experienced when I first saw those flowers spilling into the stream was mine forever. We bought fudge, ate lunch at Blossom, and browsed the shops we were coming to know and love. The Salmon Falls Lavender Festival would go on as planned, with a memorial service at the park, and we promised to attend. I'd hoped to catch Desiree at Blossom or the B&B, but her front desk manager told us she was heading to Seattle, to visit her mother, whose condition had improved.

"I'm so glad she told you," I said. "It's easier when you don't have to carry the burden alone."

"Oh, we knew," came the reply. "We pretended we didn't, because that's what she wanted, and we told Joe. Sheriff Aguilar. He warned me you might be coming by, and to keep up the pretense."

The day I'd seen him leaving by the side door, before I'd gotten a tour of the place.

"But you're right," she went on. "The scary things aren't so scary when you put them out in the light and share them."

We canceled the room reservation I had never intended to keep—somehow, she'd figured that, too, but she made clear I was welcome any time.

Then we drove to the lavender farm. Desiree was pulling out as we drove in, and she smiled and waved.

The greenhouse repairs were almost complete, the ground prepped for its expansion. Abby greeted me with open arms, radiant with her hair in braids and a pink stick-on heart at the corner of her eye. No hiking clothes for her; she wore a knee-length gingham dress over tights and short work boots.

"Prairie garden witch," I said. "It suits you. Hey, I was surprised to see Desiree here."

"Me, too. She came out to apologize for firing me. She suggested setting up farm tours and hands-on events for her B&B guests, and she wants to use our lavender soap and lotion in her guest rooms."

I don't believe that bad things happen to teach us lessons, but I am convinced that we have an obligation to learn from them. And it looked like Desiree agreed.

Leslie Budewitz · 223

Then Abby introduced Orion. Twenty-eight, give or take, slender, his brown hair highlighted by the summer sun, watching her with pure adoration. I'd lumped him in with the other men I'd met recently who didn't want to grow up. Danny Heilman in Salmon Falls. Logan Bradshaw in the Market, who had developed a bad habit of borrowing the flower ladies' cart without telling them and leaving it where it didn't belong. And who had accidentally given me the defensive weapon I'd needed.

But about Orion, I'd been wrong. You can be a responsible adult and a free spirit at the same time. Think of it as your own personal work-life fit.

"My goodness," my mother said, holding out her hand, palm down, to the dog beside him. "You must be Brambo."

"He's a big, slobbery goof," Orion said. The reddish-brown Pudelpointer licked Mom's hand and let her pet him, then stretched out his front paws and lowered his head, haunches high, back elongated in a picture-perfect version of downward dog pose.

"Your alibi," I said. My distinctive car had made me a target. His distinctive dog had convinced the sheriff to drop his suspicions.

"I'm grateful for all you did, for me, and for Abby," Orion said. "And for Liz."

"Speaking of Liz," Cayenne said to Abby. "We decided yes."

I frowned. What were they talking about?

I found out a moment later when Orion hoisted the cat carrier, Sir tucked safely inside, into the back seat of the Mustang.

"Abby's allergic," Cayenne said. "We've wanted a cat. It's perfect."

I had to agree. Two women making things happen.

To all our surprise, the day Liz had come downtown, when she and I met for coffee, she hadn't just met with a banker, as she'd told me, to finance her expansion. She'd also met with a lawyer to update her will. While she'd left a few heirlooms to the cousin back east, she had left the farm and business to Abby.

"It's going to be a lot of work," Abby said, gesturing to the acres of plants in full bloom, the hives, the cottage, the greenhouse. "But Orion and I are in this together. My mom will help. It's what Liz wanted, and I'm going to make it happen."

224 · *Lavender Lies Bleeding*

I tried sniffing back the tears. Didn't work.

Some things really are worth crying over.

THE NEXT WEEKEND, the Spice Shop was Lavender Central. The weather cooperated, always a good omen. Whether it was the advance publicity the shops had done, the snippet that ran on TV Friday evening, or the photo on the front page of the Saturday morning paper showing the balloon artist in a purple and white striped clown suit tying purple and white balloon animals for a gaggle of children, I couldn't say. But our little festival was a big draw.

"Good job," Yolande from the PDA said around a mouthful of lavender shortbread. "Can I get the recipe?"

That was about as close to eating her words as the property manager was likely to get. I handed her a recipe card, then tucked a few cookies in a small paper bag. When you're dealing with decision makers, it never hurts to sweeten the pot.

Late morning Saturday, Kristen and I popped down to the Atrium in the Economy Market. A pair of florists were teaching the art of arranging a farm-fresh bouquet. Savannah and the soap maker's daughter were helping a group of tweens make lavender wands and no-sew sachets for their dresser drawers.

"You should be so proud of her," I told Kristen.

"I am. I tried to tell her this morning, but she just rolled her eyes."

We were training the next generation, sowing the seeds of a life-long love of herbs and flowers and fragrance. Sweet.

On our way back to the shop, we stopped at the flower ladies' tables. Sara was helping her aunt.

She came around the end of the table to greet me. "Sorry I missed you when you came out to Salmon Falls. I'd gone with Preston and the other board members to meet with Mindy Jarrett and her family. And the banker you sent us to—Laura Long. It's going to happen, Pepper. It's really going to happen. Thanks to you."

"Not me," I said. "Thanks to Nate, who had the idea, and to Mindy."

The Jarretts and the Alliance had agreed to form a partnership. The winery would buy Salter Farm from Scott—from jail, Danny had given him power of attorney, meaning full authority to sell if he chose. They would fix up the barn, repair the irrigation system, and plant a good chunk of the acreage in wine grapes. The rest would be leased long-term to the Alliance for the use of small growers. Patches of hops, sweet corn, pumpkins, breadseed poppies, herbs, and flowers—and yes, lavender—would prosper where weeds now grew. No more worries about being tossed off the land they sweated over to grow food for people who had no idea of the hardships behind their lettuce and tomatoes. No more temporary greenhouses made from pallets and roofed with discarded plastic panels. No more digging up flower bulbs and scrambling for new ground.

"Did you hear the rest?" Sara asked. "Scott Salter agreed to lease the lot in town to the Whites, with an agreement to sell once all the legal wrangling is done. Desiree will have more space to host weddings and other events at the B&B. The Alliance will manage part of it for themselves and part for the B&B. Brides will have their rose bower. The cook will have her fresh produce. And town will have a community garden."

The experience Desiree had wanted to create all along. Could we have gotten to this point without all the rancor and destruction, the death and rage? I didn't know. It would be easy to chalk all this loss up to Monica Salter's skewed perspective. Easy, but too simple. She'd been motivated, I'd come to believe, by a contradictory mix of envy and resentment. She'd craved personal and financial security, but ultimately, she'd destroyed herself and all that she had wanted.

Kristen read my mind as we walked away, cradling the giant bouquets of farm-fresh flowers Cua had pressed into our arms. "Killing Liz was unforgivable. And spurring her brother-in-law to take aim at you—I have no words. But of all the things Monica Salter did, the worst might be what she's done to her own family. Scott and the boys."

I had to agree.

"A group of families got together this week to coordinate helping them out with meals and rides and other stuff," she continued.

"After everything she said? The fury she flung at you and the other parents?"

"We're not doing it for her. Or even, as she might think, to salve our guilty consciences."

226 · *Lavender Lies Bleeding*

"Guilty of what? Working hard and having something to show for it?"

My bestie wisely ignored my outburst. "Those boys don't deserve the hell she's brought down on them."

Just as Monica had not deserved the chaos and shame she'd grown up with. In trying to escape it, she had recreated it.

Humans. We're idiots sometimes.

THE NEXT SATURDAY, we closed the shop early. But we didn't go our separate ways, in search of our own versions of work-life fit. Instead, we threw another party, this one for ourselves.

'CONGRATULATIONS, GRADUATE!' read the banner hastily hung over the front windows. Reed Locke had worked in the shop longer than any of us except Sandra, ever since he was a teenager. He was a child of Pike Place, son of the acupuncturist who was one of the last medical practitioners in the Market. His parents and grandfather had brought the cake that now sat on the counter.

"I don't know what we're going to do without you," I said, cupping his sweet face in my hands.

"Live long and prosper," he said, making the hand gesture to match.

Kristen and Sandra had speed decorated the nook for a baby shower, the table piled high with gifts. Not for Cayenne, not due until October, but for Hayden and Laura, whose first baby was due later in the month. They were a hard-working young couple without much, and we three older women had gone all out for them. The production staff were there, along with the warehouse manager, Joy and her husband, and a few other warehouse tenants.

Even Detectives Spencer and Tracy came, Mike Tracy with his wife. I had not seen Elena Tracy since I too had been a police officer's wife. A sparky, petite Black woman, she pulled gift bag after gift bag out of her tote, like a magician pulling silk scarves from the circle of his thumb and forefinger.

I was not surprised to see Vinny, Matt, Jamie Alexander, Mary Jean, the Orchard Girls, and other Market friends. Vinny and Matt had brought champagne, and began the ritual of popping corks and handing out glasses.

Leslie Budewitz · 227

But when my own parents arrived, along with my brother, sister-in-law, and their kids, I suspected we were not in Kansas anymore. Up went a third banner: 'HAPPY BIRTHDAY, PEPPER!'

I grabbed a coffee mug and thrust it toward Vinny. "I think I'm going to need a bigger glass."

The toasts and roasts were just the right blend of silly and serious. Reed's gifts were fit for a young man starting his first post-college job as a research intern for a company evaluating historic properties: a fountain pen and ink, obscure books on Seattle history, and an ORCA card filled to the max for easy public transportation.

We oohed and ahhed as we nibbled lavender fudge and spread lavender goat cheese on crackers and watched the parents-to-be open their gifts. Everyone loved the baby T-shirts and onesies I'd had made, showing a stork catching a baby dropped from a saltshaker. Nate and I had stopped at Aimee's Rainy Day Vintage shop to pick up gift certificates. She's got an amazing collection of vintage baby quilts and clothes, and I had not been able to resist the mobiles hung with darling baby animals made from cardboard and paper.

Sara Vu came, too, wearing a bright blue jacket, a wide ribbon embroidered in a colorful cross-stitch pattern on the placket and cuffs. I'd seen similar embroidery in the shops in Salmon Falls, and on Hmong participants in Lunar New Year celebrations. She handed a small flat box to each expectant mother. "I know this party is for Hayden and Laura," she said to Cayenne. "But after all that's happened, we wanted you both to have something from us. From the flower ladies. And me."

Cayenne opened her box first, and lifted out a small, crocheted cap hung with gold and silver discs.

"Cua made it," Sara said. "It's a traditional Hmong baby cap. Those are Hmong coins, for good luck and health, and a long, happy life."

"I'll treasure it always," Cayenne said, and the tears that had been threatening me since we switched from work mode to party time filled my eyes.

"Now for Pepper," Sandra said.

"Why are we celebrating my birthday?" I asked. "It was almost a week ago. Kristen already gave me a present."

228 · *Lavender Lies Bleeding*

"If I hadn't," Kristen said, "you'd have known for sure something was up."

She had that right.

My gifts were more sedate than the baby gifts, but all wonderful. Wine. Chocolates. A vintage Fiestaware plate to replace one I'd broken. A Brother Cadfael mystery I hadn't been able to find, and *Brother Cadfael's Herb Garden*, an illustrated companion setting out the history of the old monk's herbs, with quotes to remind the reader how he'd used them and in which books.

And then my dad handed me an envelope. Not the size or shape for a birthday card, but a standard business envelope with my name typed on the front. My legal name.

"What's this?" I said, slipping a finger in the gap to open it. I slid out a heavy, rough-textured sheet of paper. Frowned. "The title to the Mustang? You paid for my new car?"

"Yep."

"Oh, my gosh. You and Laura Long at the bank—you had this in the works the whole time. You sent me to her to get a loan on purpose. It was fake!" I didn't have to ask if Nate and my mother had known; their grins gave them away.

"Why, Dad? I mean, I appreciate it, but I can take care of myself."

"I know that, Pepper," he said, his voice gruff with emotion. "You proved that out on Mrs. Luedtke Road. Idiot that I am sometimes, it took me too long to grasp that you hadn't put yourself or your mother in danger. Someone else did that. What you did was keep two of the people I love the most safe."

Then the tears fell, and I did not stop them.

SUNDAY MORNING, the sun shone brightly. Nate suggested we go out for brunch at Fishermen's Terminal, the place where we'd met almost a year ago.

It was an inspired choice. We sat by the water, the dog at our feet, talking about everything and nothing. I was a lucky woman and I knew it.

Our plates came, my Greek omelet fluffy and yummy. Nate had finally gotten the chance to order smoked salmon eggs Benedict, with fresh dill and dilly biscuits. He took the first bite. Set

Leslie Budewitz · 229

down his fork. "Whoever Benedict was, he—or she—had a heck of a good idea."

Afterward, we walked down to the boat. It was still old and rickety, but its woodwork gleamed. Javier had taught Nate well.

"Do you ever miss living down here?" I asked. "On the boat."

"Nope." He took my hand and we headed home.

On our way up from the basement parking garage, Nate led the way to a different set of stairs, one I rarely took. The stairs where Glenn had seen him not long ago.

"Where are we going?"

"You'll see."

The door to the rooftop was already open. His hydrangea and Liz's lavender plant sat next to our bistro table and chairs, hauled up from the veranda. On the table sat an ice bucket, holding a bottle of champagne and two glasses. And next to it, beside a stainless steel bowl of dog water, was the three-foot high Kuan Yin figure I'd seen in Aimee's shop. The one I'd pointed out to Nate when we stopped to pick up baby gifts. The one I'd held off buying because who knew if or when I'd ever have a garden, on a roof top or somewhere else.

"What is all this? You bought the Kuan Yin?"

"She is the goddess of compassion," Nate said. "The protector of women, children, and the poor. Anyone in trouble. Even sailors." He gave me the smile I love so much. "I read that Buddha gave her a thousand arms because she was so busy helping so many people that she needed them."

His Adam's apple bobbed as he swallowed and I thought he had never looked more handsome, more earnest and beautiful.

"Your arms are all the arms I need. When we got in trouble off the coast . . . When you called to tell me what happened in Salmon Falls, and then what happened at the cattle ramp . . . When I realized what could have happened if you hadn't been so strong and so determined, I knew I didn't want to be anywhere but here with you. All the time. No more weeks and months away. Just you, me, the dog—"

The dog who now lay quietly on a rug someone had laid out for him.

"For the rest of my life." He pulled a small red leather box out of his pocket, his fingers trembling as he opened it to show me a

230 · *Lavender Lies Bleeding*

breathtaking diamond and platinum ring in a vintage art deco design. "Pepper, will you marry me?"

And there, on the roof on the top of our building, on the top of the world, with my dog and my guy, beneath a cloudless blue sky, I said yes.

Yes. Now and forever, yes.

Recipes and Spice Notes

The Seattle Spice Shop recommends...

Find the recipe for Pepper's variation on the classic herbes de Provence in *Assault & Pepper*. The Lemon Thyme Shortbread in *Killing Thyme* can easily be made with lavender; simply swap crushed, dried lavender buds for the thyme, or add them to your favorite shortbread recipe. You'll find Edgar's Baked Paprika Cheese in *Chai Another Day*, and the Lavender Bay Salt in *The Solace of Bay Leaves*. Five Spice Apple Cake debuts in *Between a Wok and a Dead Place*. The recipes for Creamy Asparagus Soup with Cumin and Kristen's Four-Ingredient Asparagus Tart appear in *To Err is Cumin*.

LAVENDER LEMON PEPPER BLEND

Cayenne was inspired to create this lavender lemon pepper blend after seeing the many ways cooks in Salmon Falls used their favorite local crop. It's great on grilled salmon, or any white fish, roasted vegetables, baked potatoes, and more!

For a simple version, take your favorite lemon pepper and add crushed lavender and garlic salt.

1 teaspoon freshly ground black pepper
1 teaspoon dried lemon zest
1 teaspoon crushed dried lavender buds
¼ to ½ teaspoon kosher salt
¼ to ½ teaspoon dried minced garlic (if you use garlic powder, start with less and adjust to taste)

To make the lemon zest: Heat your oven to its lowest setting, 150 to 175 degrees. Wash and pat dry one lemon. Zest it, using a microplane, on to parchment paper on a small baking sheet or pie plate. Dry in 5-minute increments, stirring between each. One lemon will take 15–20 minutes; more will take longer. Watch carefully, as it burns quickly. Allow to cool thoroughly, separating the zest with a spoon or your fingers and crumbling it a bit. Make sure it is fully dehydrated, to avoid mold.

Store tightly covered.

To make the blend: Combine all ingredients in a small bowl or jar. Adjust to taste. Store tightly covered.

Makes about 1 tablespoon.

Remember to use a culinary variety of lavender, grown without pesticides. If you grow your own, cut the stems when the buds are about 25 percent open, bundle, and dry in open air, for about a week. (Pop the stems in a vase, without water, to enjoy them and their fragrance as they dry.) When dry, stem them by rubbing bundled stems between your hands over a strainer or colander set on a bowl or tray. Store dried buds in a jar with a tight lid.

To crush lavender, grind dried buds with a mortar and pestle, or the back of a wooden spoon in a bowl.

Leslie Budewitz · 233

Tasty Drinks Made with Lavender

LAVENDER SYRUP

Add a taste of summer to your hot or cold drinks any time of year!

1 cup water
1 cup sugar
1 tablespoon dried lavender

Combine ingredients in a small saucepan. Bring to a boil, stirring until sugar dissolves. Simmer 1 minute. Remove from heat and steep 30 minutes, then strain into a glass jar or bottle to cool.
Store in the refrigerator. Keeps 3-4 weeks.

Lavender Latte: Add 1 to 3 teaspoons lavender syrup to a double shot of espresso, to suit your sweet tooth, and add steamed milk.

Lavender Americano: Make your Americano and add 1 to 3 teaspoons lavender syrup, to suit your taste. Add milk or cream if you like.

Lavender London Fog: *The classic London Fog uses vanilla syrup. Switch it up with lavender for a taste of summer, any time of year.*
Make a strong cup of Earl Grey tea, from a bag or loose-leaf tea. Stir in 1½ teaspoons lavender syrup and top with stiff steamed milk.

For an iced version of any of these drinks, pour coffee or tea and syrup over a handful of ice cubes and add steamed milk or cream. Stir and enjoy!

Lavender Italian Soda: Place a cup of ice in a 12-ounce glass. Pour in 1-2 ounces of lavender syrup, to your taste. Add 8 ounces club soda or sparkling water and a dash of cream. Stir; adjust to taste if needed.

Prosecco à Lavande: *Pepper believes that almost everything— including Prosecco—is a little better with the right dash of spicery or herbery. And remember, when uncorking sparkling wine, turn the bottle, not the cork, to avoid splashing!*

234 • *Lavender Lies Bleeding*

lavender syrup
chilled Prosecco or other sparkling wine
lavender stalks, fresh or dried, for garnish (optional)

Place ½ to 1 teaspoon of lavender syrup in a champagne flute. Add 4 ounces chilled Prosecco. Swirl or stir to mix. Garnish with lavender.

Increase amount of syrup based on your taste and the sweetness of your wine. Start small, as lavender's distinctive flavor can easily overpower other flavors.

Salute!

Leslie Budewitz · 235

Lavender Treats from Pepper's Pals

LAVENDER LIMEADE

A perennial favorite in Salmon Falls and beyond.

6 cups water (divided use)
1¾ cups white sugar
¼ cup dried lavender
1 teaspoon grated lime zest
1 cup freshly squeezed lime juice
lime slices (optional garnish)
lavender flowers (optional garnish)

Make the simple syrup: In a 2-quart saucepan, combine 2 cups water, sugar, dried lavender, and lime zest. Bring to a boil. Reduce heat to low and simmer, stirring until sugar dissolves. Remove pan from heat and let syrup stand 10 minutes. Strain the liquid and discard the lavender.

Make the limeade: In a large pitcher, stir together the remaining 4 cups of water, the lavender syrup, and the lime juice. Serve over ice, adding lime slices or lavender flowers for garnish, if you'd like.
   Makes about six cups.

For a cocktail: Place ice in a rocks glass. Pour in a jigger of tequila or vodka, and add lavender limeade. Top with a slice of lime.

236 · *Lavender Lies Bleeding*

LAVENDER BUTTERMILK SCONES

These scones are light and fluffy with a subtle touch of lavender. Grating the butter is genius, and chilling the scones before baking helps keep them from spreading too much.

For the scones:

2 cups all-purpose flour, plus more for hands and work
   surface
½ cup granulated sugar
2½ teaspoons baking powder
2 teaspoons dried lavender, crushed with a mortar and pestle
zest of 1 lemon
½ teaspoon kosher salt
½ cup (1 stick) unsalted butter, cold or frozen
½ cup buttermilk
1 large egg
1½ teaspoons vanilla extract
2 tablespoons milk or buttermilk, for brushing
sparkling sugar for topping, optional

For the lavender lemon icing:

¼ cup milk or half and half
1 teaspoon dried lavender, crushed
2 teaspoons fresh lemon juice
1¼ cups powdered (confectioners') sugar

In a large bowl, combine the flour, sugar, baking powder, lavender, lemon zest, and salt. Grate the chilled butter with a box grater. (Using the paper wrapper to hold the stick of butter makes the job less messy.) Add butter to flour mixture and combine with a pastry cutter, two forks, or your fingers until the mixture comes together in pea-sized crumbs.

In a small bowl, stir or whisk the buttermilk, egg, and vanilla extract. Pour into flour mixture and mix until fully moistened.

Place a silicon liner on a baking sheet. Lightly flour a large cutting board and your hands.

Leslie Budewitz · 237

Use your hands to finish mixing in any dry bits in the bottom of the bowl. Divide the dough in half and place each ball on the floured work surface. If the dough feels too sticky, work in a little extra flour; if too dry, work in a little extra buttermilk. Press each ball into a 5-6-inch disc. Use a large knife to cut into eight wedges, cutting the disc first in half, then diagonally in quarters, and so on. Place scones on the lined baking sheet, 2-3 inches apart.

Brush scones with milk and if you'd like, top with coarse sparkling sugar. Refrigerate pan for 15 minutes; this helps prevent excess spreading.

Meanwhile, heat oven to 400 degrees and start the icing. In a small saucepan, heat the milk or half and half over low, until it reaches a simmer. Remove from heat and add the crushed lavender. Allow to steep while the scones bake.

Bake scones 18-20 minutes or until golden brown around the edges and lightly browned on top. Remove from oven and cool slightly, while you finish the icing.

Use a mesh sieve to strain the lavender milk into a small bowl. Stir or whisk in the lemon juice and confectioners' sugar. If the icing is too thick, thin with dribbles of additional milk. Drizzle over warm scones and serve.

Store leftover scones in a well sealed container at room temperature for 2 days or in the refrigerator for 5 days.

LAVENDER SUGAR SCRUB

Nothing says "relax" quite like lavender in the bath! Unless there's a killer outside. If you'd like a more invigorating scrub, use peppermint oil instead of the lavender and skip the flower buds.

½ cup coconut oil
¼ cup granulated sugar plus more if needed
¼ teaspoon (about 20–25 drops) lavender essential oil
1 teaspoon or more dried lavender buds

In a wide-mouth glass jar, mix coconut oil, sugar, essential oil, and flower buds; no need to melt the coconut oil first, as stirring will liquify it enough to mix with the sugar. If the mixture is too thin for your liking, add more sugar. Store in a closed container; keeps as long as you need it.

Use in the bath or shower on your elbows, feet, or other rough spots to exfoliate and moisturize.

For a room or linen spray: Add a few drops of essential oil to distilled water, in a pump spray bottle.

And remember that essential oils are not safe to eat or drink, and should not be used in cooking.

Leslie Budewitz · 239

Spice up your life with Pepper and the Flick Chicks!

LAVENDER GOAT CHEESE SPREAD

Perfect on crackers or toasted slices of baguette—or serve a dollop on top of egg-filled crepes or an omelet. It's addictive—put a bowl on your charcuterie tray at your next gathering and watch it disappear!

10-ounce log of plain goat cheese
1 tablespoon honey
1 teaspoon fresh or ½ teaspoon dried lavender buds
lavender flowers for garnish (optional)

Place the goat cheese in a bowl to soften, about 30 minutes. If the lavender is fresh, chop it; if dried, grind it coarsely with a mortar and pestle.

Add the honey and lavender to the softened goat cheese and blend thoroughly with an immersion blender or a small food processor 3–5 minutes, until smooth. Thin if necessary with a few drops of milk or half and half.

Transfer to a small serving bowl and garnish with lavender flowers.

Serve with crackers or slices of baguette. Leftovers can be refrigerated, covered, and kept up to 2 days.

240 · *Lavender Lies Bleeding*

GREEN SALAD WITH FETA, PEACHES, AND BLUEBERRIES

A great salad for a late-summer gathering—or just for you! Make your own honey-roasted pecans or buy them ready to eat.

For the honey-roasted pecans:

½ cup honey-roasted pecans

OR

1 cup pecan halves, or halves and pieces
½ tablespoon honey, or more if needed
flake salt

To roast the pecans: Heat oven to 350 degrees. In a pie plate or other small baking dish, toss the pecans and honey until well coated. Roast 10-12 minutes, or until well caramelized. Remove from oven and sprinkle with the flake salt. Remember that nuts will continue to brown as they cool. Store extras in a sealed container. Or just eat 'em.

For the dressing:

2 teaspoons Dijon-style mustard
1 tablespoon honey
1 tablespoon fresh lemon juice
1 tablespoon olive oil
2 tablespoons orange juice
kosher salt and fresh ground pepper, to taste

Whisk together in a small bowl or shake well in a sealed jar.

For the salad:

6–8 ounces fresh greens, washed and cut or torn
½ pint fresh blueberries, washed and stemmed
1 peach, diced
½ English or seedless cucumber, diced (no need to peel)

½ cup crumbled feta, or more to taste
1 tablespoon fresh basil, chopped

Place the greens in your serving bowl. Combine remaining ingredients in a medium bowl, then add to the greens. Add the dressing and top with the honey-roasted pecans.

242 · Lavender Lies Bleeding

At Home with Pepper

INDIAN BUTTER CHICKEN

This dish sounds more complicated than it is. Bonus: leftovers! Pepper uses a mild cayenne; if you'd like to tone down the heat, use ground chilis (note that typical American chili powder may include other spices) or skip it entirely. Garam masala is a classic Indian blend without much heat—buy a blend or make your own using the recipe in Guilty as Cinnamon. *Note that the chicken really should sit in the marinade for at least 3 hours.*

For the marinade:

½ cup plain yogurt
1 tablespoon lemon juice
1 teaspoon ground turmeric
2 teaspoons garam masala
½ teaspoon ground chilis or cayenne
1 teaspoon ground cumin
1 tablespoon ginger, freshly grated or jarred
2 cloves garlic, crushed or minced
1 ½ to 2 pounds chicken breasts, cut into bite size pieces

For cooking and for the sauce:

2 tablespoons butter
1 cup tomato sauce or crushed tomatoes
1 cup cream or half and half
1 tablespoon sugar
1¼ teaspoon salt
2 tablespoons butter (additional)

For serving:

Jasmine or Basmati rice, cooked
fresh cilantro leaves, chopped (optional)

Leslie Budewitz · 243

Make the marinade: Combine the marinade ingredients in a bowl or casserole dish with a lid. Mix well. Add the chicken and stir to coat. Cover and refrigerate at least 3 hours, or up to 24 hours.

To cook the chicken and sauce: White rice usually takes 20–25 minutes to cook, on the stove or in a rice cooker, so start it before you cook the chicken.

In a large sauté pan, heat the butter over medium to medium-high. Use a fork or slotted spoon to remove the chicken pieces from the marinade and place in the pan. (Keep the leftover marinade in the bowl for a later step.)

Cook the chicken 3-5 minutes, until it appears whitish—because of the marinade, it won't appear to actually brown.

Add the tomatoes, cream or half and half, sugar, and salt. Scrape in any marinade left in the bowl. Stir well, then reduce heat and simmer for 20 minutes. Taste and adjust seasonings if necessary. Just before serving, stir in the additional two tablespoons of butter.

Serve over rice. Garnish with cilantro, if you'd like.

Serves 6.

244 · *Lavender Lies Bleeding*

ASPARAGUS WITH GOAT CHEESE VINAIGRETTE

Pepper's tip: Cook just the amount of asparagus you want to eat, and make the full amount of vinaigrette. Cooked asparagus will suffer and wrinkle in the fridge, and it's easy to cook quickly and allow to chill while you make the rest of dinner. The vinaigrette holds nicely, and can be used with any vegetable or salad. It's especially tasty on roasted asparagus and cherry tomatoes, or on warm, roasted potatoes.

> 2 pounds asparagus
> 4–5 scallions
> ¼ cup pine nuts or sliced or blanched, slivered almonds
> ½ cup rice wine vinegar (unseasoned)
> 3–4 tablespoons chèvre (fresh goat cheese)
> 2 tablespoons lemon juice
> 2 teaspoons Dijon mustard
> ½ teaspoon thyme leaves
> 1 small shallot, peeled and sliced
> 1 clove garlic, peeled and sliced
> neutral vegetable oil, such as canola, about 1 cup
> Salt and freshly ground black pepper (to taste)
> zest of 1 lemon

Rinse the asparagus in cold water. Trim off the tough end of each stalk. Blanch in salted boiling water until it is cooked but still has a bit of crunch, 2-3 minutes. Immediately rinse well in cold water to stop the cooking. Drain, dry, and refrigerate.

Rinse the scallions, trimming off the roots and any ragged ends of the greens. Slice thinly, including some of the greens.

Toast the pine nuts in a dry pan over medium heat 5-10 minutes, or in the oven at 300 degrees, 8-10 minutes. (Watch carefully, as they can burn quickly. They will continue to cook and brown as they cool.)

Combine the vinegar, chèvre, lemon juice, mustard, thyme, shallot, and garlic in a blender or with an immersion blender. Puree. Slowly add the oil and continue to blend until the vinaigrette emulsifies; you may not need the full cup. Taste. The vinaigrette should have a bright acid profile. Correct the seasoning with salt and fresh ground pepper as needed.

Arrange the asparagus on four salad plates or on a serving platter. Drizzle with vinaigrette to taste. Sprinkle with nuts and scallions, and top with the lemon zest.

Serves 4 as a first course.

LAVENDER ORANGE CRÊME BRULÉE

A friend of Pepper's says forget what they say about cake—crême brulée is the angels' favorite dessert. Who can argue with the angels?

2 cups heavy cream or half and half
½ cup white sugar (divided use)
zest of 1 orange, removed in wide strips with a peeler or
    channel knife
3 tablespoons dried lavender buds
4 egg yolks
½ teaspoon vanilla extract
4 teaspoons turbinado sugar, for topping
strips of orange peel or lavender sprigs for garnish (optional)

Heat the oven to 325 degrees. In a small saucepan, combine the cream, ¼ cup sugar, and orange zest. Lightly crush the lavender buds between your palms, over the pan, to release the essential oils, then toss the buds into the pan. Whisk to combine. Bring the mixture to a boil, then remove from the heat and strain into a bowl to cool. (This step infuses the cream with the aromatics—the orange zest and lavender buds.)

In a large bowl, whisk together the egg yolks, remaining ¼ cup sugar, and vanilla. When the infused cream is cooled to the touch, slowly pour it into the egg mixture and whisk to combine. (Cooling the cream avoids curdling the eggs.)

Place four 4-ounce ramekins or custard cups in a large baking dish or roasting pan. Carefully fill the ramekins with the custard mixture. Place the dish in the oven and carefully pour hot water into the pan, till it reaches about halfway up the sides of the ramekins.

Bake until the custard is set around the edges and slightly jiggly in the center, about 35 minutes.

Remove the baking dish from the oven. Lift out the ramekins—tongs work nicely—and cool on a rack at room temperature. (Don't leave them in the hot water, as the heat would continue to cook the mixture.) When cool, move ramekins to refrigerator to chill for at least an hour before the next step. Just before serving, sprinkle a teaspoon

Leslie Budewitz · 247

of turbinado sugar evenly over the top of each dish. Caramelize the sugar with a kitchen torch. The sugar will harden, turn golden, and become crunchy. If you don't have a torch, raise the rack in your oven and broil the dishes 2-3 minutes until the sugar forms a crisp, golden top. Garnish with a curvy strip of orange peel or a sprig of lavender.

Serves 4.

READERS, it's a treat to hear from you. Drop me a line at Leslie@LeslieBudewitz.com, connect with me on Facebook at LeslieBudewitzAuthor, or join my mailing list for book news, free short stories, and more. (Sign up on my website, www.LeslieBudewitz.com.) Reader reviews and recommendations are a big boost to authors; if you've enjoyed my books, please tell your friends, in person and online. A book is but marks on paper until you read these pages and make the story yours.

Thank you.

Acknowledgments

SALMON FALLS AND THE SURROUNDING FARM COUNTRY ARE my invention. If you know Western Washington and you picture Carnation, North Bend, or LaConner, you wouldn't be wrong, especially if you picture them as they were twenty years ago. Mrs. Luedtke Road is one of those names that stuck in my brain until I needed it. The real road is outside Cut Bank, Montana, a farm and ranch community on Montana's Hi-Line whose library was one of the first to invite me, when my first mystery was published. If you think of Lower Valley Road outside Kalispell, Montana, Foothill Road between Kalispell and Bigfork, Chuckanut Road south of Bellingham, Washington, or any scenic, two-lane, country road that makes your heart sing, again, you wouldn't be wrong.

While there is a lavender grower in the Pike Place Market, she is not Liz, who sprang fully formed from my imagination. Thanks to the lavender growers here in northwest Montana who kindly gave me tours of their farms and retail shops, and shared their knowledge and love of the plant: Mike, Cathy, and Jaime Sullivan at Longview Lavender Farm in Somers, and Deb Davis at Purple Mountain Lavender in Lakeside. If you're in the area, do visit them.

Propagating plants and running a wholesale nursery operation is much more involved than I've portrayed here. Mistakes are my own.

In the summer of 2024, after years of work by a wide web of volunteers, my town, Bigfork, Montana, finally got the spacious, modern library it deserves. At a magical final fundraising auction, Kay Stone and Keith and Debra McCormick bid generously on the right to name a character in this book, and helped close the funding

250 · *Lavender Lies Bleeding*

gap. Kay chose to honor her late sister, Laura Long, a long-time Bigfork resident and library supporter. Dot and Dash, the dock kittens, are named for Laura's cats. The McCormicks chose to honor Keith's late bird dog and hunting partner, a Pudelpointer named Brambo. I am honored to include Laura and Brambo in these pages, and grateful for the generosity they inspired.

Much as I loved working as a teenage bookseller, I did not expect that being a published author would turn me back into a bookseller, selling at libraries, festivals, and other events, and stocking the gift shops who fill the void in a town with no bookshop of its own. Impossible without the help of author-bookseller extraordinaire Laura Beard Hayden, of Author!Author! Books. She's wrangled shipping delays, damaged books, the odd substitution of a case of a Japanese graphic (and I do mean graphic) novel for one of my cozies, and more. The Spice Shop's warehouse manager Hayden and his wife Laura bear her name as my thanks.

Over the years, readers have contributed to the stories and settings in many ways. Thanks to reader Jennifer Gallagher and her pup, Polo, for naming the doggy daycare in this book. Arf and I are bouncing with joy!

I was inspired to write about the shelter clinic and the prison dog training programs by a series of articles in the *Seattle Times*. Whether you live in a small town or a large one, please support your local newspaper. An independent newspaper is critical to the life of a community; my fictional newspaper editor Nina is nasty just for fun.

Readers often ask where the recipes come from. Although Pepper does find a pair of books on lavender on her trip to Salmon Falls, and I own and recommend both, the recipes in this book are my own. Pepper's Asparagus with Goat Cheese Vinaigrette is my adaptation of a recipe from Le Pichet, a French bistro in Seattle, originally shared by the restaurant's former owner and published in the *Seattle Times*.

Thanks to the Facebook and Instagram group leaders and members who share their love of the cozy mystery. There are too many to name, but I want to shout out Heather Doyle Harrisson and her crew at Cozy Mystery Party; Kelly Vaiman and her crew at Cozies, Conversations, and More; the readers and authors of Cozy Town Sleuth; and my sister bloggers and the readers of Mystery

Leslie Budewitz · 251

Lovers' Kitchen, where our motto is "mystery writers cooking up crime . . . and recipes!"

I've been beyond lucky to have thriller author Debbie Burke as my longtime critique partner, although lately, I've benefitted more from the partnership than she has. Debbie gave me the memory I gave Chuck Reece, of the grandmother who smelled of lavender and cigarette smoke, and taught her to read.

Thanks to my editor Rene Sears, Ashley Calvano, publicist Wiley Saichek, and everyone at Seventh Street Books who helps make these books better and get them into your hands.

Pepper has Kristen and I have Lita Artis, who's walked and driven many miles with me, researching these books. It was on a drive with her from a tulip garden into the town of LaConner, north of Seattle, that I spotted the red azalea tumbling into a stream, sparking my image of Salter Farm.

How anyone writes without a supportive spouse, I can't imagine. Add in a love of travel, eating, and cooking, and a font of medical knowledge, and it all makes Don Beans truly my "Mr. Right."

Finally, thanks to you, readers, for buying the books, for reading and listening and checking them out of libraries, for passing them on to your friends. For sending me exactly the right notes at exactly the right time. For taking my imaginary friends into your hearts and making them real. Stories truly are the spice of life.

About the Author

LESLIE BUDEWITZ IS PASSIONATE ABOUT FOOD, GREAT mysteries, and the Northwest, the setting for her national-bestselling Spice Shop Mysteries and Food Lovers' Village Mysteries. She also writes contemporary and historical short stories. Her latest books are *Lavender Lies Bleeding*, the ninth Spice Shop mystery, and *All God's Sparrows and Other Stories: A Stagecoach Mary Fields Collection*, featuring a remarkable real-life woman born into slavery who spent her last thirty years in Montana.

As Alicia Beckman, she writes moody suspense set in the Northwest.

Leslie is a three-time Agatha Award winner: 2011 Best Nonfiction for *Books, Crooks & Counselors: How to Write Accurately About Criminal Law and Courtroom Procedure* (Linden/Quill Driver Books); 2013 Best First Novel for *Death al Dente* (Berkley Prime Crime), first in the Food Lovers' Village Mysteries; and 2018 Best Short Story for "All God's Sparrows" (Alfred Hitchcock Mystery Magazine). Her books and stories have also won or been nominated for Spur, Derringer, Anthony, and Macavity awards. A lawyer by trade, she has served as president of Sisters in Crime and on the board of Mystery Writers of America.

Leslie loves to cook, eat, hike, travel, garden, and paint—not necessarily in that order. She lives in Northwest Montana with her husband, Don Beans, a musician and doctor of natural medicine.

Visit her online at www.LeslieBudewitz.com, where you'll find maps, recipes, discussion questions, links to her short stories, and more.